D0394274

A Beeline to
MURDER

A Beeline to
MURDER

Meera
Lester

KENSINGTON BOOKS
www.kensingtonbooks.com

KENSINGTON BOOKS are published by

Kensington Publishing Corp.
119 West 40th Street
New York, NY 10018

All Kensington titles, imprints and distributed lines are available at special quantity discounts for bulk purchases for sales promotion, premiums, fund-raising, educational or institutional use.

Special book excerpts or customized printings can also be created to fit specific needs. For details, write or phone the office of the Kensington Special Sales Manager: Kensington Publishing Corp., 119 West 40th Street, New York, NY, 10018. Attn. Special Sales Department. Phone: 1-800-221-2647.

Kensington and the K logo Reg. U.S. Pat. & TM Off.

Library of Congress Control Number: 2015937827

ISBN-13: 978-1-61773-909-5
ISBN-10: 1-61773-909-X
First Kensington Hardcover Edition: October 2015

eISBN-13: 978-1-61773-910-1
eISBN-10: 1-61773-910-3
First Kensington Electronic Edition: October 2015

10 9 8 7 6 5 4 3 2 1

Printed in the United States of America

For my Scribe Tribe,
my readers,
and all the mystery writers—past and present—whose
books have inspired me.

Chapter 1

A drone (male honeybee) must be able to fly
fifty feet straight up, or he will miss the chance
to mate with the queen; it is nature's way of
ensuring a robust gene pool.

—*Henny Penny Farmette Almanac*

Abigail Mackenzie pushed the trowel deep into the soft, loamy earth where she had been planting lavender from gallon pots. She rocked back on her heels and cocked her head to one side, listening intently. The low-pitched drone could mean only one thing. Removing her gloves, Abby pushed a tangle of reddish-gold hair off her face and yanked up a hemmed corner of her faded work shirt to wipe the perspiration from her forehead. Squinting up into the dappled sunlit branches, she spotted them: thousands of honeybees writhing in a toffee-colored mass in the crotch of the apricot tree.

"Arghh," Abby groaned. "Would it have killed you to wait another day?"

The sound of honeybees swarming ordinarily would have lifted Abby's spirits; it meant an additional hive for her growing colony of bees. But today that buzzing pushed her stress level as high as the cloudless May sky. The queen and her entourage had left the hive en masse, and unless Abby acted quickly, they would follow their winged scouts to a suitable new home, even if that home was five to eight miles away. To rescue the bees, she would have to don her beekeeper's suit, position a hive beneath the swarm, tie a rope around the apricot limb, and shake it with enough force to dislodge the bees into the open box—all adding up to precious minutes that she would have to shave from her already over-scheduled morning.

Watching the bees coalesce into a thickening corpus, Abby pondered the remote possibility that the bees might also hang around. But, for certain, the lavender wasn't going to plant itself. More importantly, she couldn't postpone delivering that file to the district attorney's office before noon if she expected to get paid for her part-time investigative work. And, of course, she had better get those ten jars of honey to the chef at the Las Flores Patisserie by eight thirty or risk another dressing-down, although the chef's cursing in French somehow rendered it less offensive.

Blowing a puff of air between her lips in exasperation, Abby threw down the trowel. The lavender and the bees would have to wait. Chef Jean-Louis Bonheur could be a tyrant or a charmer, and his moods seemed to swing without warning. She could only hope that today he'd be happy to see her. He was paying her well—twenty-two dollars for a sixteen-ounce jar. With her first delivery of lavender-flavored honey, the chef had convinced her to also sample his delectable pastries and had even invited her to watch him work. Abby recalled how she had enjoyed the role of observer—he was definitely eye candy, with thick brown hair, large brown eyes, and a buffed physique. It didn't hurt that he oozed personality. What woman wouldn't fall for that combination? But Jean-

Louis was gay, and his hair-trigger temper had already become legendary along Main Street. So she vowed today to skip the banter and just deliver her honey, get paid, and stick to her schedule.

After guiding the Jeep into the parking space at number three Lemon Lane, the alley behind the patisserie, which faced Main Street, Abby checked her watch and smiled. Five minutes early. Not like last time, when she'd arrived late because of a flat tire to find Chef Jean-Louis in his kitchen, pacing and swearing under his breath. He'd shocked her by throwing a pastry bag of batter that he'd been piping onto a parchment-lined baking sheet with such force, it knocked over a bowl of chocolate ganache. And later, while counting out cash to pay her for the delivery, he'd launched into another tirade, punctuating his French exclamations with incredulous glares, his hands wildly gesticulating in the air. As she hurriedly pocketed the money and made her way to back door, he'd called out an apology, or so she'd thought. His words stuck with her. "It is not you, AHbee." She'd never get used to his pronunciation of her name. "Non, c'est Etienne. Il est en retard." Apparently, she hadn't been the only person that day to violate the chef's obsession with punctuality.

Now with minutes to spare, Abby hoisted the box containing the sixteen-ounce jars of honey into her arms and scampered to the pastry shop back door, which stood slightly open.

"Chef?" Abby called cheerfully through the crack. "Chef Jean-Louis. It's Abigail Mackenzie. I've got your honey order here."

Abby pushed the box against the door. It swung open. Inside, the sudden hum of the motor of the chef's commercial-size, stainless-steel refrigerator kicked on. The sound pierced the silence of the empty kitchen. On the long center island, metal sheets of pastries on cooling racks awaited icing, filling, and drizzling. Cream horn and madeleine molds, pastry slabs, baking liners, mats, and cannoli tubes littered the counter space. Next to a large mixing bowl of royal icing lay a pastry bag filled with icing that had hardened from its wide tip. The ovens were still on, and the burnt smell of cake permeated the room.

Abby frowned. Something was terribly wrong with this scene. Setting the box of honey on the island, she instinctively grabbed a pot holder and turned off the oven. The law enforcement training she had gone through while at the academy and during her seven years with the Las Flores Police Department had honed her senses. Now, like back in the day, when she was often the first at the scene of a crime, her stomach knotted in that old familiar way. Why would the chef leave the premises with the back door open? Why was the CD player not on, when the chef, a fan of opera, always listened to his favorite arias while he worked? And why was his workstation so messy, when the chef took great pride in keeping his kitchen clean and organized to be as efficient as possible? Where was Chef Jean-Louis?

Abby's pulse quickened. Her muscles tightened. *What's going on here?* Abby tensed as she looked around. "Jean-Louis," she called. And then again more loudly, "Hello, Chef. Are you here?"

No answer.

Abby moved the box of honey in jars over to the cupboard where the chef usually stored them, since his pantry was often overflowing with supplies. Turning back, she walked slowly to the other side of the large island and rounded the corner. Her breath caught in her throat. There lay the chef, near the pantry door—eyes open, body not moving.

"Oh, my God in heaven!" Abby knelt and felt his wrist. No pulse. She leaned against his chest, desperately hoping to detect a breath. His open eyes were dull and cloudy. The ashen pallor of his skin, the bluish-colored lips, and the nonreactive and dilated pupils told Abby he was gone. She looked for signs that would tell her *how* he'd died. Instinctively, she peered at his neck and the narrow ligature mark it bore. Her senses flew into high alert.

Scanning the room for any sign of movement, Abby slowly rose. So what happened here? Had he killed himself? Or had he been the victim of foul play? She glanced at the pantry door, which was not completely closed. Could a killer be hiding on the premises? Heart pounding, adrenaline racing, Abby took out her cell and tapped the speed dial for her old boss.

"Chief Bob Allen, please," Abby said in a low voice. When he answered, she replied softly, "It's Abigail Mackenzie. I want to report a death. It's Chef Jean-Louis Bonheur . . . and it looks suspicious. You might want to send a unit to his pastry shop on Main. I entered through the rear, facing Lemon Lane."

Abby stared at the pantry door. Spotting a box of latex gloves on the counter, which the staff used to handle pastries, Abby took two and slipped her hands into them. She slowly, firmly grasped the pantry doorknob. Held her breath and yanked hard. She flipped on the light switch. Seeing no one, she exhaled in relief and pivoted slightly and noticed a length of knotted twine tied to the inside knob. The loose end had been cleanly cut and lay on the tile floor. An icy shiver ran up her spine. It looked like suicide, but who'd cut down the body?

Abby understood that she'd unwittingly stumbled into a crime scene. She knew how quickly the officers could respond to a call, especially to the pastry shop, which was located just ten blocks from the police station. Police headquarters occupied the first floor of the Dillingham Dairy Building, a century-old, two-story brick building situated at the end of Main Street, next to the city offices of the mayor, the town council, and the district attorney. Abby didn't want to contaminate the scene in any way, but her instincts told her to take in the details.

Gazing down upon the chef's dim, unanimated eyes, their once snappy brilliance forever quelled, Abby felt a twinge of sadness. She noted that the sleeves of his chef's jacket were rolled almost to the elbows and that his left forearm was tattooed with what looked to be an interlocked nine and six. Siren screams ended Abby's observations. She quickly peeled off the gloves and tucked them into her jeans pockets.

A tall, blond-haired uniformed officer, her gun and nightstick holstered on her duty belt and her black boots shining, apparently from a recent polishing, stepped in through the back door. Abby relaxed and grinned. So the police chief had sent Officer Katerina Petrovsky to investigate. Kat had been Abby's best friend since they met at the Napa Police Academy. Abby had been invited as a guest speaker when Kat was still a cadet. Finding themselves seated together during the lunch that preceded Abby's talk and again afterward, Abby and Kat had promised to stay in touch. Later, after Kat had been hired by the Las Flores Police Department, Abby had served as her field training officer.

Before the two friends could say hello, a malnourished woman with matted gray hair and bright blue eyes banged her metal shopping cart filled with stuffed plastic bags against the wall before shuffling in through the open back door. Abby instantly recognized Dora; she was one of Las Flores's more colorful eccentrics.

"Where's my coffee?" she asked. "The chef always gives me coffee."

"Not today, Dora," Kat replied.

Abby watched Dora try to undo the covered button of her once stylish, threadbare gray sweater—the task made more difficult since Dora seemed intent on not removing her 1940s-style cotton gloves. Abby remembered meeting a much younger Dora years ago at the historical cemetery, when the nearby, newly constructed crematorium had caught fire. That was before Shadyside Funeral Home was built; before the Las Flores Creek had flooded, prompting the town council to prohibit the building of any new cemetery within city limits; and long before Dora's chestnut-colored hair had turned gray and she had taken to sleeping at the homeless encampment beneath the bridge by the creek.

"I want my coffee."

"The chef can't give you coffee today," Kat explained. "You have to leave."

"No, he told me, 'Later. Come back later.'"

"When did he tell you that?" asked Kat.

"He always tells me that."

"Okay, well, there is no coffee today. So out you go." The officer took Dora by the arm and escorted her through the back door.

"You should talk to her. She gets around," Abby said when Kat had reentered the kitchen. Abby pulled another pair of gloves from the box on the counter and slipped them on.

Kat looked at her with a wary eye. "Yeah, but *usually* her conversations are with those voices inside her head, so I'll get right on that, girlfriend, but I'd like to see the body first."

"Over there." Abby pointed to the opposite side of the island.

"And why, may I ask, were *you* here?"

"Delivering my honey. What else? When I got here, Kat, he was already dead, lying just like that. I swear."

"Uh-huh. And of course you didn't touch anything, did you?"

Abby had anticipated the question. "I promise you won't find my fingerprints on anything here except my honey jars."

"Good." Kat walked over to view the body more closely. She scanned the scene, taking special note of the area where the chef lay on the black-and-white tile floor.

"No blood, no splatter, unless you count stipples of frosting," Abby observed.

"So how did he die?" Kat asked. Unsnapping the fastener on the small pouch of her duty belt, Kat removed a pair of latex gloves. Sliding her hands into them, she knelt to look closely at the body. She leaned in to see the ligature marks on the neck. "What could he have possibly done to anyone to get himself killed?"

"Well, he could have killed himself. Take a look at the pantry doorknob . . . on the inside."

Kat stood and walked to the pantry. "I see what you mean. So if he hung himself, who took the ligature from around his neck and laid out his body on the floor? And what did he use to stand on?"

"All good questions I've been asking myself," said Abby. "Since the only chair in here holds a ten-pound bag of meringue powder, I'm guessing he didn't use it to stand on. Maybe a café chair from the other room?"

"Yeah," Kat said with a peculiar look. "And I guess after he hung himself, he got up and moved it back?"

"Well, someone else was here. When I arrived, the back door was ajar. Perhaps someone he knew."

Kat's expression grew more incredulous. "Would that be the someone who couldn't bear to see him hanging? Or the someone who wanted to tidy up after murdering him?"

Abby chuckled. "I see you haven't lost your sense of humor. Clearly, if he was murdered, there would have to be a motive."

"Pretty much everyone on Main Street has experienced the chef's temper."

"Yeah," admitted Abby. "Even I have felt the brunt of his temper. But he was also generous to a fault. I mean, he doled out coffee and sweets to unemployed vets and the homeless." Abby watched as Kat surveyed the kitchen before strolling into the adjacent room, where glass display cases and small wooden café tables and chairs filled the cramped space. Fleur-de-lis wallpaper above dark wainscoting was partially obscured by the numerous black-and-white posters of Parisian scenes. Above the cash register a memento board hung slightly askew. Its crisscrossed red ribbon secured photographs of customers and friends posing with the chef.

Kat leaned in for a closer look.

"I've come through that door many a morning while his ovens were still on and the smell of freshly baked dough permeated the place," said Abby. "People would line up outside, all the way down to the antique store. Well, you know, he always had free coffee and fresh pastries for us cops. He liked having law enforcement around."

"For being in such a small space and open for only two and a half years, his business seemed to be booming."

"True, but you and I both know that things aren't always as they appear."

"Uh-huh." Kat walked toward the restroom, which was tucked off the kitchen, and flicked on the overhead light to look around.

"Is his apron in there?" Abby asked. "He never worked without one."

"You don't say. Now, what made you think of a detail like that?"

"Lest you forget, I notice little things like that."

"Does anything else come to mind?"

"Not really. I just remember how he always tucked a towel into his apron strings. Makes sense if you're wiping your hands often. You'll notice he doesn't have dough or icing or flour on his clothes, so he must have worn an apron if he worked all night in the kitchen. And I don't see it."

Kat looked behind the restroom door. "Not here." She walked back to the body, where she halted, finger against her radio call button. She pushed the button, and dispatch answered. "We've got a DOA at number three Lemon Lane. Notify the coroner and get me backup."

"Need help documenting this?" Abby asked.

"I ain't sayin' no. Just me and Otto working the streets this week."

"I thought Chief Bob Allen had hired some new recruits."

"Yeah, but three are in San Francisco for defensive tactics training, two are getting recertified at the firearm range, and our crime-scene photographer is in L.A. all week."

Abby winced. She knew working short staffed could be grueling, what with patrol work, traffic stops, ticket and report writing, court appearances, and the like. God forbid anything more serious, like a robbery or a murder, should happen. When she and Kat had worked together, their beat was the downtown district. They had worked mostly petty crimes, which ranged from the occasional burglary to high school pranks and shoplifting.

Las Flores was ethnically mixed, mirroring Northern California's Bay Area and wine country towns, and without much crime. The outskirts and rural areas were populated by farmers, ranchers, and young, upwardly mobile urbanites who favored family-friendly businesses and all things organic. Like any other town in America, Las Flores had its share of hotheads, rednecks, gangbangers, and retirees. But the vast majority of folks were decent and hardworking. Abby knew that the largest number of traffic tickets went mainly to nonresidents of Las Flores who used Main Street as a shortcut from the cities in the valley to the beach towns on the other side of the coastal mountains. But with a state prison only twenty-five miles to the north of town, just outside the county, Las Flores also got its share of shady characters passing through—convicted felons, parolees, and gang members, who frequented the local watering hole, the Black Witch Bar. Anything could happen on any day, but especially over the weekends, when out-of-towners cruised through.

Abby and Kat had witnessed plenty of public drunkenness and brawls at the bar, a favorite of bikers, who frequently stopped in for one last cool drink after a long day of riding in the mountains or visiting wineries. The bar and the dead chef's pastry shop shared space in the same building that also housed Cineflicks, the local theater. Occasionally, the business owners along Main Street would complain of the stench of urine, sure that the culprits were bar patrons. Having worked the streets for years, Abby had seen many crimes and criminals during her tenure in the downtown, but homicides—those were few and far between in Las Flores.

Abby sighed, "What about the county sheriff? Couldn't Chief Bob Allen request some extra officers from him?"

Kat shot an incredulous look at her. "Are you kidding? Chief Bob Allen threatened to withhold our uniform-cleaning allowance to reduce departmental spending. That is, until the comptroller told him he couldn't do that. Ask for outside help? No way."

Abby frowned. "Well, what if I take the crime-scene pictures for you . . . ? I've got my camera in the Jeep."

Kat rubbed an earlobe between her thumb and finger as she weighed Abby's offer. "You know the rules. I'm supposed to say no. But seeing as how it's you, I don't think the chief could get too flipped out."

"Just trying to help," Abby said. "I've got to deliver a file to the DA's office by noon and head back to the farmette. If I don't rescue my bee swarm, they'll take off for parts unknown. So if you want pictures, speak up, or I'm out of here."

"Oh, what the heck! Let me grab the crime-scene tape from my cruiser." Kat turned and walked to the back door.

Following her to the parking lot, Abby opened the door of her Jeep and rummaged through the glove compartment until she located her digital camera. She slammed shut the door and, with camera in hand, said, "Just like old times."

"Yep," Kat replied. "Let's start inside and work our way out. I'll bag and tag everything on the countertop."

"I suppose you'll want me to get some shots of the scene, the body, and close-ups of the ligature mark on his neck."

"Uh-huh." Kat's gaze swept the room, as though she was searching for something, anything that could help her understand what had happened here that had resulted in the death of the town's award-winning chef. Once the crime-scene tape had been strung, and evidence collected and labeled, Abby pulled the camera from her shirt pocket. "Besides the interior photos and the body, anything else you want me to shoot?"

Kat motioned toward the kitchen's back door. "In the café, get some shots of the baker's rack and close-ups of items on the shelves like the recipe binders and that box up there, but don't remove anything."

"Okay," Abby replied.

Kat looked around. "I want images of the blue metal Dumpster between the pastry shop and the theater, a shot of the back door of the pastry shop all the way to the biker bar, and a panorama shot of the back of the building, since those two other businesses share common walls with the pastry shop."

"You got it. Are you thinking that somebody from the theater or the bar might have had a run-in with our chef?"

"We can't rule out anything at this point," Kat said. "I think a Dumpster search for a rope or the apron might be in order. The murderer could have tossed them, unless, of course, the chef hung himself, which I'm not buying."

Abby walked across the alley and turned to face the building's back side. She took several shots of the weather-beaten, stucco-covered grand ole lady, which the townsfolk considered a landmark of sorts. Built in the 1930s, it had remained unchanged as businesses emerged and closed while the town evolved into a chic little enclave of stylish shops and restaurants. The old building had endured the October 17, 1989, earthquake in the Bay Area, with only a few horizontal fissures to prove it, but the city engineers had found it stable enough to leave it standing.

Other buildings in town had not been so lucky. Bright red CONDEMNED notices had been tacked or taped to them, indicating they were to be torn down. The replacements, such as the row of small office buildings on the opposite side of the Lemon Lane alleyway behind the pastry shop, provided commercial tenants more functionality, but without any of the charm or character of the older buildings, which reflected the pre– and post–World War II architecture of Las Flores.

Returning to the chef's kitchen, Abby determined the best angles for her shots. She wanted clear and focused images for the investigation. Police chief Bob Allen didn't need another reason to be angry or upset with Kat . . . or her.

To establish the distance and relationship of the back door to the island and the restroom, she positioned herself at the back entrance to the kitchen. Later, she shot images from the opposite direction. Then, climbing on a chair next to a tall wire baker's rack, Abby clicked off a couple more photos. When she leaned into the last one, she nearly lost her balance. Grabbing the top of the baker's rack to steady herself, she knocked over a basket of dusty faux ivy that concealed a small security camera. Dismounting from the chair, she sidestepped the camera until Kat could bag and tag it, tugged a pencil from her pocket, and used it to pick up a plastic cup that had tumbled to the floor. Before setting it aside for Kat, Abby sniffed it and made a mental note to tell Kat about the booze smell in the cup.

Working the room, Abby photographed from every conceivable direction and angle. As she zeroed in on the area occupied by the body, Abby recalled the first homicide she and Kat had worked together. The victim had been a local divorcée who had met a man for drinks at the Black Witch. The man had driven the woman home. The next morning, the woman's boyfriend had found her on the floor of her cottage. She had been strangled and sexually assaulted.

The victim's boyfriend had called police. When his alibi had checked out, he'd been eliminated as a suspect. Strangely, it was the boyfriend who had noticed the woman's colorful patterned rug had gone missing. He gave a description of it to police. Then Kat, a flea market addict, spotted the rug a month later. Las Flores cops began surveillance of their new suspect, a Turkish immigrant whose family had ties to carpet weaving in the old country. He had a good eye and had, apparently, recognized the rug as a Ladik prayer rug from central Anatolia. Abby and Kat arrested him for selling stolen property and, after having the rug tested for trace evidence relating to the homicide, charged him with the woman's murder.

Abby knelt and took some shots of the chef's body. She noticed tiny particles of dough on the cuticles of the first and second fingers on his right hand. She also noted the lividity, or discoloration, from blood pooling in the parts of the body touching the floor. Pressing a gloved finger against the chef's right hand where it rested upon the tile, Abby realized that although the chef's body was not yet cold, it was stiff. She surmised that the corpse was in the early stages of rigor mortis. Abby knew that blanching would not occur after four hours from the time of death, so she deduced that Jean-Louis was probably killed sometime within the past few hours or just before dawn. Her estimate, she knew, was rough; the coroner would give a more accurate time of death.

Putting the camera back into her shirt pocket and removing the gloves, Abby walked outside, to where Kat was leaning against the wall, jotting notes in a spiral notebook. A white van pulled in and stopped just behind the flares. The van sported the blue coroner's department logo and insignia—stalks of wheat curved into a half circle.

"She's new," said Kat as she watched the young woman, in her late twenties and wearing her chestnut hair pulled back in a short ponytail, hop out of the driver's side.

"What happened to Millie?" asked Abby.

"Maternity leave."

"Oh, gotcha." Abby recalled Millie, with whom she had worked over the years. Her chirpy voice and quick smile for first responders—regardless of how grisly the scene was—somehow made the scenes of death more bearable.

"Millie married the son of the fire chief, didn't she?"

"Yep."

"Liked her."

"Me, too," Kat replied. "Dunno about this one."

The young woman slammed the van door and introduced herself in a loud voice. "Dr. Greta Figelson, assistant investigator with the coroner's office." She flipped her hand in a backward motion over her shoulder to a young black man with an Afro, who seemed hesitant to exit the van. "My driver, Virgil . . ." She couldn't seem to recall the rest of the man's name.

"Smith," the driver called out through his open window to finish her sentence.

Abby looked down and suppressed a smile. *Yeah, Smith's so darn hard to remember.* Kat jotted their names in her notebook.

Dr. Figelson marched over. Abby wondered why the coroner's assistant had even bothered to come with such an attitude. Two workers were needed to handle the gurney, although Abby recalled that the newer gurneys had electric controls and could be operated by one person. Maybe one of the workers had called in sick and the doc had to fill in, doing grunt work along with her regular duties today.

"So, where's the body?" Dr. Figelson asked, pulling a yellow mask with white ties from her khaki pants pocket. "I'm just here to pronounce him. Don't have all day."

Kat jerked her thumb in the direction of the kitchen. "In there." She stepped aside to allow Dr. Figelson to pass.

Dr. Figelson disappeared inside the pastry shop.

Finally, Kat's backup arrived. The second cruiser, red light flashing and siren screaming, wheeled into the empty parking space next to Kat's police car.

Kat called out, "Really, Otto? You needed lights and siren? Seriously?"

Otto Nowicki, a hefty, balding man with skin the color of an unbaked pie crust, hoisted himself out of the seat. Once upright, he spent two minutes adjusting and readjusting his gear, guns, and nightstick on his duty belt. Abby knew Otto was always talking about becoming police chief one day. He had a thing about looking and acting official. Both she and Kat believed it was unlikely, since Chief Bob Allen had no plans to leave and would never be pushed out, but Otto kept on acting like *he* was in charge.

"Ya thinkin' pastry shop . . . doughnuts?" Kat winked at Abby.

"Uh, *no*," Otto replied, running his hand across his spare tire of a belly. "I'm on a diet. Wife says I gotta eat more like a caveman and stay away from sugar."

"That right?" Kat quipped. "Does your wife know about the four teaspoons in your coffee at roll call every morning?"

Otto grinned sheepishly. "Jeez, the station's coffee is like drinking turpentine. I've got to put something in it, or it doesn't go down." He hooked his thumbs into his duty belt, sucked in his belly, and stood a little straighter.

Abby noticed Otto had lost a little more hair and had gained a few more pounds from when they had last worked together. His pate was bald except for a few sprigs of gray-brown hair standing up like beleaguered dried grass on the California hills during the dog days of summer.

Kat lifted the yellow crime-scene tape, allowing Otto to enter.

He trained his eyes on Abby. With a deadpan expression

and a slow drawl, he greeted her. "Hello, Abby. Seen ya around. You don't drop by the station anymore. Don't you miss us?"

Abby inhaled deeply before answering. "You know, Otto, I kind of do miss the work, but then again, there are some things I don't miss."

"Yeah? Like what?" Otto asked.

"Well . . . for starters, being micromanaged by Chief Bob Allen. In my new life, I'm the boss. I like it that way."

Otto nodded. "Know whatcha mean. So how's the hand?"

Abby winced. Otto never shrank away from asking the direct questions. He was good in the interrogation room. He was the one who made the bad guys squirm.

"Healed. Thank you," she said, sliding her hand into her jacket pocket. Abby turned and walked through the back door. Standing just inside, she let go a deep sigh.

There was no need to share her medical history with Otto. He certainly didn't need to see the scars left by her surgery, which the doctors had hoped would repair the ligaments of her right thumb. The surgery hadn't worked out the way she'd hoped. To shoot her gun, her thumb had to be consistently stable. Hers wasn't. And she didn't want to talk about it anymore to anyone, least of all to Otto, whose tongue had a tendency to wag in gossip about as much as it did when licking doughnut sugar from his thin lips. Still, to his credit, he could also shut down and clam up, especially in matters involving police business.

From where she had been examining the body, Dr. Figelson stood up and untied her mask. "I'm finished."

Abby wasn't wearing a police uniform, and she was pretty sure the assistant investigator to the coroner would resist telling her anything, but she asked, anyway. "Time of death?"

Kat entered through the back door.

Dr. Figelson ignored Abby's question. She said, "Get my driver. Tell him to tag the body with a blue label, wrap the hands, and let him know that I've authorized the removal. You've no knowledge of any infectious diseases here or any involving the deceased, have you?"

Abby looked at her wordlessly. She shrugged. *Now, how would I?*

"Good. See to it, then."

Abby's forehead creased in a frown.

Dr. Figelson addressed Kat. "Obviously, he's dead. Did he have a regular physician I can talk with?"

Kat shrugged. Abby shook her head.

"Our office will do a limited investigation," Dr. Figelson said. After writing on a form, she handed it to Kat. "Here's the release number and my contact information. Now I've got a call to make."

Abby didn't like the assistant's attitude. Generally, the coroner's office and the police adhered to an agreeable level of professionalism. This woman was irritating. When Dr. Figelson brushed past, boot heels in paper covers clicking against the black-and-white porcelain tiles, Abby looked at Kat and shook her head. *What arrogance. Oh, well.* Helping the coroner's driver to remove the body would present an opportunity to take a closer look. On the other hand, Abby wasn't a police detective anymore, but even when she was, her pesky curiosity had gotten her into trouble more times than not. Still, she reached for the box of gloves on the counter, grabbed two more, slipped them on, walked to the door, and motioned for Virgil to come inside.

Virgil slid out of the driver's seat and dropped to the ground. He looked taller perched behind the wheel than standing at full height. Abby guessed he was a head taller than her own five feet three inches. He scampered over.

Abby tapped her watch. "Your partner says it's time to load and go. Oh, and she said to wrap the hands."

Virgil's blue-black forehead and cheeks glistened with sweat. He glanced furtively at the body lying on the floor next to the counter and swallowed hard. Twice.

"Oh, come on. Don't tell me you're new, too?" Abby asked.

"Uh-huh." His complexion assumed a greenish cast.

"Why don't you go get into your protective gear and bring the sterile sheet, the hand wraps, and a body bag?" Abby said.

He nodded, but then cried out weakly, "Toilet!" His hands flew to his throat. He doubled over.

"No. Do not vomit. Not now. Not here." Abby pushed him in the direction of the restroom. "There." For the next several minutes, Abby clenched her jaw and waited for the disgusting sounds from the restroom to cease. *Newbie.* Another reason why she didn't miss police work.

Tips for Maintaining a Strong, Healthy Beehive

- Plant lavender, sunflowers, and such herbs as basil, thyme, and sage near your honeybee hive. When the food source is close to the hive, the hive tends to grow robustly in less time than if the bees have to fly off in search of food. Also, flowering food sources keep the bees on or near your property, where they will pollinate your garden vegetables, flowers, and fruit trees.

- Avoid using pesticides to control pest infestations on your flowers, as the chemicals will poison your honeybees.

- Place the hive on an elevated stand or platform, and off the damp ground, to aid with air circulation, help prevent frames from molding, and keep marauding animals from molesting your bees. And don't forget to control ants.

- Keep the hive dry, and face it toward the east and southeast for warmth, dryness, and light.

- Use a screened bottom board under the hive. It allows mites (which harm bees) to fall through to the ground, thus ensuring the mites will perish and will not reenter the hive.

- Feed your bees, especially if the autumn and winter seasons have been harsh, to prevent starvation.

Chapter 2

An herbal tea made of meadowsweet,
chamomile, or peppermint can calm an
upset stomach.

—*Henny Penny Farmette Almanac*

Abby watched as Virgil Smith wiped his mouth on a paper towel from the toilet's dispenser as he dashed past her and through the back door of the pastry shop to the van. *Poor guy . . . looks pitiful. Newbie driver for a newbie coroner's investigator . . . I wonder how that's working out for the county.*

When Virgil returned, his face still had not lost its greenish cast, but at least he had donned examination gloves and slipped sanitary booties over his shoes. He rolled in the gurney, fingers clamped over the sterile body drape, the hand wraps, and the body bag. Once he neared the corpse, he seemed dumbfounded as to how to get the body from the floor onto the gurney.

Exchanging a look with Kat, Abby already knew what her former partner was thinking . . . and it was best left unsaid. Virgil didn't seem cut out for this line of work. He probably wouldn't last too long as a driver of the dead. His lack of experience might also explain the assistant's foul mood.

"Well, with the coroner's go-ahead for the transport, shall we help Virgil get the body on the gurney?" Abby asked.

Kat nodded.

"We'll do a three-man lift. I'll take his feet," Abby said, dropping to the floor, onto one knee. She slipped her hands around the chef's ankles and tightened her grip. Kat and Otto positioned themselves on either side of the chef's shoulders. Virgil secured the gurney.

"Ready?" Abby asked. "On the count of three. One, two, and three."

As they shifted the body upward, onto the gurney, a ping sounded against the tile floor. Otto huffed to catch his breath, while Kat helped Virgil adjust the body on the transport bed. Kat then joined Abby, who'd already dropped back down on her hands and knees to examine the floor.

What had caused that sound? Where was it? Abby ran her gloved hand as far as she could under the stainless-steel island, feeling back and forth with her fingers as they advanced as far as they could under the structure, while Kat searched the other end with her flashlight. Finally, Abby felt something—a small object.

"Feels like maybe a screw," she said to Kat. "Bring over your light."

Kat grunted as she pinched the object between her latex thumb and first finger, and held on to it until she was again standing upright. Abby, Kat, and Otto stared at the object, an earring stud, its prongs securing a faceted clear stone.

The stud appeared similar to the pair of earrings Abby's maternal grandmother, Rose, had given her on her eighteenth birthday. The delicate filigree setting reminded Abby of heirloom or vintage jewelry. "Old mine cut," her grandmother had explained when Abby had asked her why, if the earrings her grandmother had given her were real diamonds, their shine seemed so lackluster. Grandma Rose had explained that at the turn of the century, diamonds used in jewelry were far rougher. Few jewelers could afford expensive faceting machines in those days, and many of the stones had large inclusions and so looked muddied.

Kat held the stud up toward the ceiling light. *More fire than my earrings have,* Abby thought. *Might be a diamond. Could be glass. A jeweler would know.*

Abby said, "You might want to check the body for piercings, see if this was maybe his."

While Otto examined the chef's rather petite ears, left and right, and his prominent nose, Abby and Kat studied the earring.

"Apparently, Chef Jean-Louis wasn't into piercing," Otto declared.

Abby peered at the stud. "It's missing its backing. Let me have your flashlight, Otto."

From his duty belt, Otto peeled off the small flashlight and handed it to Abby. "If you find it, don't touch it. Custody of evidence and all that being sacrosanct."

"Yeah, I know the drill." Abby ran the light back and forth under the island. Finally, she rose, switched off the light, and handed it back to the big boy. "Nothing there but a lot of dust."

Kat slipped the earring into a paper evidence bag and jotted the relevant identifying information on it. Her radio came on, and the dispatcher's voice informed her that the police chief needed an update. "Again?" Kat rolled her eyes at Abby. She pushed her two-way.

Chief Bob Allen's voice cut through. "What have you got, Petrovsky?"

"Well, the vic is definitely the pastry chef Jean-Louis Bonheur."

"Keep talking," said the chief.

"The scene's contained. Otto's here, and a new assistant to the coroner, her driver, and Mackenzie, who, as you know, found the body. Two possibilities at this point, Chief. Looks like he could have strung himself up or he could have been murdered. That homeless woman, Dora, has been by already, looking for free coffee. I want to talk with her because I'm thinking maybe she came by even earlier. If she cut him down, then I'd lean toward it being a possible suicide, but it's early."

"All right. Keep me posted," the chief commanded. "I'm out for a meeting with the mayor, but I'll want a full briefing when you're finished there."

"Right, Boss," Kat said, sounding respectfully subordinate. With the call ended, she turned her attention back to the body, studying the dead man's neck area.

"What material do you think made that mark?" Kat asked.

Otto and Abby jockeyed for a better position, both leaning in for a closer look.

"You mean the bruising around his neck?" Abby asked. "The twine on the doorknob looks like it might make that kind of narrow ligature."

"Well, I'm going to ask Dr. Figelson to speculate on the manner of death, but I'm not holding out any hope that she'll tell me anything until after an autopsy," said Kat. She made a sweeping motion with her arm to indicate to Virgil that he could proceed with covering the body.

"Ready, there, Virgil?" Otto looked at the wide-eyed young man, who stood a couple of feet away, with the drape for covering the corpse still pinched between his fingers. "Like some help there with that sheet?"

"Uh, yes, sir," Virgil said. His dark eyes remained riveted on the body. He proffered the unopened plastic bag containing the drape.

Otto, grinning like a monkey, winked at Abby and asked Virgil, "You scared of something? A dead body can't hurt you. It ain't like he could whack you."

"Uh-huh," Virgil muttered. His large dark eyes were fixated on Jean-Louis's lifeless face.

Abby shook her head in dismay at Otto's remark. "You had to go there."

Otto looked over at her. "Just saying."

"Oh, give it to me," Kat said impatiently. She grabbed the plastic bag, ripped it open, shook out the bright yellow drape, and covered the body with it. Abby, Kat, and Otto rolled the chef on his side to tuck the drape around and under him, then repeated this maneuver on the other side, effectively bundling him like a baby in a tightly wrapped blanket, before wrapping his hands. They then rolled the body onto one side and maneuvered it into the body bag. Virgil zipped it and, with help from Otto, maneuvered the gurney around the counter, over the wooden threshold, and out the back door to the van.

A small crowd of onlookers and local business employees was clustered around the yellow crime-scene tape, gawking and pointing at the black, zippered bag on the gurney. A young woman cried out. Appearing to be in her late teens or early twenties, she wore a dark, mid-calf peasant skirt, black leggings, and Doc Martens purple boots with miniature footprints patterned over the leather. She plucked up the crime-scene tape and darted under.

"What's happened? Is it Chef Jean-Louis?" she asked.

Abby spotted peacock tattoos over each shoulder through the see-through, sleeveless blouse the young woman was wearing over a lacy black camisole. Her brown dreadlocks had been threaded with lavender beads and pulled into a huge ponytail at the back of her head, leaving a purple forelock to hang to her chin, where it partially covered one of her heavily made-up eyes. *Strange attire and makeup for work in a pastry shop,* Abby surmised, but then again, Jean-Louis had seemed to attract unusual characters.

Kat threw her hand up and ordered the woman to stop. "The tape says, 'Do not cross.' That means *you* need to stay back."

"But I work here," the young woman replied.

"I'll come to you," Kat said. "Your name?" she asked, approaching the woman.

"Tallulah Berry. The pastry shop cashier. Has something happened to my boss, Chef Jean-Louis?"

"Why do you think something's happened to him?" Kat asked.

"He works the night shift. He sometimes forgets to lock the back door."

"Anyone work with him on the night shift?" Kat softened her tone.

"No. He works alone. Can't you tell me what's going on?"

"I need to talk with you, Tallulah, so don't go anywhere," Kat said, ignoring the young woman's question. Turning to Abby, Kat asked, "When Otto is finished helping Virgil, will you see to it that he asks Miss Berry for the names of anyone else who worked with her and the chef at the shop, along with their addresses and phone numbers? I see the coroner's assistant is getting into the van, and I need to go over a couple of things with her before she leaves."

"Sure," Abby replied.

Directing her questioning to Abby, the young woman said, "Please tell me that . . . that body bag wasn't for Chef Jean-Louis."

Abby said gently, "I'm sorry, but it is."

"No! Can't be!" Tallulah's youthful expression glazed with despair. Her light gray eyes widened, and tears began to pool. Soon they spilled over, staining her pale cheeks with black mascara. "But how? Did he have heart attack or something?"

"We don't know the details as yet." Abby put a comforting hand around Tallulah's elbow, then escorted the young woman a short distance away from the crowd. She gave Tallulah a minute to let the news sink in before asking, "Did he have a heart condition? Is that why you asked about his heart?"

"No. He was really healthy."

"Was he depressed?"

"More stressed than depressed."

"That so? Why was he stressed?"

"Money. He'd gotten loans to keep the business going, and the money was due. Chef Jean-Louis told me once to never do business with guys who would break your legs for late payment. I guess he was in pretty deep."

"Who were the guys? Do you recall their names?"

"I never heard their names, just that they are private investors. They give loans to people who can't get the funds any other way."

"Do you think those people would have exacted revenge on Chef Jean-Louis for not paying back the loans on time?" Abby asked.

Tallulah used her fingers to wipe away her tears. She sniffed. "I don't know. Sometimes they came around, had coffee and pastries, more like cousins than investors. But Chef Jean-Louis gets worked up when he can't pay the bills. He yells a lot, but it doesn't mean anything. He just vents. But the loans stressed him, and so did the problems he was having with the landlord."

"Whose name is . . . ?" Abby's brow shot up. She leaned slightly toward the young woman and waited for the answer.

"Willie Dobbs. He did not want to renew the pastry shop lease. He said he needed to refurbish the building. But Chef Jean-Louis told me Dobbs just wanted the pastry shop gone so he could get someone else in here and jack up the rent." Tallulah choked back sniffles.

Abby pulled a tissue from her jeans pocket and handed it to the young woman.

After wiping the tissue beneath each eye, Tallulah used it to blow her nose. "You know, he's nothing but a redneck bully, that Dobbs guy. I . . . I heard him and the chef arguing."

"When was that?" Abby asked.

Tallulah bit her lip and frowned in concentration. "I'm not sure. Oh, my God! I can't believe he's dead." Her face took on a stricken expression.

Abby sighed. "Sure. I understand. Take a moment to catch your breath. I wouldn't ask you if I didn't think it was important."

Tallulah's eyes welled again with tears. She wiped her nose. "Last week, I guess . . . maybe Saturday. Yeah, I think it was Saturday. I wanted to see that arty film being shown next door. The theater's last showing on Saturday was at eight p.m. We usually close the shop at six. The last customer had left. Just me and the chef . . . He'd come in early to work a split shift, instead of his usual midnight schedule. I was closing the shop."

"Go on," Abby urged.

"Well, that's when I heard voices in the kitchen. Mr. Dobbs had come around back to talk with my boss. Chef Jean-Louis had just turned off his CD player, so I could hear them really clearly." She wiped her nose again. "You know, the chef, he loves opera."

Abby smiled. "Yes, I know. . . . Can you remember what they said?"

Tallulah bit her lip. "Um, let me think. I had just finished wiping down the counters and was refilling the napkin holders. Mr. Dobbs sounded really mad. The two of them were shouting, talking over each other. Chef didn't back down, even after Dobbs made threats."

"Threats? Like what?" Abby knew Otto should be and would be asking these questions, but she couldn't just turn off her instinct to probe—she had cared about the chef, too.

"He told Chef that their lease deal was not valid. He sent Jean-Louis to hell and said that the renovation was going to happen whether Chef Jean-Louis liked it or not. But Mr. Dobbs was pushing out only the pastry shop."

"And you know this because. . . ."

"Chef Jean-Louis spoke with the proprietors of the theater and the biker bar. Mr. Dobbs hadn't asked either of those tenants to vacate."

"So what else did Dobbs say?"

"He told Chef Jean-Louis that the pastry shop's lease would be broken, even if he—that is, Mr. Dobbs—had to ice him."

"*Ice?* He really used that word? Goodness, sounds like Mr. Dobbs has been watching too many mafia shows," said Abby.

"I avoid people like him." Tallulah shifted from foot to foot, swayed from side to side, as if the rhythmic movement could somehow help her cope. "That horrible man is nothing but a selfish bully with a giant ego, a hothead with a big mouth." Tallulah pushed the purple forelock from her eye. "I'm a pacifist, like Gandhi and Reverend King. I hate arguments. But that night I had to get my purse from the kitchen, where they were going at it. The tension in there was terrible. Shaking off that kind of negative energy, it's hard for people like me."

"What do you mean by 'like me'?"

"Empathic."

Abby shot her a quizzical look.

"I feel other people's energy. The chef and Dobbs . . . their energies were intense. I mean, off the charts. We're talking major testosterone. Chef had gotten right into Dobbs's face. I could feel electricity streaming out of his head. We empaths feel emotional energy more than other people. My intuition is as finely tuned as a crystal, receiving and magnifying energy, positive and negative."

"And so you went to the pastry shop kitchen to get your purse?" Abby asked, sidestepping what she considered the bogus hocus-pocus.

Tallulah pressed fingers against the corners of her eyes, where new tears were forming. "He just can't be dead," she said. "This doesn't happen in real life . . . does it?"

Abby sighed. "Unfortunately, it does." She waited a beat. "And so you went to get your purse, and then what?"

"It was hanging on the coat rack. I snagged it and beat the heck outta there. I don't think either of them even noticed me."

"So you didn't hear anything else? Did Dobbs or Jean-Louis say anything as you were leaving?"

"Nope. They were just evil eyeing each other, kind of like fighting dogs panting before the next onslaught, if you know what I mean."

Abby noticed the small studs in Tallulah's earlobes, along with a ring of tiny hoops going up her left ear. "You've got pierced ears. Lost an earring lately?"

"No, I rarely lose my earrings. I use the screw-on safety backs. Only thing is, you have to tighten them on all the way. Oh, occasionally one will pop off."

Abby nodded. "The police will want your statement, Tallulah. Just tell them everything you can recall, okay? That way we can figure out what happened to our chef."

Tallulah put three fingers against her lips, as if doing so would hold back the sob building inside.

Abby stepped forward and wrapped her arms around Tallulah's bony shoulders. "I'm sorry, sweetie. It's quite a shock, I know." She pointed toward Otto, who had lifted the Dumpster lid and was peering in at the contents. "Come on. I'll introduce you to one of the officers who'll want to talk with you."

Abby led Tallulah over to the blue Dumpster and waited until Otto had lowered the lid.

"Sergeant Otto Nowicki, meet Tallulah Berry. She worked for the chef in the pastry shop. Says the chef had a visitor on Saturday and they argued."

Otto sized up Tallulah. "Are you willing to come down to the station and give us a statement?"

"If you think it would help, sure. But it won't take long, will it? I want to light a candle for the chef and see if I can tune in to his spirit . . . help with the crossing over, if you know what I mean."

Abby smiled at Otto, curious as to how he would respond.

"It won't take long at all, Miss Berry," Otto said after a beat, taking Tallulah by the arm. "Not long at all." He led her in the direction of his police car.

Abby glanced over at the van, where Dr. Figelson had taken her seat and Virgil was turning on the ignition. Kat was giving directions to Virgil.

"Head that way," she said, pointing left. "Lemon Lane

goes all the way down and exits out onto Chestnut. Chestnut connects to Main Street."

Virgil slowly backed up the van and then inched it down the alleyway. After turning the corner, the van disappeared from sight.

Abby watched in silence and said a mental good-bye to Chef Jean-Louis Bonheur. Their colorful, madcap, illustrious chef was gone. He had blessed Las Flores with his savory tarts, sugar-dusted *oreillettes,* and delectable honey-almond madeleines. She smiled, recalling how she had wheedled the madeleine recipe out of him, but she knew deep down hers would never taste like his. He had had the gift.

Whoever had taken Jean-Louis's life had robbed Las Flores of its culinary genius. For a split second, Abby found herself wishing she were back on the force, one of the team members who would get to the bottom of his mysterious death. But when she heard Kat's radio go off and Chief Bob Allen's clipped voice demanding yet another update, she just as quickly surrendered the wish.

Walking toward her Jeep, Abby called out to Kat and Otto, "Catch you all later. I don't want to be late for my meeting with the district attorney. I've got reports to turn in and a check to collect."

"When can I get a look at those photos?" Kat called back, walking toward Abby.

"Soon. Let me off-load them onto a thumb drive. Question. What's the coroner's estimated time of death?"

"Based on body temp, she's giving it a window. Between three and five this morning."

Abby slid into the driver's seat of her Jeep.

"Choir practice later?" Kat called out.

Kat had used their secret code for "drink after work." Abby knew that if Otto overheard their plans for a drink, he would insist on joining them. She didn't mind Otto so much. He seemed starved for company, in spite of being married. His wife was the West Coast regional director of an ambulance company and was gone more than she was home. Otto hung out mostly with Bernie, the annoying skirt chaser who worked in the evidence room. When those guys swilled more than a couple of beers, they turned into Village Idiot One and Two. They unabashedly flirted with the usual barflies and the more respectable ladies, who would just laugh at them as the men one-upped each other with stupid pickup lines.

Abby cringed as she recalled one Saint Patrick's Day when some of her fellow officers had finished their shifts and met up at the Black Witch for green beer. Bernie and Otto had shown up, too. She had let Bernie convince her to join him for a new dance step he'd learned. She only had to hold out her arm straight and steady, with her fingers locked with his. Abby hadn't been too sure she believed Bernie's story about recently taking Argentine tango lessons, but she'd reluctantly complied. More like a teenager instead of a fourteen-year veteran of the police force, Bernie had awkwardly twirled himself in, blocked her leg, lost his balance, and crashed, taking her down with him.

Disentangling her legs from his beefy body and searching for the shoe that had flow off her foot when she hit the floor, Abby had winced at the laughter of the patrons and had hissed at Bernie, "Never again." *Never.*

"So whaddya say?" Kat asked.

"You buying?"

"My turn?" Kat grinned.

"Yep," Abby replied, handing her a sprig of lavender from the tied bunch lying on the passenger seat. "It clears the nose when you've had to smell something unpleasant, like a dead body."

"Why, thank you. So about tonight . . . my shift ends at seven . . . half hour to get to the cottage. What say we review the crime-scene images after we eat? I'll make sandwiches."

"Sounds good." Abby turned the key in the ignition. "Oh, and I'll be interested in what you find on the surveillance camera behind the faux ivy that was on the baker's rack. The plastic cup that fell off the rack is still there. Smells of booze."

Pulling away, Abby glanced in the rearview mirror to see Kat racing back into the pastry shop. She hoped that the video had the killer's mug on it or something else that could point the investigation in the right direction.

Honey-Almond Madeleines

Ingredients:
3 large egg whites, at room temperature
1 cup powdered sugar, sifted
½ cup unbleached all-purpose flour, sifted
⅓ cup finely ground blanched almonds
6 tablespoons unsalted butter, softened (almost melted), plus extra for greasing 2 madeleine baking tins
1 tablespoon honey

Directions:
Preheat the oven to 400°F. Grease 2 madeleine baking tins with butter.

In a large stainless-steel or copper bowl, beat the egg whites to soft peaks. Add the powdered sugar and beat the whites to stiff peaks. Gently fold the flour and almonds into the whites in 4 additions.

In a small bowl, combine the butter and honey and mix well. Gently fold the honey butter into the almond–egg white mixture.

Spoon the batter into the prepared molds, filling them about two-thirds full. Bake for 8 to 10 minutes, or until the outer edges of the madeleines are golden brown.

Remove the madeleines from the oven and allow them to cool in the tins for 5 minutes. Then remove them from the molds and arrange them on a wire rack to cool completely.

Makes 3 dozen cookies

Chapter 3

To get stronger eggshells, feed your chickens
extra calcium.

—*Henny Penny Farmette Almanac*

Kat's cottage squatted behind a three-story Victorian with ornate gingerbread trim and a large wraparound porch with a swing. Unlatching the iron side gate, Abby swung it open and followed the gray stone walkway through drifts of silver maiden grass leaning over a low-growing row of mounding native violets. The scent of wild hedge roses and eucalyptus tinged the air with a spicy pungency that Abby loved.

She hadn't done a whole lot of socializing after leaving the force, that is, until Clay entered her life. But even he preferred nights in—cooking together and dancing through the unfinished kitchen—to dining out. After he left, friends had accused Abby of becoming a hermit. Tonight, it felt rather nice to slip into a girly dress and stylish heels for a change. But each precarious step on the gray paving stones tested Abby's ability to steer the two-inch silver pencil heels of her taupe-colored Anne Kleins away from the cracks.

After limping to the red door with the brass kick plate and antique Victorian knocker, Abby leaned against it and removed her high heels. Holding them with two fingers of one hand, she tucked her clutch bag under her arm and raised the fist-shaped striker. The knocker was one of Kat's prized flea market finds.

She banged the striker twice.

"I'm in the kitchen," Kat called out.

Abby pushed open the heavy oak door, then entered the living room and dropped her heels next to Kat's steel-toed duty boots. The cottage's cozy interior, its biscuit-colored walls and soft furnishings in muted hues, offered a warm—and eclectic—charm. Though she was a twenty-eight-year-old, Kat surrounded herself with old things found at white elephant sales, antique and consignment shops, architectural salvage yards, and, of course, flea markets. Finding unusual items from bygone eras was an interest that she and Abby shared.

Sinking into a cushion of Kat's saddleback couch, Abby opened her clutch to remove the thumb drive containing the crime-scene photos. She stood, dropped her clutch on the couch, slipped the thumb drive into her pocket, and maneuvered through the cramped space between an accent chair, covered in needlepoint embroidery depicting young lovers surrounded by turtledoves, and a mahogany tea table, its doily-covered surface crowded with assorted china pieces. Passing the ornate floor lamp with way too much fringe hanging from its rose silk shade, she quickly gazed beyond the arched doorway and trained her eyes on the modest-size kitchen, where Kat was busily arranging sandwiches on a platter.

"Something smells good."

"French onion soup," Kat replied, grabbing a spoon to stir the steaming pot on the back burner. "Nothing fancy . . .

just takeout from Whole Eats. I didn't have time to make the real deal." After putting down the spoon, Kat reached for the lid of the deli mustard jar and screwed it in place. She opened the refrigerator, and placed the jar on a shelf of the door. "Iced tea okay?" she asked, removing the pitcher.

"Sure," Abby replied, lifting up one small square of crustless bread on a sandwich from the platter on the table and examining the spread under it.

"Chicken salad with cucumber," Kat said, refilling her own tall glass with cubes of ice and tea and pouring one for Abby.

"I can see that. My favorite."

After returning the pitcher to the fridge and closing the door, Kat turned to face Abby and quickly scrutinized her attire. "Jeez, I haven't seen you dressed up this much since when Clay was around. Looking pretty good for a farm girl. Forget the shoes?"

"No. Left them by the front door. Seemed like a good idea when I put them on, but I think I've forgotten how to walk in heels."

Kat smiled. "I know what you mean," she said, sipping tea and motioning for Abby to sit. "My two cents . . . the lower the heel, the better. Who says women look best on stilts? I'm all about comfort."

Abby nodded. She slid into one of the mismatched chairs at the cherrywood table. "I doubt this little black dress would look as lovely paired with my ladybug clod-hoppers," Abby deadpanned.

"Uh, no, you didn't say that! But I get what you're saying about comfort." Kat set her tea glass on the table and fetched the one for Abby. "This pantsuit is a relic, but it's so easy to move in, and I got it for a great price. You think it looks dated? I could change."

"Nah. The retro look suits your figure, and the apple-green color is nice on you. Lots of blondes wear that shade."

"Tell the truth now. You just like it because it reminds you of that organic lettuce you grow."

"Okay. Maybe it's that, too. Speaking of vegetables, I've got a thing for onions. Is that soup ready? I'm famished." Abby reached for the empty tureen on the table and admired the flow blue iris pattern for a moment before handing it to Kat.

Pouring the soup from the stainless-steel pot into her prized china tureen, Kat turned her head away from the vapor cloud, which threatened to steam off her makeup. She ladled a generous helping into Abby's bowl before filling her own dish. After fastidiously wiping the edge of the tureen with a tea towel and placing it on the white Battenberg lace tablecloth, she dropped into the chair that Abby had pushed out for her. "You know that surveillance video from the pastry shop?" Kat asked. "Didn't have anything on it."

"You mean it didn't show the murder or the killer's face?"

"No, I mean there was nothing on it. It's like Chef Jean-Louis hooked the camera up to test it and never turned it on again."

"Really?" Abby shook her head in disbelief. "With the heated arguments going on in that kitchen, you'd think he would have wanted to capture them. You know, in case he ever needed to prove a point. But why even buy a camera if you are not going to use it?"

"Who knows? Las Flores might be a stone's throw from Silicon Valley, but it might surprise you to learn that not everyone is into technology," Kat said. "Anyway, if you are in a state to end your life, you probably aren't thinking about turning on a camera."

"So you think it was suicide?" Abby lifted a sandwich from the platter and placed it on her plate.

"Not necessarily. You know we have to rule out the possibility it was murder."

Abby nodded, pinched off a portion of her chicken sandwich, and placed it in her mouth. Slowly chewing, she pondered what she really knew about the pastry chef. She soon realized it wasn't much. "You think you know people," she murmured.

Kat nodded and sipped the broth on her soup spoon. Looking up, she said, "I don't get it. Hanging yourself isn't exactly easy. And if someone else took his life, wouldn't it be even more difficult? I mean, he would fight back. Why not just shoot him?"

Abby swallowed a mouthful of iced tea and wiped the bottom of the sweating glass with a napkin before setting it back on the tablecloth. "Well, hanging tells us two things. It's so hands on, it's personal, and it's unlikely to have been done by a woman, unless she had a lot of strength. I could see a woman using a gun, a knife, or a blunt object—"

"Let's not forget poison," said Kat.

"Or poison. And statistics bear that out. So I'm betting that if Jean-Louis did not do this to himself, our killer is a guy." Dabbing her lips with the napkin, Abby added, "Makes you wonder who has a motive for murder besides those loan sharks and the landlord."

"We've cleared the loan sharks. They were attending a convention in Sacramento."

"Really? Since when do loan sharks attend conventions?"

"When they are investment counselors, too. They have hotel receipts and time-stamped tickets from the parking garage," Kat said. "We're taking a close look at his lovers, family members, disgruntled employees, the usual suspects," she added after a moment.

Abby finished eating her sandwich in silence, staring absentmindedly past Kat at a poster on the wall depicting various breads and pastries. She pictured in her mind Chef Jean-Louis standing in his pastry shop kitchen, dusting mini Bundt cakes with powdered sugar, and singing along with a CD of Maria Callas belting out Puccini's "O mio babbino caro." That image seemed so incongruous with the image of the chef with a rope around his neck.

Kat's voice intruded. "Apparently, he took that video camera out of the box and stuck it up there on the shelf, behind the ivy, but never used it."

"What about the decorative box that was up there, too? Find anything in that?"

"Just personal items. Mainly recipes that looked like they'd been copied . . . some on napkins and paper towels. The paperwork for that award he won last year . . . You remember that televised bake-off in Las Vegas, don't you?"

Abby nodded. "Watched it on TV, like everyone else. Quite an honor for Jean-Louis and Las Flores . . . but he clearly had created a spectacular dessert, and that sugar embellishment was the crowning touch. That plaque hangs on the wall in his shop."

"You'd think with all the hoopla, and it being Las Vegas and all, the award could have been a little nicer, maybe a crystal bowl or an eggbeater with a jewel-studded handle or something like that," said Kat. "But for all his creative genius, fabulous recipes, and hard work, they gave him an ugly little plaque with his name and the title 'Best Pastry Chef.'"

"It's the honor, not the plaque," said Abby.

"I know, but, Abby, in that box I got a look at some of his amazing handwritten recipes. Well, technically, the handwriting appears to be his, but we are taking a closer look."

Abby sipped a spoonful of broth before posing another question. "Anything else in that box?"

"Family pictures and a letter of agreement between the chef and a guy named Etienne. The contract had a secrecy clause that forbade Etienne from revealing or exploiting the recipes the chef created, and threatened legal action if he did."

"No kidding. So only Etienne? Were there similar contracts with others?" asked Abby.

"Nope."

"So why had the chef singled out Etienne?"

"Apparently, Chef Jean-Louis was mentoring him," explained Kat. "That is, until he fired him two weeks ago. According to Otto, who questioned him, Etienne went from liking his boss to thinking he was a master manipulator who exploited people and circumstances to get what he wanted in life."

"Well, that's not a very nice thing to say. Let me guess. Etienne has felt the brunt of the chef's hot temper?"

"Pretty much. Etienne said he quit, but Talullah says Etienne was fired."

"Could be a motive."

"Yes, but Etienne has an alibi."

A frown creased Abby's forehead. "Okay, let's back up. The chef was working. His kitchen light was on. No signs of forced entry. Someone walked in."

Kat rubbed her temple. "Whoever went into the kitchen area must have entered through the back door, somehow subdued the chef, and killed him."

Abby voiced her thoughts. "I found him on the floor without his apron and with twine on the pantry door. The ovens were on, and cakes were burning. It was daylight, for goodness' sake, and the back door stood ajar, yet no one, apparently, knew he was lying there in his kitchen, dead." She inhaled deeply. What she needed was more oxygen to her own brain. She was beginning to feel incapable of clear and logical thinking. "Okay, that means we have to put together a timeline, find someone who saw the chef come to work, locate folks who might recall seeing the chef during the last twenty-four hours."

Kat nodded. "And we've already started working on that." She polished off the last of her soup. Wiping her mouth with the edge of her napkin, she said, "There was an opportunity for a robbery. The killer could have grabbed the money out of the cash register but didn't. We did a walk-through with Tallulah, who makes the bank deposits on Wednesdays and Fridays, and she said that although they didn't keep much money in the cash drawer, it didn't appear as though any had been taken."

Abby bit into another chicken salad sandwich square. "So if robbery wasn't the motive, was it a crime of opportunity? One in which the killer used as a murder weapon anything close at hand, maybe the strings of the apron? But then why take the apron? Doesn't make a lot of sense, unless that is really what happened and the killer was concerned about his or her epithelials still on the apron ties."

Kat ran a finger through the film of moisture that had formed at the top of her tea glass.

Straightening in her chair, Abby closed her eyes for a moment to collect her thoughts. Then, looking straight at Kat, she said, "Okay, so what if the killer wanted something else . . . something they could steal and sell for drugs or whatever? Maybe it was a burglary."

Kat looked at her. "What if the scene was just made to look like a burglary, but the motive was personal vengeance?"

"That works, too," said Abby. "Although," she added, "when murder is payback, it's usually for something really egregious. What could Chef Jean-Louis have done to anyone that would rise to that level?"

Kat chewed her lip. "Good question."

Abby wiped her fingers on her napkin while she considered other options. "So who would want to exact revenge and for what? An ex-lover, maybe?"

"Possibly," said Kat. "But who hasn't been dumped? You get over it. You don't kill the other person."

"Not if you're in your right mind. But love makes you crazy." Abby folded the napkin and set it back on the table. She pushed her fingers through her hair, absentmindedly adjusting the comb above her right ear. "Tallulah said Chef Jean-Louis argued with his landlord over the lease renewal."

"And the landlord's motive for murder would be what? When you want a tenant out, you evict."

"True," Abby replied. "I don't know. . . . Maybe it wasn't the landlord but someone who wanted to humiliate the chef. Or maybe he took his own life. People do hang themselves. But then, as I think about it, that doesn't work, either. . . . He put cakes in the ovens and hid his apron and then hung himself."

"Good point." Kat leaned back and laced her fingers together at the back of her neck. A stumped expression crossed her face.

Abby closed her eyes and mentally reviewed the facts for the umpteenth time, noting the holes. Finally, she looked over at Kat. "I know it's not my official business, Kat, but I admit to being fascinated . . . and deadly curious, so to speak."

Kat smiled and shook her head. "And that's just like you to say something like that."

"I find this case puzzling," said Abby. "We can speculate all we want, but we're short on facts. So, to fill in the blanks, let's take a look at the photos I snapped of the scene. Then, tomorrow, you and your partner can continue with your knock and talk with people in the neighborhood, and you can find out the names of all Jean-Louis's former lovers, friends, and enemies. Let's determine who saw him on the last day and night so we can keep working the time-line, and then let's find out what the coroner's investigation turned up."

While Kat cleared the kitchen table, Abby loaded the file of digital images onto Kat's laptop. Then Kat sat down and methodically clicked through the images. When she got to one particular photo, Kat zoomed in and pointed to the abrasion marks around the chef's neck. She clicked to the next picture, a close-up of the chef's forearm tattoo, which looked like the number ninety-six.

She and Abby both leaned in for a closer look.

"Do you think it's some kind of baking symbol?" Abby asked.

"We have a file of gang tattoos, but when we can't identify them, we take pictures of them to the guys who actually do the inking."

"Tattoo artists?" Abby asked.

"Some call themselves ink masters."

"Wait a minute," said Abby. "We're looking at this upside down. It's actually more like sixty-nine, but with the numerals on their sides. I've seen that symbol before." Her brow furrowed. "Yes, I think, in the horoscope column of the *Weekly*. Isn't it the symbol of the crab's claws? Cancer. People born in the last week of June and the first three weeks of July are Cancers, aren't they?"

Kat smiled. "Well, that would fit with the chef's birth-day of July eighteenth."

They stared at the next image—a photo of the chef in the kitchen, surrounded by his employees that apparently had been taken at some earlier time.

"You said the chef barked at you some time ago and then apologized, explaining that he had been upset with Etienne. I wonder which one of the faces in that photograph is Etienne's."

Abby peered intently. "Hmm, good question." She stopped on the next image to explain. "I snapped this photo of a photo because it hung on the wall behind the cash register, and I wondered if any of the people, once identified, could help in the investigation. Clearly, that's Jean-Louis there front and center. It's hard to make out the young man with the shaved head. The other two guys in suits look out of place. Why not see if Tallulah can identify the men in this photo?"

"Sure," Kat said, bobbing her head.

"You know," Abby mused, "the chef's business partner could give you access to personnel records."

"Otto is already doing database cross-checking of the people the chef knew and worked with."

"Good." Abby studied the image on the screen, as if doing so could somehow reveal more than what her eyes could actually see. Her intuitive sense was both a blessing and a curse, one that had surely been passed from her grandmother Rose after skipping a generation. Rose could be briskly walking hand in hand with Abby, late to church, only to change direction to avoid crossing paths with someone she sensed bore an ill temper.

When Abby was only four years old, she had rightly discerned that the messenger knocking on her grandmother's door was bringing devastating news. Rose's husband, Mac, Abby's grandfather, had been thrown from the horse he'd been riding to inspect the farm fences. Grandma Rose had warned him not to get on that horse, but Mac had laughed off her worry as just a woman's prattling. In the accident he had injured his back in two places and had broken several bones. The vet had had to put down the mare. It took nearly a year for Mac to mend, and after he did recover, he never saddled up again without first checking with his wife.

Kat said, "Whatever else went on, those ligature marks make it pretty clear Jean-Louis passed away from asphyxiation by hanging."

"It's so late. Should we still have that nightcap?"

Kat tilted her head toward the door. "I'm up for it if you are."

"Uh-huh. I'll have one glass of wine and then head home. First thing tomorrow, I've got to pick up a truckload of compost."

"Again?"

"Yep. I'm going to put in some plants just for the bees."

"But I thought that's what you did last year, when I helped you plant all that rosemary and lavender."

"Yes, but bees need year-round food sources, so I keep thinking of new flowers, blooming trees, and bulbs that the bees will love and that will impart good flavor to the honey they produce. I get the dark amber honey that tastes earthy and comes from the pollen of the early blooming eucalyptus and the long flowering stems of lavender, but not until late summer. I'm already thinking ahead to next spring." Abby's voice bubbled with perkiness, as it always did whenever she talked about her bees. "Kat, just imagine the palest golden honey, harvested in early spring, that tastes exquisitely like the earliest woodland wildflowers."

Kat regarded her longtime friend with a bemused expression. "A truckload of compost sounds like a lot."

"The farmette soil is clay, like concrete. It might take a couple of truck-bed loads, along with some gypsum, to get the soil amended correctly. Then I'm going to plant a couple of fast-growing eucalyptus trees. I've been coveting the ones with the green-gray leaves and the creamy white flowers that bloom from spring through summer, like those on that land adjacent to mine. Although, back there, other varieties of eucalyptus have pink, wispy blossoms that bloom in late September. Oh, the bees will love that flower, and Chef Jean-Louis will love—" The words caught in Abby's throat. She bit her lower lip and heaved an audible sigh upon realizing the chef was gone . . . truly gone.

"He would surely have loved your spring honey, girlfriend. I guess now you can sell it to other pastry shops."

Abby looked at her darkly and girded herself with resolve. "No. I can't do that. I promised Jean-Louis that I wouldn't." She thought for a moment before revealing to Kat, "You know, I haven't yet told the bees that Jean-Louis is gone."

Kat raised an eyebrow. "Now you're sounding kooky."

"No, listen. The chef actually came out to the farmette to inspect the bees. He wasn't afraid. He just walked to the hives and stood there, watching and listening, as if he was tuning in to the bees and allowing the bees to sense him. He tasted the honey, loved it, and told me he wanted regular deliveries."

"Hmm," Kat murmured, shaking her head, as if she wasn't fully comprehending but was thinking that perhaps it didn't matter. "I'd still love a swig of red, if you don't mind. What say we make it a quick one?"

Abby found the crowd at the Black Witch Bar unusually animated for a work night. As she and Kat pushed past people to a table at the back, Abby overheard some at the bar wildly speculating.

"Do you think it was murder? Or did the chef kill himself because of depression over a lover's spat?"

"Did his business partner do him in?"

"Is the killer on the loose in Las Flores?"

The chef's demise had become heady leavening for local whispers. Gossip had increased in volume like a loaf of yeasted dough resting in the sun. The chatter annoyed Abby, and she tried not to listen to the conversations around the room by checking her watch against the clock on the back wall, next to the bathrooms. Both timepieces affirmed what her body was already telling her: 11:30 p.m., well past her usual time for bed. Houdini would be sounding his cock-a-doodle-doo long before dawn.

The din of the bar had gotten so loud that Abby dreaded the thought of even trying to talk. Three bikers in leather club jackets and jeans, one with a Hells Angels insignia, began a game of darts in the alcove at the end of the bar. Elsewhere, tall bistro tables and wooden booths—gouged, carved, and burned with initials, hearts, peace symbols, and other graffiti—served as conversation pits for the rough crowd of locals who had drifted in and anyone else seeking companionship in a social setting that included alcohol.

On the large flat-screen TV mounted on the wall opposite the bar, a perfectly coiffed blonde with large lips painted hot pink and wearing an indigo suit, a white blouse, and a fuchsia scarf, offered a sound bite to the local television crew about her plan for fiscal change and jailhouse reform when she was elected mayor. Abby leaned toward Kat.

"Isn't that the councilwoman in the mayor's race?"

"Sure is. Her name's Eva Lennahan. Already acting like she's governor. Her detractors say she has a huge ego and is politically driven. But others love her for her charity work. She has quite a few supporters, and . . . guess what? Our very own Chief Bob Allen is one of them."

"Airbrushed makeup. Perfect hair. Her own entourage," said Abby. "She must have dough."

"More money than God. She's married to a venture cap-
italist, you know. He keeps a low profile, but I'm guessing
he's just like the others who build McMansions and think
they can do whatever they want, whether or not it's good
for the rest of us or our local environment."

Abby was about to ask Eva's husband's name when the
waitress hustled over to take their drink order. The old gal
was wearing a low-cut top that showed a little too much
of her aging boobs, which resembled wrinkled goose eggs.
The cheap perfume she wore did little to mask the smell of
tobacco smoke. The overpowering scent was almost more
than Abby could bear in the poorly ventilated room.

"I know you ladies need a glass of something. What can
I get you?" the waitress asked in a gravelly voice.

"I'll have the house merlot," Abby said, then leaned forward to read the woman's name and added, "Toots."

Kat chimed in, "Oh, make it two."

"Coming right up," said the overly cheerful waitress,
turning away.

Abby watched as the woman balanced her tray and
cruised by two other tables before scurrying back to the
bar with new orders. With her thoughts drifting back to
the case, Abby said, "If the cause of death is undetermined
or suicide, the police department will close the case, Kat.
But if it is homicide or manslaughter, I guess you'll be
working it for a while, won't you?"

Kat nodded and said, "I love a good puzzle as much as
you." She laid a twenty-dollar bill on the table and reached
for the wineglass the cocktail waitress had set before her.

"My turn next time," said Abby.

"Ah, that's okay. I know how tight finances are for you.
I wish that farmette of yours wasn't such a money pit,"
Kat said. She clinked her glass against Abby's. After a sip,

she changed the subject. "The part I hate about this job is notifying the first of kin."

Abby only half heard Kat's comment; her attention had been diverted to a bar patron's foulmouthed complaints rising over the din. She heard the man clearly say, "Why don't you fairies beat it? No one wants you here. It's your kind that's ruining this town."

Kat turned to look in the same direction. "Know him?"

"No," Abby replied. "But I'd wager he is *not* a card-carrying member of the LGBT coalition." She listened as the man's rhetoric became increasingly inflammatory.

"I try to have a pleasant off-duty moment, and now I have to deal with a jerk," Kat said, sliding off her stool. "Better find out why he's so angry."

They picked their way through the crowd, toward the man who stood at the bar near the front door, sipping from a beer mug. His sleeveless, faded work shirt revealed a heavily tattooed arm, shoulder to wrist. Abby soon figured out that the man's diatribe was directed at two young men nearby who clearly were more interested in each other than they were the crusty biker spewing vitriol.

"Is there a problem?" Kat asked the biker.

Before Abby could hear his reply, she tripped. Her high heel had caught in a mesh gym bag on the floor. Trying to regain her balance, she knocked bar napkins to the floor and fell against the troublemaker, causing his beer to slosh across his mouth, coat his mustache and chin, and dribble down his leather vest. In one fluid motion, the man slid his beer mug onto the bar and drew back his tattooed arm to lodge a blow. Apparently realizing at the last possible moment that he was about to hit a woman, he dropped his fist and glared at Abby.

Abby stood her ground. For a middle-aged biker, out of

shape most likely from hard living, drugs, and booze, this guy seemed as tense as a new spring on a screen door. She wobbled backward on her heel and grabbed onto the bar. Holding the bar with one hand, she used the other to disentangle her heel from the mesh. Then she locked eyes with the biker. "Sorry. My fault. I didn't see the bag."

Impaling her with his gaze, the biker swiped the beer from his mustache with a single downward stroke of his hand. Addressing the two gay men, he said, "Why don't one of you get up and give a real lady a place to sit?"

"No," Abby insisted. "Stay where you are. That's okay." The two young men, who looked like bankers in their dark suits and pastel shirts, huddled as still as statues, their eyes frozen on the mirror behind the bartender, where they could see the other tough guys in the room without turning around. They seemed frozen with fear, apparently too afraid even to sip their cocktails.

The bartender wiped his hands on a towel and pointed to the other end of the bar while he addressed the foul-mouthed biker. "Two seats at the end, Harlan. I can serve you there just as easily as here."

The biker shook his head in defiance. "Screw you. I ain't going nowhere. This is where I always sit. Except this fairy is in my seat."

"Suit yourself," the bartender replied and returned to wiping down the counter.

"Sir." Kat addressed Harlan in her most authoritative tone. "These men have every right to be here."

"These aren't men. They're sissies." The biker pivoted his large frame awkwardly to lock eyes with Kat. "And who the hell are you, anyway? Why don't you just keep movin' toward that there door?" Harlan said. "Or I'll give you a reason to wish you had. Show you what a real man can do." He stepped forward in his steel-toed boots. "This is none of your freaking business, little lady."

"Actually, it is," Kat replied coldly. "What say, let's share some ID?" She opened her purse and flashed her badge at Harlan and the barkeep. "So, I've shown you mine. Let's have a look at yours."

"Cop. Shoulda known." Harlan gave a yank on the chain attached to the wallet in his rear pocket. He removed his identification and handed it to Kat.

"Your name, sir?" Kat asked, glancing over at the bartender, who held up eight fingers, apparently one for each beer Harlan had downed.

"You can see right there, it's Sweeney. Harlan Sweeney."

"Well, Harlan Sweeney, are you drunk?"

"Maybe. Free country. I gotta right to drink and to express my opinion."

"Just the same, Mr. Sweeney." Kat handed back the ID. "You are harassing these men. Here's your choice. . . . You can go back to your own crib or the jail."

He seemed at a loss for words. The din dropped to a murmur. Everyone's attention was now on the biker and Kat. A few patrons, apparently not wanting to hang around for a police action, dashed for the door.

Abby watched the man, thinking maybe Kat should have called for backup before confronting him. Abby knew from experience that showing the bad guys your badge always seemed to piss them off. But she also suspected that Kat was packing a concealed weapon, in case things got too out of control. As the man slid his wallet back into his jeans pocket, Abby's gaze followed his hand's movement. She noted the narrow strip, which resembled twine, threaded through the biker's belt loops.

"I get claustrophobic in tight places," the man finally

drawled, stepping back to let Kat pass. "Besides . . ." He drilled his eyes into Abby's and cocked his head toward the two young banker types. "You never know who has sprawled on those jail cots." His wink at Abby was unmistakable even in bar light. "I hate boozin' with fairies." His forced laugh was as coarse as sanded grout.

Abby flinched. She knew better than to comment. Kat told the bartender to call a cab for Mr. Sweeney and said she'd get a cruiser out to make sure the guy actually got home. Abby followed Kat past Sweeney, but he reached out and grabbed her arm.

"Next time," he said, addressing Abby, "why don't you and I have a drink together? Get to know each other better?"

"In your dreams," she hissed, wrenching free of his grasp.

Outside, Abby watched the bar door, while Kat called in the disturbance. They waited until they saw the cruiser pull up. Kat briefly exchanged words with the officer. Then she and Abby walked in lockstep past the dozen or so motorcycles parked at the meters in front of the bar. They strode at a brisk clip past the pizza parlor, the antique shop, and the quilting store, then finally turned the corner onto Church Street, where they stopped momentarily in front of the padlocked wrought-iron gates of the Church of the Holy Names. Holding on to the gate, Abby removed her left high heel to rub her foot.

"You let him off easy," she said.

"Seriously, you think me and you and Toots could've taken him?"

"Not in heels," Abby joked.

"A guy like that is easy to find. He mouths off too much. We'll get around to questioning him, if not in this case, then in another one."

Tips for Growing Lavender

- Pick the right type of lavender for your gardening purposes and for your area's microclimate.

- Grow the lavender in raised beds in which pea-sized gravel, sand, or chicken grit has been incorporated.

- Add aged manure to the soil for extra nutrients.

- Give the lavender plants room to spread out. This will ensure adequate air circulation as they grow upward.

- Keep the soil slightly acidic and don't overwater the lavender.

- Clip back the lavender as needed to avoid a heavy pruning. But prune tall varieties roughly a third of their height in early spring.

Chapter 4

Producing manure is easy; it's the moving of it
that takes patience and the right shovel.

—*Henny Penny Farmette Almanac*

Abby leaned on the wooden handle of the utility broom
and stared at the small mountain of black compost
she'd swept from the truck bed onto the ground. Pulling
the broad brim of her straw hat down to shield her eyes
from the sun, she proffered silent thanks for friends like
Lucas Crawford, who had given her the key to his 1958
Ford pickup and permission to use it whenever she needed
to haul supplies or building materials. Lucas had lovingly
restored it but hardly used the truck anymore. Most people who knew him figured Lucas saw his truck as part of
the past. . . . And Lucas was trying to forget the past.

For years, Lucas and his red truck with CRAWFORD FEED
AND FARM SUPPLIES emblazoned on the doors were as much
a part of the landscape as the two-lane roads that crisscrossed Las Flores. Lucas delivered bales of hay, various
types of feed, salt licks, and even baby chicks throughout
the county and sometimes across the county line. After he
married, Lucas's feed-store employees joked that he had

fixed up that old truck—which matched his wife's hair color—so that if Lucas, who seemed to be a woman magnet, was ever tempted to dally, he'd see the truck and fear the wrath of that little redhead to whom he'd hitched his destiny.

Abby stiffened at the thought of the tragedy that had befallen Lucas in the past year. Business had been so good that when Lucas found out he was about to become a father, he and his wife had purchased a prime piece of real estate in the southern part of the county. There they planned to build their dream home. Six weeks after the building started, Lucas's wife, who was recovering from the flu and was feeling well enough to visit the construction site, suffered a relapse. Fungal spores in the dust out there, which were known to cause valley fever, increased the load on the poor woman's weakened immune system. Pneumonia set in. Her passing had shocked everyone.

After the burial, Lucas wanted nothing to do with the south county property. He secluded himself on the ranch up the hill from Abby's place. Back at the feed store, where Abby bought her chicken pellets, customers and staff gossiped about how his wife's death had pushed Lucas off purpose with the life he had planned. Abby felt sorry for Lucas but refused to be another one of the town's unmarried ladies who delivered casseroles to the poor guy. He had lost his wife and unborn child and needed time to grieve. Lucas, everyone said, showed up for work as punctually as ever but kept to himself. He seemed to have lost his passion for everything, including his prized red truck. Most days, it could be seen parked in front of the old gray barn at the entrance to the Crawford property—one hill away from Abby's farmette.

That was where Abby had found it when she needed to haul the compost. Just as she'd expected, it was Houdini's crow—not the alarm she'd set—that had awakened her before six o'clock. Fifteen minutes later, she'd arrived at the Crawford place. A raccoon had left a pattern of fresh paw prints across the truck's dusty hood. Abby had smiled when she'd seen it, and had reminded herself to wash the truck before returning it. Back in the day, Lucas had kept that truck spotless. She figured it was the least she could do after using it at the Go Green and Recycle facility where she'd gotten the load of aged manure.

Now, back at the farmette, with the compost swept from the truck bed, she would have the rest of the morning and the greater part of the afternoon to ferry the earthy-scented black mound from the front of the property to the back garden. Tossing the broom to the ground, Abby jumped off the tailgate, latched it, and marched through the big wooden gate with the broken hinge to retrieve the faded blue wheelbarrow that was behind her house.

Abby's high spirits sank when she spotted the wheelbarrow's flat tire. Grimacing, she realized that not only would she would have to fix the tire, but she would also have to plant those six raspberry vines. Their roots remained suspended in the galvanized bucket of water that sat in the wheelbarrow bin, right where she'd left them the day the DA called. That was the day before Jean-Louis died.

"Arghhh," she growled under her breath. *Serves me right for thinking I was going to catch up. The vines, the tire, the truck . . . Better do them in that order.* Resigned to the tasks ahead of her, Abby turned and stiffly marched to the tool-shed to fetch the shovel, a tire patch, and the bicycle pump. When her cell phone chimed in her jeans pocket, Abby jumped. *Now what?* After removing a glove, she retrieved the phone, pushed the side button, swiped her finger across the screen, and lifted the phone to her ear.

"Etienne *is* in that picture . . . but is not one of the guys in a suit. . . . He is the one with the shaved head." Kat's voice sounded matter-of-fact.

"Whatever happened to saying hello first?" Abby asked en route to the toolshed. Noticing the profusion of leafy grapevines spilling over the fence into weeds that threatened to dwarf the toolshed, Abby blew air between her lips. *Pull weeds. Oh, and by hand, too, seeing as how the weed whacker is broken.* She uttered a barely audible "Rats!"

"Abby?"

"I'm here. Just . . . here," Abby said with resignation.

"I know that tone of voice," Kat said. "You're annoyed about something . . . or everything. . . . What died, broke down, or can't be fixed on the farmette today?"

Abby kept silent. What was the point in giving more power to Kat, who insisted that the farmette was a headache and a money eater . . . even if it was true? Better to keep silent. One did that for best friends who could never truly grasp one's infatuation with the scent of loamy earth, the sight of flower spikes swaying in a vagrant breeze, and the screech of a scrub jay hidden in a bush, or one's delight at the first bite of a ripe persimmon plucked from your own tree.

"Okay," Kat said. "Let's start again. Good morning, girlfriend. Is all well on the farmette?"

"Just dealing with the usual annoyances," Abby replied.

"I know you don't want to hear this again," Kat said, "but, honestly, Abby, you're living like an old lady. You seem to have forgotten that there is a whole world of things you used to love . . . going down to McGillicutty's to listen to the Irish fiddle music or over to the theater to watch the latest foreign film. You never want to have dinner at Zazi's anymore, because you worry that if you don't make it home before sundown, the hawks will carry off your chickens. You're thirty-seven, Abby, and single. There's plenty of time to be sixty-seven in about three decades! Girl, your chickens get more action than you do."

"You think?" Abby didn't hide her irritation at being reminded of what she clearly knew.

"Look, I tell you these things only because you're my friend and I care about you."

"I know . . . and I'm sorry the farmette is so labor-intensive right now. But, Kat, I'm empire building here—one plant, one tree, and one jar of honey at a time. I can socialize once I'm through with this intense period of work and the farmette is supporting me." Abby quickly changed the subject. "So let's get to why you called. You've identified Etienne?"

"Yes. When Otto interviewed him, he had hair, but Tallulah says that shaved-headed guy in the picture is Etienne. His real name is Steve Flanders, and Chef Jean-Louis was the only person to ever call him Etienne. Steve, she said, was always reinventing himself and thought the name had more culinary cachet than his given name. Apparently, this is his French phase. Oh, and get this. . . . Tallulah said she suspected the chef and Etienne had a little pas de deux going on, until Etienne stopped showing up for work. Tallulah said Chef Jean-Louis suspected Etienne of sticking his fingers in the cash register, where they didn't belong, and the chef was tired of it and canned him."

"That so? We know the killer didn't hit the cash register, so Etienne's firing becomes his motive for murder? Doesn't seem like a strong enough reason." Abby turned away from the toolshed and continued down a gravel path to the apricot tree where she had propped supports under the limbs heavy with nearly ripe fruit. "Anyway, you said Etienne had an alibi. Is it airtight?"

"Not a hundred percent. Checking it out right after I leave here."

"So where are you?"

"At the county health department." Kat lowered her voice. "With Chief Bob Allen. Lordy, he's all over this. Even canceled a meeting this morning to be here. Just like when you and I were partners, and he never wanted one of us to tell the other anything until we had told him first. The chief still insists on not just being in the loop but also being the first to know everything. I was thinking that he could actually help us by steering the investigation, because, you know, we don't get that many deaths with unusual circumstances here, and then he goes and gets all jellylike while taking a call from Miss I'm Going to Be the Next Mayor . . . or governor. Like we're not investigating a serious situation here. Hello."

Imagining the chief smitten, Abby suppressed a smile.

"He must be in a midlife crisis or something," said Kat. "He turned to glare at me and then walked out of earshot."

"But he's married—"

"To a sweetheart of a woman, whose volunteer work is sewing prayer blankets for sick kids. Chief Bob Allen, for the brainiac he claims to be, doesn't seem to appreciate what he's got at home. Know what I mean?"

"Uh-huh. Like a lot of guys." Abby knew that Kat found the police chief irritating and often abrasive.

Kat continued her diatribe. "The way I see him right now is with his knuckles dragging the ground, Abby. Totally Neanderthal. Now, why do you think he's behaving like a stupid teenager?"

"Well, I'll venture a guess. Chief Bob Allen is like an artichoke—you've got to peel back a lot of layers of ego to discover who or what is hiding underneath. Might be a little boy cowering in a corner, with a huge inferiority complex, or a man consumed with self-loathing."

"Uh-oh. He's coming. One more thing . . . I almost forgot. A neighbor of the pastry chef called us. He's an independent consultant and works from home, but he's leaving town on a business trip tomorrow, and he's got Sugar, Jean-Louis's dog. Any chance you could take her for a few days? The animal shelter is overpopulated right now and begged us to find someone who would foster the dog until they could take her for adoption, or they'll have to place her with another rescue operation somewhere. I mean, you've got all that room out there, and you could use a watchdog, right?"

"I guess so. I'm not really into pets, other than my chickens and my bees. Maybe the chef's neighbor can take the dog back when he returns from his business trip?"

Kat's voice dropped to a whisper. "Got to go."

By the time Abby had finished all the chores for the day, the sun had dropped behind the hillside, leaving in its path wispy streaks of pale pink and gold. She had patched and inflated the wheel on the wheelbarrow, planted the raspberry vines, and ferried the compost to the garden and then tilled it into the soil. The weeds would wait for another day. She had also washed Lucas Crawford's truck and returned it, with a jar of honey and a thank-you note tied to the steering wheel with gingham ribbon. And finally, she'd made it into Las Flores to take charge of the pastry chef's dog, Sugar.

Sugar was a two-year-old mixed breed. According to the neighbor, Jean-Louis had told him that the dog had some English pointer, beagle, and whippet in her, showing up in rounded eyes, long legs, a lean body, and a short-haired white coat with liver-colored freckles and spots. She also had a long, sloping neck and a thick tail. Abby worried that the dog might be highly energetic, needing to hunt and run every day—a concern borne out by the neighbor, who had said he was marathon runner and had taken the dog with him on his daily practice runs. What if the dog went after the wild birds that were attracted to the feeders she'd hung around her property? That would never do. On the upside, maybe the pooch's mixed breeding had tempered an aggressive hunting tendency. In the final analysis, Abby reminded herself that the arrangement would be temporary—she'd be the foster parent to Sugar, but only until other arrangements could be made.

After latching the chicken-house door, Abby trudged back to the kitchen as the clock struck nine bells. She flipped on the light and opened the fridge, then stared at the contents— a jar of jam and a plastic tray with six eggs. Dinner could wait, too. What she really longed for was muscular hands to massage her aching back, a glass of wine, and a long hot bath.

Sugar looked up at Abby with big brown eyes, her tail wagging, as if to say, "What about chasing some birds or running up Farm Hill Road? Or is it time to eat yet?"

Abby stared back at the dog. "I don't speak dog. How are we going to learn each other's signals? Oh, Lord, what was I thinking? I don't need a dog." She took a bowl from the cupboard and poured some dog food in it from the bag that Jean-Louis's neighbor had given her. After putting down the bowl of dog food and a bowl of fresh water, Abby said, "Well, go ahead. Have at it."

Sugar contented herself with crunching on the doggy nuggets and slurping water until Abby trudged over to the antique Queen Anne chest, where she kept an unopened bottle of California cabernet sauvignon. Sugar leapt up against the antique chest and began pawing it, as if the old piece of furniture hadn't already been scarred enough over the past hundred years.

"Oh, no, you don't. Down. Get down now!" Abby immediately regretted how loud and mean she sounded. She mentally chastised herself for being unduly harsh with the poor creature.

The dog dropped to all fours, but its body quivered.

Abby sank to her knees. "I'm sorry, Sugar. I didn't mean to yell at you. It's just this chest is one of the few things I have left from my grandmother. It's irreplaceable. Oh, I do hope you understand."

Sugar began to bark, seemingly as loudly as Abby had shouted.

"Okay, okay. I get it that you're upset. Let's just let this go for now."

If Sugar seemed unmanageable, Abby could understand why: she wasn't the best choice for a dog foster parent. And this dog had been through a lot of changes lately. Sugar's owner had died, and the neighbor had tried to do a good deed, until his job had required him to leave. Now the poor animal was stuck with someone who had never been a dog owner. They hadn't had time to bond, and Abby didn't know if they ever would. In her heart, Abby knew she wasn't doing a very good job of reassuring the dog and making the fosterling feel secure.

After standing and inspecting the chest for scratches, Abby looked down at the dog. "I'm not mad at you, Sugar. You just need to learn the boundaries."

Sugar stopped barking and lay on her tummy, waiting, apparently, for Abby to make the next move.

Abby reached for the bottle of cabernet. She had intended to open the wine after she sold her first case of homemade jam, but that wouldn't happen until stone fruit season next month. The bottle stood next to Clay's picture in its silver frame. She swallowed hard against the lump that always formed in her throat whenever she gazed at his image. She'd stuck the picture there months ago so she wouldn't have to see it as often. And today, after grueling hours in the garden, dealing with the necessary chores, and amassing a growing list of challenges she'd have to address—including caring for a dog now—Abby reached for the picture and turned it facedown. Her muscles hurt. Even her eyelids felt tired. No point in being reminded of shattered dreams that would make her heart ache, as well.

Although she hated the old shower and tub combo, with its chipped porcelain and leaky faucet, Abby felt her body relaxing once she had eased into the hot, soapy water. After the restorative bath, she dried off, slipped into her big girl panties and a T-shirt, and opened the bottle of wine. Sugar had fallen asleep on the bed while watching Abby bathe, since there was no door hanging and not even a frame between the master bedroom and the master bathroom yet. Soon the dog was snoring, and her lean legs moved restlessly, as if she was dreaming of chasing a rabbit.

After splashing a bit of the red liquid into a crystal wineglass that had survived the move, Abby traipsed out to the patio and dropped onto the seat of her grandmother's cane rocker. The rocking motion soothed her spirit as she sipped the wine in the gathering violet dusk. Crickets and bullfrogs serenaded her in a throaty chorus. Abby welcomed their unseen company. Her thoughts drifted to Clay. Getting used to the solitude hadn't been difficult, but she sorely missed his physical presence, his boyish laughter, and his sweet kisses. Why had he told her he loved her if he knew deep down that someday, when the timing was right and a new challenge beckoned, he would walk out of her life the same way he'd walked in?

Abby forgave him. It wasn't like he hadn't told her about his past. Clay built tunnels under freeways and airports and even through mountains. He moved around a lot, probably had a girl in every town he'd worked in, and there'd been many towns. She had pressured him to stay on in California—half believing he would—when he had finished working on the new bore through the mountain that linked the eastern inland valley towns to the Northern California beach towns. When the job offer came through to oversee the construction of a tunnel beneath a major airport in the Southeast, he hadn't even tried to hide his excitement from her. He had loaded up his sticker-covered hard hat, secured his pickax, thrown his suitcase in the cab of his truck, and left . . . on Valentine's Day!

Abby flinched as she recalled how she had driven around aimlessly the morning Clay had left, not wanting to be in the house, where she'd hidden a bottle of champagne and a heart-shaped cake. Half blinded by tears, Abby had finally wheeled into the lot of Crawford's feed store, parked her Jeep in front of a hay bale, and sobbed uncontrollably. And later, back at home, she'd tossed the cake into the garbage can.

Clay had loved sitting in the dark with her, spinning dreams. He had often asked her to imagine the kind of farm they would build together. Olive trees would line the driveway. He would tunnel into the earth to create a wine cave, would plant a vineyard, and would build her a home with a thousand windows so she could see the heaven on earth they would create together. Now, as Abby rocked in the darkness, with her bare toes touching the cold patio tiles, she pushed her fingers against the corners of her eyes to hold back the new threat of tears. Finally, gazing up at the star-splashed sky, she lifted her glass. *To you, Clay, wherever you are . . . You once said, if ever there was no me . . . or no you, then there would be no us. . . . You might have led me on with lies of omission, but you didn't lie about that.*

A loud crash—like shattered glass—cut through the silence. Abby shot out of the chair. *What the hey?* She froze. Heart racing, adrenaline pumping, she dropped to a squat, taking cover.

There, behind the portable barbecue, she cocked an ear in the direction the sound had come from. A barn owl screeched a raspy scream for about two seconds as it batted its wings in flight to the tallest eucalyptus tree on the property behind hers. Abby peered into the darkness. She could faintly make out the black silhouette of the cinder-block house that had been the sanctuary of its owner until his death, a year before Abby had moved to the farmette. Now, although she didn't see them, Abby believed snakes, rats, skunks, and raccoons crawled through the empty rooms and climbed the gnarly dead limbs of the ancient oak that towered over the old house. Yet, despite the haven the old house afforded wildlife, some local teens had only the month before broken into it to drink beer and do drugs. Abby had called county dispatch, and the responding officers had broken up the party. The property owner's daughter and her husband had returned and padlocked the iron entrance gates but had left any type of cleanup or maintenance for another day.

Okay. Overreacting. Calm down. Abby inhaled a long, slow breath. Slowing her breath would slow her heart rate, and her heart was racing faster than the lead car in a drag race. She might be overreacting, but the chef's sudden death had everyone on edge. And that vacant house, hidden by weeds and trees, was a recipe for trouble.

Abby crept into the dark kitchen of her house. She heard Sugar spring off the bed and pad down the hallway to her side. Rested, the dog apparently sensed excitement and jumped up on Abby.

"Some watchdog you are, snoozing away while there's a murderer on the loose. No jumping. Get down." Sugar wasn't taking no for an answer and covered Abby's face in wet licks. "No means no!" Abby reiterated. She felt for the tea towel she kept draped over the oven door handle. Tying it in a knot and pitching it away from the kitchen, Abby prayed that Sugar would run after it.

With the dog bounding to the living room in search of the knotted towel, Abby took the opportunity to close, lock, and shutter the patio door before groping her way to the bedroom. There, she stealthily opened the drawer to the bedside table and pulled out her Ruger LCP 380 semi-automatic pistol and its magazine. Though it was lighter than her service revolver, the weight of the small gun in her hand had a calming effect. She might have a gimpy thumb, but her two-handed aim was still good. She slipped the magazine into the gun and inhaled deeply, then slowly let go of the breath. Crouched on high alert in the darkness, stroking Sugar's neck to keep her silent, Abby remembered the crates of jars and wine bottles awaiting removal by the property's heirs and considered the possibility that a roaming wild animal had knocked them over. As the clock on the wall ticked away minutes and Abby heard no other racket, she concluded that maybe she'd been spooked by something wild, and not necessarily the two-legged kind. All the same, she decided to sleep with her gun within arm's reach. The dog didn't seem particularly interested in the doggy toys or her own bed, a folded blanket. Nor had Sugar yet learned that Abby's bed was off-limits.

Tip for Using Honey for Optimum Health

One to two teaspoons of raw honey eaten each day helps to strengthen the immune system, according to modern science and medical doctors. Regarded as a super food, raw honey is beneficial to your health and healing. The ancient Greek physician Hippocrates advocated the use of honey as medicine. In the ancient world, honey was used to treat a variety of medical problems owing to its antibacterial properties: it kills germs and thus promotes healing. Honey doesn't go bad. If honey in a jar crystallizes, simply place the jar in hot water to liquefy the contents.

Chapter 5

Sow plants that produce aboveground crops
during a waxing moon and plants that produce
belowground crops during a waning moon.

—*Henny Penny Farmette Almanac*

At a quarter to six, Abby awoke to the *kuk-kuk-kuk* chatter of a squirrel in the Black Mission fig tree that towered over the north side of her house. Houdini was already engaged in a crow-off with a neighborhood rooster. Somewhere down Farm Hill Road, a dog barked nonstop at what sounded like a garbage truck, its engine revving for starts and its brakes squeaking for stops as it lumbered along its route. Sugar leaped from the foot of Abby's bed to engage fully in her role as watchdog. The pooch stood on point beneath the window and barked without letup.

Abby rubbed her eyes, yawned, and stretched, taking notice of how energetic she felt. *Hormones.* There were times of the month when she hated her hormones, but then there were other times, like today, when she felt like a world-class gymnast in a thirty-seven-year-old goddess body. *Feel like jogging up the mountain. Ten miles over, dip in the Pacific, ten back. Could be fun . . . but then again, those heirloom beans aren't going to plant themselves.*

"All right. Stop with the barking, already. You've made your point, big girl." After throwing back the covers, springing from the bed, thrusting feet to the floor, Abby bounded to the dresser and rummaged through the drawers, searching for something to wear. She pulled out a pair of denim jeans, a white camisole to wear under her work shirt, and a pair of ankle socks. They were her last clean pair and not the best, because of the lace edging, but serviceable nevertheless. She hated hair hanging in her face and decided that the green bandanna in the top drawer was a practical solution to controlling her curly mass.

Sugar busied herself with the pile of unwashed laundry. She especially liked Abby's underwear and used towels. Abby groaned with the realization that with Sugar around, she would no longer be able to leave clothing on the floor, the gate open, or a half-eaten sandwich on a chair while she watered her plants. After putting away the laundry basket, Abby sprinted to the kitchen to swallow a few swigs of hot coffee, even though she didn't need help waking up this morning. Abby reached for her cell phone, which was lying next to her pocketknife on the kitchen counter. She disconnected the phone from the charger and slipped it and the knife into her back pocket. She hated the interruptions cell phones always brought. *But then again, maybe I don't want any calls to interrupt me today.*

Abby wiggled the phone back out of her hip pocket and laid it back down on the plywood that served as the countertop until she could get the real thing. Surely she could be unavailable by phone for a few hours. Kat and the other officers eventually would get to the bottom of what had happened to Jean-Louis. They knew how to do their jobs. If anything really important turned up and the cops needed her insight, Abby knew Kat would call and leave a message. Feeling justified at disconnecting the phone, literally, from her hip, Abby marched outside with Sugar on the leash. Nothing was going to stop her from getting those beans in the ground today!

Abby closed the fence gate dividing the front of her property from the back yard before letting Sugar off the leash, then shook the pebbles from her ladybug-patterned gardening shoes and set off for the drying shed. Sugar headed straight for the wild birds balancing on the cosmos blooms, flitting among the sunflowers, and perching in the apple tree. The dog showed a special interest in the yellow finches pecking at the Nyjer seed in one of the feeders that Abby had suspended by a rope from the pole braced between the peppertree and olive tree.

"Point and bark all you want, but no hurting those birds," Abby admonished before returning to her beans.

In the drying shed, Abby seized upon a spool of orange string, a hammer, and a five-gallon bucket of stakes. Next, she gathered packages of beans with exotic names like Turkey Craw, an heirloom from Tennessee, and Hutterite Soup, an heirloom bean grown by a Hutterite communal sect of Anabaptists in North Dakota. If the latter bean lived up to its reputation of making a magnificent white soup, she might be able to convince Zazi's to buy some of her crop.

After hammering the first stake into the earth and tying the loose end of the string around it, Abby paced off twenty-five steps to the other side of the garden and repeated the hammering process. She wound the spool of string around the stake, pulled out her pocketknife, cut the string, and tied the loose end. When she had completed ten straight rows, she sank to her knees in the dirt and began to plant the beans in one-inch-deep holes two inches apart. She speared the empty packages onto stakes and stuck them at the end of each row to identify the bean type. *I know you babies are going to grow and produce. With the money I'll make selling you, the honey, and my jams, maybe . . . just maybe I'll be able to fix up this old place. A granite countertop in the kitchen would be nice, for starters.*

Abby hummed while she worked, and the work went swiftly. With the beans finished, she retrieved the flats of herbs she'd been growing on the patio and began planting them. She lost track of time, but her skin felt prickly from the sun beating down on her. When she stopped to dab perspiration from her forehead using the tails of her faded work shirt, she heard a voice call out from the front of her property.

"Abby? Hey, girlfriend, you here?"

Abby groaned. *Wouldn't you know? And I'm just beginning to make headway.* Tree canopies blocked the view to the gravel driveway at the front of the property, but she recognized Kat's voice.

"Back here," Abby called out.

Kat's willowy body in her uniform emerged from the other side of the gate. "Brought someone to see you."

"Yeah? Hope he's good-looking."

"Oh, he is," Kat replied.

"I *wasn't* being serious," Abby told her.

"I *was*." Kat shot her a chimpanzee grin and took several steps toward the newly planted area before Abby asked her to stay where she was.

"Can't have you trouncing on the rows I've just planted. I'll come to you."

"Oh, gotcha," Kat said, backing up.

Abby hoisted a flat of herbs in cell packs onto one arm and slid her hand under a second flat. Balancing the two flats, she gingerly walked toward the patio. Sugar, eager to meet the new visitor, bounded between Abby's legs.

"Watch out!" Kat shrieked a millisecond too late.

Abby hit the ground, landing on the side of her face and sending cell packs of oregano, thyme, and tarragon seedlings flying in every direction.

"OMG! You all right?" Kat called out.

"Been better," Abby drawled, pushing up into a sitting position. "That dog is going to be the death of me . . . the dog and those darn twine lines."

"Why are they even there?"

"They're marking the gravel paths, which will prevent this sort of stumbling and bumbling through the garden."

"Well, girlfriend, they do make *marking paint* in spray cans now."

Abby grimaced. "Yeah, but a hand guided by the eye will never make a line as straight as a piece of string tightly strung between two stakes." Abby dabbed at the blood oozing from her left nostril.

"Can I get you some ice?" Kat offered, softening her tone.

"Forget it. This isn't serious. It's just—" Abby sucked in a breath before spitting out the word. "Stupid." She pushed herself to an upright position and dusted dirt from her clothes. Then, she began picking up the cell packs of broken seedlings, only to toss them aside. She looked at Kat, not even trying to hide the gloom she knew her face showed.

Kat shook her head. "You are going to break your neck one of these days."

"Well, if I do, just put me out of my misery, because with my gimpy thumb and a broken neck, I wouldn't make much of a farmer, would I?" Abby said and dusted dirt from her clothes.

From beyond the gate, a male voice called out, "Hello? Are you ladies back there?"

Sugar ran to the gate, which Kat had closed, pawed the boards, and barked incessantly.

"No," Abby commanded in her most authoritative voice. To her utter surprise, Sugar dropped down and trotted over to her.

"Looks like she recognizes you as the top dog," Kat said.

But the moment of pleasure Abby felt was short lived, as she watched Sugar spring to life upon spotting finches foraging in the giant sunflower near the gate. The dog sprang into the air in a flying leap. She thrust her weight against the stalk, taking down Abby's prized sunflower. From the head of this one flower, Abby had hoped to harvest seeds enough to sell alongside her honey at the farmers' market. Abby shot a grimacing look at Kat.

"I'm so over that animal," Abby lamented. "Why couldn't the chef have been a cat lover instead?"

"She just needs training, and you need time to bond with her," said Kat. Then, turning her attention to the voice calling to them, she replied, "Be right there, Mr. Bonheur."

"Bonheur?" Abby arched her brow questioningly. "A relative of the pastry chef?"

Kat nodded, grinned. "Brother."

"Is he here to take the dog? Oh, thank goodness!"

"No. He's here to see you."

"Why me?"

"Well, if you'd answered your darn phone, I could have told you that Chief Bob Allen shared the findings of the coroner's office with Jean-Louis's brother. The death was the result of asphyxia by hanging. Then our visit to Dora under the bridge, in the homeless encampment, confirmed it for us."

"Really? How?"

"In her shopping cart, we found a bucket that matches the others in the pastry shop."

"How about the twine from around his neck?" Abby asked.

"No twine, no apron. She says she can't remember those. And, believe me, we pressed her."

"Slips in and out of lucidity, I suppose," Abby said.

"But she admitted to cutting him down. Thought if she straightened him out on the floor, he'd get up and get her coffee."

"No kidding? And when he didn't?"

"She helped herself to his heavy-duty utility bucket—the one he must have stood on, until . . . he wasn't standing anymore."

"Ladies . . . hello," the man called out again, sounding slightly impatient.

"We gotta go, but one more thing," Kat said softly as she made a sweeping gesture to invite Abby to start walking to the gate. "Two friends who knew Jean-Louis well said he struggled with professional and personal difficulties. Defaulting on loans, losing his lease, and having to fire his protégé had to be extremely stressful. Chief Bob Allen says we can't spare anyone to conduct what would amount to an unnecessary investigation, when it seems clear it was suicide, so case closed."

Abby wondered if Chief Bob Allen wasn't being premature in his decision, but she said nothing.

Kat called out, "We're coming, Mr. Bonheur."

Chief Bob Allen would want the whole ugly mess to go away, of that Abby was certain. The negative publicity would stop. Many of the shops in Las Flores depended on summer tourist dollars, and those dollars also boosted the town's economy. People on their way over the mountain to the seaside villages and beach towns often stopped in Las Flores for lunch and a bit of antiquing, but they wouldn't if a murderer was on the loose. With suicide, things could return to normal.

"So how's the brother taking the news?" Abby asked.

"Not well. He argued with Chief Bob Allen, who listened like he was the man's best friend and then told Philippe Bonheur that he'd seen plenty of cases where the family couldn't accept suicide as the finding, but that is what happened. End of discussion."

"So, how is it that my name came up?"

"That was later, when I was driving Mr. Bonheur back to his hotel. I might have mentioned your name."

"Oh, yeah? What else did you tell him?" Abby slipped her fingers under the bandanna, inched it off her head, and pushed her fingers through her hair to comb it. She must look a mess, particularly after she literally rubbed her face—and hair—in the dirt.

"Not much. Well, your track record, of course—your strength at crime solving. Oh, and I also mentioned your love of rhubarb and honey. I'm sure I told him about your luscious honey."

"Of course you did." Abby smiled and shook her head. She reached down and scratched Sugar between the ears.

Kat flashed a wide grin. "Look, Abby, you know when the chief says to back off, we can't touch it. But you could. You've solved more cases than anyone else on our force."

"But I'm not on the force, am I? I'm a farmer now. And honestly, Kat, I don't think you know how much I'm trying to do here. Don't you think I would bring in day laborers to help me if I could afford it?"

Kat's tone shifted to a tease. "You'll thank me when you find out how much money he wants to give you."

Abby arched her eyebrows. "Okay, so tell me."

Kat smiled. "And steal his thunder? Uh, *no*. I'll let him tell you." She turned and quickly marched back to the front of the house, where her cruiser was parked. Kat called out over her shoulder, "Come on. I'll introduce you."

Following Kat through the heavy wooden gate and then latching it to keep Sugar from taking off, Abby noticed a lot of bee activity on the gate's driveway side, where she had planted a circular-shaped wildflower garden. The honeybees loved the pollen in the flowers of the giant pink, red, and white cosmos. No matter what time of the day Abby went to water them, she would see the bees foraging.

Abby looked past the cosmos to the forty-something, tall, dark-haired man with silvery threads of gray at his temples. Casually dressed in jeans and penny loafers without socks, he held his sport coat in the crook of an arm while his other hand squeezed a tiny ball of fruit hanging on the two-year-old blood orange tree. The sleeves of his white shirt had been rolled up, exposing lithe forearms.

"A man that good looking has to be married," Kat whispered.

"Is he?" Abby whispered back.

Kat shrugged and kept walking.

When the man spun around to face them, Abby noted the family resemblance to Chef Jean-Louis but also that drawn, haggard look that took over a healthy face when someone suffered a shock or was grief stricken.

"Philippe Bonheur," the man said, extending his hand to Abby.

"If you'll excuse me," Kat said, "I've got to check in with dispatch." She walked a discreet distance down the gravel driveway and stopped at the mailbox, which was mounted on a fence post. Abby could tell from the way Kat was leaning her head in toward her shoulder that she was talking on the two-way.

"Pleased to meet you, Mr. Bonheur." Abby tried to say his name correctly, to pronounce it Bon-NEUR, but it didn't sound right to her. She'd nearly failed high school French. "Abigail Mackenzie." She extended her right hand but yanked it back when she noticed dirt clumped under her nails and streaks of soil still on her palm and wrist. "Sorry . . . I . . . I wasn't expecting anyone to show up at my door. I've misplaced my gardening gloves."

"It's no problem, mademoiselle." Philippe clasped her hand, then pulled it back into his and shook it firmly. His red, puffy eyes dominated his gaunt face, which sported a day-old beard and a weak smile.

"I'm so sorry for your loss, Mr. Bonheur."

"Thank you. *C'est une affaire terrible.*" His voice broke from a sudden huskiness as he lapsed into his native language.

Abby's heart sank. She hated to see an obviously strong, healthy man in such terrible pain. Empathy had been the bane of her life, especially in police work. Kat had once told Abby that her personal sense of outrage on behalf of the victims and their families was why she was so good in law enforcement. But Abby too keenly felt the pain of the victim, sometimes feeling compelled to work a case as if it were personal, when her primary task was simply to keep her personal feelings in check and just do the job.

Now, as Abby observed Philippe Bonheur struggling to show composure under the most trying of circumstances, she inhaled a long, deep breath and heard herself ask politely, "Mr. Bonheur, how can I help?"

"This Chief Bob Allen, you worked for him?"

Abby nodded. "Yes, I did."

"I will speak frankly. I do not agree with Chief Bob Allen and the coroner. Suicide? *Non.* I tell you, it was not. It was murder!"

At that moment, Kat returned. She thrust her hands into her uniform pants pockets and leaned against the cruiser, swatting occasionally at a bee if it flew too close.

"But how can you be so sure?" Abby looked directly into his eyes, thinking their hue lighter than the new leaves on her apple tree.

"I know my brother." Philippe Bonheur reached into his white dress-shirt pocket, removed a silver lighter and a small box, and opened the box. It was lined in foil and contained cigarettes. "Mind if I smoke?" Not waiting for her reply, he plucked out a cigarette, flipped open his lighter, set fire to the cigarette tip, and inhaled a deep, long drag.

Abby took a step backward. *Seriously?*

A sheepish expression claimed Philippe's countenance, as if he had picked up on her thought and now felt awkward about smoking.

"You Californians, you do not like smoking, *c'est vrai?*"

Abby nodded. "Some of us don't."

Philippe took another long drag of the cigarette and then flipped it to the ground. "Jean-Louis tells me on the phone about a man named Dobbs. They argued about the patisserie lease."

"Yes, I know about that." Abby asked, "Was your brother assaulted by him?"

"No."

"Well, then, perhaps they ironed out their difficulties." Abby was starting to wonder if Philippe could tell her anything, anything at all, that could convince her that the case had merit.

Philippe looked at her incredulously and shook his head. "Jean-Louis, he tells me about a man who attacked him behind the patisserie."

"When did that happen?" Abby asked, looking for a response from Kat, who had folded her arms across her chest and was listening intently.

"A week . . . two or three weeks ago. My mind does not think so well now." Philippe ran his hand through his hair. He seemed to be struggling with how best to express what he wanted to say. He finally spoke. "My brother, he was not like everyone. People did not understand him. Some did not like him, because—"

Abby waited for the words that did not come. "Did Jean-Louis's family . . . did they know . . . Did you know he was gay?"

"*Oui.*" Philippe seemed relieved that she had said what perhaps he could not. "We know. Jean-Louis feared for his life sometimes. That man who attacked Jean-Louis, he rode a motorcycle. He called my brother names. Jean-Louis followed him into the bar one night. They argued. The bartender made them leave."

Abby zeroed in on that detail. "And that man assaulted Jean-Louis?"

Philippe nodded.

Abby looked over at Kat. "Police report filed?"

Kat shook her head. "Nope. First I've heard of it."

Abby addressed Philippe. "Any chance you got the name of that biker from Jean-Louis?"

"He never told me."

"How about the name of the bar?"

"The Black Wench or Witch . . . something like that."

The only bar in Las Flores. Abby considered how desperate Philippe must feel. How hard he must be searching his memory for names and situations that might prove his brother was the victim of an enemy. She gauged the distance between her dusty gardening shoes and the discarded, still smoldering cigarette, reminding herself to dispose of it properly once he and Kat had left. Unconvinced that a biker, landlord, or any local had killed Jean-Louis, Abby couldn't shake the feeling that suicide explained the death. And without a good motive or a prime suspect, there didn't seem to be any good reason for her to take the case, despite details about the local bar and its mostly biker patrons. Details anyone could know.

How she hated these situations. . . . *How many times can you say, "Sorry for your loss," before it begins to sound like it's just an excuse to end the conversation so you can go back to your life?*

Philippe inhaled deeply. "Jean-Louis. . . ." His voice became husky. "He mentions to me friends, too."

Abby smiled at him reassuringly. "I'm sure Jean-Louis had *many* friends in Las Flores."

Philippe's haggard face managed a weak smile.

"Can you recall any of his friends' names?" Abby asked.

"Charles, Joseph, Patrick, and someone he called Vieillard, 'old man' in English."

Abby shot a quizzical look at Kat, who had flipped open a small notebook to jot down the names. Abby wondered if the word might mean a man who was older than Jean-Louis or if the chef had used the word as a term of endearment.

"Did your brother often use pet names for friends?" asked Abby.

"Oui. Vieillard. A nickname, perhaps?" Philippe brushed his fingers against a tuft of hair over an ear, where a honeybee had just alighted.

"Don't move," Abby quickly cautioned. "Just try to be still. If you swat at it, it will sting you."

"Arghh," Philippe growled. He followed her directions, staring intently into her eyes, apparently awaiting a sign that the bee might depart.

Abby moved a step closer to him, watching closely as the bee took its time exploring. The insect must have found Philippe's cologne to its liking. And what wasn't to like? High notes of mint and basil counterbalanced with a woodsy undertone and a hint of musk. Attractive to her, attractive to the bees. Abby considered what it would feel like to have her face as close to Philippe Bonheur's as the bee was. She slowly lifted her hand, thinking of how she might help the little insect on its way, but at just that moment the bee's tiny body waggled. The honeybee flew upward, turned in midcourse, and headed in the direction of the hive behind the weathered wooden fence.

Philippe relaxed his posture; his attention again became fixed on Abby. "Surely, you do not raise these . . . these *abeilles?*"

Abby nodded. "Honeybees."

"It is dangerous, n'est-ce pas?" He looked over at Kat. Kat shrugged, as if she couldn't understand Abby's love for bees, either.

Abby smiled disarmingly. "No. It's not dangerous. I love the bees and their honey. Actually, no one appreciated their honey more than Jean-Louis." She decided to ask a point-blank question. "Was there someone who disliked Jean-Louis enough to want him dead?"

Philippe rubbed an unshaven cheek, as though thinking about the question. "Jean-Louis, he tells me he thinks his business partner or someone—how do you say?—*détourné de l'argent.*"

Abby searched her memory for the meaning of the phrase and then proffered an alternative in English. "Embezzled money?"

"Oui, embezzle, but Jean-Louis, he could not prove it."

Abby sighed. *Suspicion. Not the same as proof.* She lifted the collar of her work shirt and shook it slightly to allow a bit of air to circulate over her flushed skin. "Truly, I wish I could help." She knew it was not what the man wanted to hear. To avoid what she was sure would be a pleading gaze, Abby glanced over at Kat, who was staring at the ground, as if not wanting to telegraph her personal feelings about the case. "Look, we really don't have much to work with here." Abby straightened her spine, as if standing taller and stiffer would make her appear more resolute. "I try not to insert myself into police business. Chief Bob Allen would not welcome my intrusion, and, besides, he and I are not exactly buddies."

A long and brittle silence ensued before Philippe said coldly, "It is not police business, not anymore. My brother, he tells me he was going to the Caribbean for his birthday. His good friend Vieillard had access to a yacht on the southeast coast of the Dominican Republic, near Casa de Campo. So, pardon me, mademoiselle, but does that sound like he intended to end his life?"

Logic compelled her to agree with Philippe Bonheur. People who were about to check out usually did not take a vacation first.

"Remind me of when Jean-Louis's birthday is," Abby said.

"July eighteenth." Philippe glanced at Kat, apparently in an effort to gauge whose side she was on, but Kat remained silent, still staring stone-faced at the ground. An awkward and tense silence ensued.

"You are repairing this place, oui?" Philippe asked, apparently wanting to shift the direction of the conversation. He slid his fingers, with manicured nails, into his pants pocket and drew forth a folded piece of paper. He handed the paper to Abby. "It is not complicated." His tone warmed slightly. "You help me. I help you."

Abby opened the folded paper and stared at a check in the amount of ten thousand dollars. She took a quick, sharp breath. *Granite countertops!* Her heart raced as she pondered the possibilities of what else she could accomplish with that amount of money. *Replace the shower-tub combo. Buy a rototiller. Pay the second installment of the property tax bill without having to sell the 1929 Duncan Phyfe dining table and chairs. Hire some help.* As her mental list grew, so did Abby's excitement, but she tried not to show it.

Running her fingers along the crease of the check, Abby thought about how Philippe Bonheur must have written that check before even meeting her. That could mean only that he and Kat had discussed what a money pit the farmette had become. Abby's cheeks grew hot with humiliation. She'd have a chat with Kat later. For now, she reasoned she would take Philippe's money as a fair wage for the time she would have to put into the investigation. And she would certainly ask him to take responsibility for Sugar—surely he would want to keep his brother's dog.

"If I take your money, Mr. Bonheur, I ask only that you not talk about the case with anyone else. If your brother's death *is* a homicide, we don't want the murderer to know we are looking into this, at least not yet."

A warm smile made its way across Philippe's face. His eyes crinkled in an expression of joyful relief. "We have a deal?"

Abby nodded. "Seems so."

"Oh, *merci beaucoup.*"

Abby needed to tell him that her investigation would stop if she discovered proof that his brother's death was *not* due to foul play. But maybe now was not the time to go over her conditions. The poor man surely needed a bright spot in the darkness he was enduring.

"Look, I'm not making any promises, Mr. Bonheur, but—"

He interrupted, "S'il vous plaît, Philippe. We are friends now, non?"

Abby nodded. *Suppose associates might be more correct, but whatever.* "My friends call me Abby. I hope you will, too."

Kat was already in the cruiser when Philippe extended his hand and surprised Abby with a vigorous, firm handshake. "Au revoir, Abby."

Abby smiled sweetly. *Okay, so bring up the dog issue next time.*

As Philippe slid into the passenger seat of the black-and-white cruiser, Abby caught a quick glimpse of a honeybee riding in on the back side of his shirtsleeve. Not wanting to race down the driveway after the police car, Abby hesitated briefly. She didn't like the idea of Philippe swatting away at the poor insect, either, so she sprinted, calling out in her loudest voice, "Roll down the window." But the cruiser had already passed the mailbox, turned onto Farm Hill Road, and sped away.

Tips for Relocating Bees

- Do not move a hive of bees until you've fulfilled the necessary requirements for them at the new location: a water supply with a pump, a platform on which the hive will rest, and a waterproof covering to protect the hive from rain.

- Make sure the hive faces east or southeast for maximum light, warmth, and dryness.

- Always move bees at night, after they have settled into their abodes.

- Insert pieces of foam in the mouth of the hive to seal the bees inside before the move.

- Remove the foam before you leave the new site so the bees can begin exploring and foraging with the first light of dawn.

Chapter 6

The simplest treatment for a bee sting is to get
the stinger out.

—*Henny Penny Farmette Almanac*

Abby patted a fingertip of red-tinted gloss on her lips
before adjusting the clip holding her swooped-up hair.
By her estimation, she had transformed her usual farm-
friendly look, perfect for selling her wares at the farmers'
market and visiting the feed store, into that of a fashion-
able sleuthing professional, or at least a reasonable facsim-
ile. For the 1:00 p.m. meeting with Philippe, she didn't feel
a need to get too crazy with her hair and makeup. She had
given a muscular brushing to her coarse, thick hair and
had toned down her sunburned cheeks and nose-bridge
freckles with pearlescent finishing powder.

Clothes were another matter. Farmwork was hard on
clothes. Abby had a few nice things, but mostly her wardrobe
consisted of jeans and T-shirts. She had two black suits for
her sessions with the DA, several dresses, and a few skirts.
She didn't want to look too casual or too formal for her
meeting with Philippe. After trying on several outfits,
she'd selected her skinny, boot-cut black jeans, a crisp
white blouse, a black jacket with red piping trim, and

rooster-red flats. But, as she slid out of the driver's seat in the parking lot of the Las Flores Lodge and looked at the sky, she regretted not grabbing an umbrella and different shoes. The red, silky fabric of the skimmers made them a pretty complement to her outfit, but they were not suited for the late May rain.

Slamming the Jeep door, Abby searched the sky for signs of impending sprinkles, which had been forecast for the afternoon. She could only hope that the showers would stay north of the Golden Gate Bridge, but in the last hour, high wisps of vapor had thickened into chunky, layer-like cotton batting, which had increased in bulk until only a smattering of holes afforded glimpses of the blue sky behind.

Abby strolled toward the wide Spanish-style veranda of the lodge, where lemon trees potted in Italian terra-cotta lined the entrance. She half expected to see Philippe pacing. She was not immune to his physical attractiveness, but she found his impatience and indignant emotional fervor off-putting. A murder investigation required a calm, focused mind. Unrestrained emotions served only to muddle one's memory, logic, and problem-solving ability. However, she reminded herself, he was duly grieving and deserving of her patience and understanding.

In her peripheral vision, something moved. She heard "Out of the way!" and jumped back against her Jeep. A bicyclist jangled a handlebar bell nonstop. The bike flew past. A small dog cowered in a basket in front of the bike seat and another little pooch perched precariously inside a wooden box mounted behind the bike seat. Despite the bicyclist maneuvering the bike around a curve at the end of the flat driveway, the dogs remained upright. The bike, the man, and his canine passengers disappeared after turning into the bike lane on Las Flores Boulevard beyond the gate. *Those poor dogs.* Abby thought fiercely about what she could do *now* to deal with the man. Finally, in resigned exasperation, she sighed. *Don't think I won't report you, you idiot!*

"Abby, bonjour. Comment allez-vous?" Philippe called to her over the racket of hammers and heavy equipment. The lodge was ground zero for construction, as some new bungalows were being built around its garden and pool. She turned and saw Philippe descending the stone steps, gesticulating wildly.

"*Mon Dieu! Pouvez-vous me recommander un bon médecin?*" he asked, shaking his hand, as if to dislodge something stuck to it.

"English, Philippe," Abby told him. "In English, please."

"Look." He held out his right hand. It was swollen, like a latex glove turned into a water balloon.

"You were stung?"

"Oui."

"When?"

"Yesterday . . . at your farm."

"Ouch . . . Have you ever been stung before?"

"Non."

"And that's why you want me to recommend a good doctor?"

"Oui. This hand, I need."

"Well, I'm certain you need both your hands. What you mean is that you favor your right hand for writing and other tasks, correct?"

He nodded.

"Well, I rather doubt a doctor will be necessary, but let me have a look." Abby examined the red dot on Philippe's swollen right hand. "Well, it appears the stinger is out."

"Stinger?"

Abby looked into Philippe's large light eyes. She cleared her throat. Wished she'd paid more attention in her French class. *So . . . the French word for "stinger." Let me see. Barbed lancets, venom, bee gut rupture, death . . . death. I know that one.* La petite mort . . . *No, no, that's not right. That's a euphemism for "orgasm." Must be* décès. *Yes, that's it.* "*Décès!*" Abby exclaimed aloud.

"Décès? I'm going to die?" Philippe's expression conveyed alarm.

"No, no, no, Philippe. I meant the bee. . . . The bee dies . . . died. Not you. You're fine. Well, except for . . ." She took a deep breath. *Not going well. Try something else.* "So, I've got an analgesic cream in my car. It'll make your hand feel better." She pointed to her Jeep.

Philippe nodded and followed her to her car.

Abby rummaged around in the glove compartment until she finally located the analgesic, histamine-blocking cream. After removing the cap and squeezing a pea-size dollop onto a finger, she rubbed it on Philippe's hand, at the site of the sting, and then smoothed some over his hand, up to his Cartier watchband. She could feel the heat in his hand. Her own skin prickled. Her heart hammered hard. When she looked up at him, those sparkling pale green eyes were gazing back at her.

Abby quickly tightened the cap on the tube. "You okay to meet Chief Bob Allen?"

Philippe nodded.

"He's expecting us in twenty minutes." She tossed the tube of analgesic cream back in the glove compartment and turned to find Philippe planted in the same spot.

His face took on a silly grin. He used one finger to open his jacket pocket. "My hand, it is useless for tying my necktie. Do you mind?"

Abby leaned over to see a tie lodged in his pocket. As she withdrew the tie, Philippe moved so close to her, their toes nearly touched. He was close enough for her to smell his cologne and feel his breath against her face. He stood a head taller than she and was about the height of Clay. *Don't think about him right now.* Abby flipped up Philippe's dress shirt collar, slipped the Italian red, patterned silk tie under it, and flipped the collar back down. Standing directly in front of him, she began to perform the sequence of knotting the tie. *Over, under, around, and through.* Clay had taught her that. As she was tightening and adjusting the position of the knot, Philippe placed his hands on her shoulders. Electricity shot through her. She pulled the narrow part of the tie down and pushed the knot upward in one swift motion. Philippe stepped backward and coughed against the tightness of the knot.

"There. Looks great!" Abby exclaimed. "Time to go." She walked around to the driver's side and climbed in the Jeep.

Philippe slid into the passenger's seat. His eyes held a bemused merriment as he reached for the seat belt and looked over at her. "This . . . I can do this myself."

Abby laughed. "Good. Pull it tight. Wouldn't want you breaking the law. I'd have to make a citizen's arrest and hand you over to the authorities."

Philippe grinned and snapped the belt into the buckle.

When they arrived, Abby felt a familiar flicker of apprehension as she stepped inside the Las Flores Police Department. Her former place of employment held a lot of memories. Some were not so good. Catching the attention of the two dispatchers stationed behind the massive glass enclosure of the county communication center, Abby strolled over and waved. Both women nodded, but their eyes were focused on Philippe. It was not often that a handsome, debonair man walked into the station, or anywhere in Las Flores.

Abby walked past a second glass window, which separated the waiting area from the office cubicles, the locked property room, and the interrogation rooms. She saw the department's female crime-scene investigator hobbling toward her on crutches. They met on opposite sides of the security door.

The woman pushed open the heavy door, and Abby and Philippe walked through. "Goodness, Nettie. You're injured. Line of duty?"

Nettie Sherman snorted. "If you want to call it that. Chief Allen didn't want to buy a new desk and chair for me, so he dragged in his brother-in-law's old metal desk and had a chair brought up from the basement, where, as you know, stuff goes when it's broken. First day in it, I leaned forward and heard that chair crack like someone had snapped a bullwhip. Next thing I know, my body was flying into a file drawer." Nettie adjusted the crutches under her arms and glanced down at her right leg. "My knee had an old injury. Now it has a new one."

Abby couldn't suppress a laugh. "Oh, Nettie, I'm so sorry." She clamped a hand over her mouth. "It's not funny, but you're such a fabulous storyteller."

"Well," Nettie continued, "I'm stuck with that dang dinosaur of a desk, but I did get a new chair."

Abby chuckled. "What happened to the old one?"

Nettie rolled her eyes. "Where else? Back to the basement." She pointed down to the end of the corridor. "Chief is expecting you."

"Yes." Abby drew in a deep breath and tried to exhale the tension that had suddenly claimed her body.

"I'm supposed to escort you there, so follow me." Nettie hobbled on her crutches ahead of Abby for a few steps and then stopped to whisper, "What is it? Twenty-five feet? I could have watched you walk there from here. But he won't bend the rules for anyone."

"Of course he won't," Abby replied, following Nettie again as she hobbled ahead.

Before Abby could say another word, the chief's office door flew open from the inside. He glowered from the doorway. "Mackenzie, you're late. Your fault . . . or Nettie's for yammering on about that knee of hers?"

"Mine," Abby said. "I apologize, Chief. Mr. Bonheur and I were unavoidably delayed."

Chief Bob Allen uttered one of his customary grunts, spun around, and marched back to his desk. "Take a seat." He gestured to the two black metal institutional chairs in front of his desk, then sat down in his own chair.

"Chief," Abby said, knowing that the chief preferred to set the agenda and that by speaking first, she was pre-empting his privilege. "You've met Mr. Bonheur, and you know we are here because he has asked me to dig a little deeper into his brother's untimely death."

"Waste of time. We've closed it." The chief leaned back in his chair and turned a steely-eyed stare upon Abby. "It's what we do when it's a suicide. You know that, Mackenzie."

"Yes, sir, you're very likely right, but we would like to review the police file as soon as it is possible."

"It hasn't been redacted yet."

"When can we expect that to be completed?"

"We're shorthanded," he said, leaning forward and narrowing his eyes.

Abby met his gaze . . . waited.

"A few more days," he finally offered. The chief then addressed Philippe. "As I said before, Mr. Bonheur, we're sorry for your loss. You can hire Ms. Mackenzie here if you want to, but there is no great mystery to unravel, so delving further into this would be a waste of Mackenzie's time and your money."

"Thank you, Chief, but my family has many questions. I believe Ms. Mackenzie will help me answer those questions."

"Up to you." Chief Bob Allen leaned back in his chair again, then laced his fingers together over his stomach. "Are we done here?"

Abby stood up. "Not quite. I'd like to review that surveillance tape the officers acquired from the pastry shop and any tapes from other businesses in the area. Philippe and I will also be compiling a list of the chef's known associates. Your officers would already have started such a list. I'd like a copy of that. Finally, we'd like to take with us any property the department has belonging to Jean-Louis Bonheur."

Chief Allen rose.

Abby understood how the chief would see that for him to remain seated while she stood put him in an inferior position.

Chief Bob Allen addressed Abby directly. "Like I said, it was a limited investigation. When the coroner ruled the death a suicide, we closed the case." The chief seemed to take particular satisfaction in emphasizing the word *suicide*. He walked around the desk and shot a steely-eyed stare at Abby. "You know how this works, Mackenzie. Find something my people can take to the DA, and I'll take another look at it. Otherwise, don't waste my time."

He slid a hand into his pants pocket and extended the other to Philippe. "There's no delicate way to put this. Up behind your brother's left ear was the mark made by the knot in the ligature he used to hang himself. His brain got no oxygen because of his strangulation. That was how the coroner's investigator put it." The chief's words hung in the air.

Philippe rose, grasped Chief Bob Allen's extended hand, and shook it. "And do you have this knot?"

"We have a large section of the twine he used. We found it on the doorknob of his pantry."

"You are paid by the people of this community, n'est-ce pas? You protect them, oui?"

Chief Bob Allen raised his eyebrows and nodded, undoubtedly wondering what his visitor was getting at. "That's my job. I think I speak for our community when I say your brother's untimely death was also a loss for us. But there comes a time when we must get past it and move on."

"If my words offend, forgive me, but you did not protect my brother." Philippe's gaze darted to Abby, who remained poker-faced but pivoted slightly to face the two of them. Intensely staring at Chief Bob Allen, Philippe added, "You seem to want only to make the news of his death go away as quickly as possible. Do you not care that a murderer could be hiding in your town? Tell me, Chief Allen, how well do you sleep at night?"

"I sleep just fine, Mr. Bonheur. Just fine."

The chief strode to the door, jerked it open, and summoned Nettie with a "Come here now" hand gesture. Abby cringed. She knew Nettie would stand up to him when others wouldn't. But she could just hear him saying something like, "Good God, woman! When are you getting off those damn crutches?" Any knee-jerk reactions to his comments only made the chief come down even harder. Abby shifted her attention to the massive collection of black-and-white photographs lining the walls on either side of the door. The chief was in every photo. No surprise there. *A collection to match his ego!*

She walked over to one of the walls and studied the

photos. She knew the chief had hung them there so people would gaze at them. He liked that. *Because, after all, it is all about him.* One image showed the chief with the mayor and the town council members. In the next image the chief was in his class A uniform, his badge fitted with a black sash to show respect for a fallen officer. The occasion would have been a funeral.

In another picture, Abby spotted herself standing in a group with the chief at a promotion ceremony. Abby had worked as hard as any of them, putting in overtime, working weekends, taking on extra responsibilities, and studying for the sergeant's exam. Although her turn at a promotion had been coming—or so the chief had promised year after year, all seven of them—it had never materialized, not even when she passed the exam. But she had never given him the satisfaction of letting her disappointment show.

Nettie hobbled in.

In an authoritative tone, the chief addressed Nettie. "Give Mackenzie and Mr. Bonheur his brother's belongings and any evidence we took from the pastry shop during our investigation. Oh, and she wants a copy of the police report, too, when it's ready. Make sure we get a signature for everything they take with them."

"Yes, sir." Nettie turned her heavy body as best she could, taking care to favor her bad knee, before leading Abby and Philippe back down the corridor. The chief's door slammed, and Abby was pretty sure she heard Nettie whisper beneath her breath, "Someday, karma's going to bite you in your chiefly butt."

Dashing into the drizzling rain, Abby and Philippe each carried a box sealed with the tape used by the police department for evidence. Once the boxes were safely stashed behind the car seats and she and Philippe had climbed in,

Abby turned the key and flipped on the windshield wipers. She looked over at Philippe and asked, "Your place or mine?"

Philippe twisted in his seat and gazed quizzically at her, as if not sure he had understood the question.

"We should go through your brother's property together. If there are photos in those boxes the police gave us, you might be able to identify who is in them. You know the saying, 'Two heads are better than one'?"

Philippe nodded. "*Alors*, in that case, shall we put our heads together in my suite?" A sheepish smile crept across his face.

"Actually, I was thinking of the lodge's library," Abby countered, in case Philippe was having ideas about something other than work. "It's a spacious room with a massive table, comfortable chairs, a fireplace—always good to take away the chill—and complimentary wine and cheese at this hour of the day. Sound good?"

A beat of silence ensued. Then, in a tone of acquiescence, Philippe replied, "Oui."

"Alrighty then."

Releasing the emergency brake, Abby guided the Jeep back down Main Street. At the theater, she pointed toward the marquee. The newest movie being shown was a French-language film. But Philippe was already looking past the theater, toward the plate-glass window of his brother's patisserie. And there was Dora. The town's eccentric homeless woman, perhaps in an effort to find refuge from the rain, had pushed her grocery cart laden with bags under the pastry shop's roof overhang. With nose pressed to the glass, and the sides of her eyes shielded with gloved hands, she stood staring into the darkened interior.

A sudden sharp twinge of sadness gripped Abby's heart. Hoping to lighten the heaviness, she quipped, "Suppose the poor woman is still waiting for that coffee Jean-Louis promised her." Abby lifted her foot to the brake and slowed. After rolling down the window, she called out, "Everything all right?"

Dora turned. The distraught look on Dora's face suggested to Abby that all was not okay. The homeless woman pulled anxiously at a tuft of matted gray hair and muttered inaudible words. Then, abruptly, she grabbed the handle of her grocery cart and turned back into the rain, heading in the opposite direction of Abby and Philippe.

Abby swiftly maneuvered a U-turn. "Sorry, Philippe, but this can't wait. I'll be back." She guided the car into a parking spot and left the engine running and the wipers slapping as she jumped out and raced to catch up to Dora. Not wanting to spook the poor woman, widely rumored to be schizophrenic, Abby strolled alongside the shopping cart until they reached the park opposite the police department.

"Can I buy you coffee, Dora?"

Dora cocked her head, as if listening to other voices.

Abby waited.

Dora finally turned a blue-eyed questioning stare toward Abby.

"You want some hot coffee, don't you, Dora? And maybe a sandwich?"

Dora nodded.

"So . . . how about I help you push your cart with all those bags to the diner over there?" Abby proffered a helping hand, but Dora adamantly pushed it away.

"Okay. You push, and I'll walk with you. We can leave the cart next to the diner window. You can see it from inside." Abby knew the way to communicate with Dora was through simple, direct sentences and nonthreatening actions. She had dealt with Dora before and understood how quickly and easily the woman became overwhelmed. Certain that Dora was more troubled than usual, Abby wondered if the chef's death haunted her.

When they got to the door of the small diner, Dora, emaciated and surely hungry, refused to go inside. Abby entered the diner, where she ordered and paid for a turkey sandwich and coffee. Then she darted back outside and stood in the rain while Dora devoured the sandwich as if it were her last meal.

Abby waited while Dora sipped the hot coffee, stroking the cup to warm her hands. Finally, she decided to broach the subject of Jean-Louis.

"Miss our pastry chef, Dora?"

The gray-haired woman nodded. "My friend."

"He gave you coffee, too, didn't he?"

Again, Dora nodded.

"You liked him, Dora. I suppose everyone liked him."

Dora shook her head. "No. Not everyone."

"Really? Who didn't like him, Dora?"

Dora didn't speak. She cocked her head, as if voices had started chattering in her ear. Abby waited her turn. A beat later, Dora tilted the paper cup and swallowed the last sip of the fragrant, hot coffee. She licked her lips and shoved the cup back at Abby.

"Good, huh? Refill? You want another?"

When Dora didn't reply, Abby figured another cup of coffee couldn't hurt. Although the poor woman's thinking might be tortured and confused, it was also possible that she saw or heard something prior to finding the body. Dora frequently slept in business doorways and alleys, as well as by the creek. In fact, she prowled about at all hours, and she knew things. Abby would be patient and kind. Dora would open up.

"I'll be right back, Dora. Don't go, okay?"

But when Abby returned with the replenished cup of coffee, she discovered that Dora, like a wild bird, had flown away—shopping cart, bags, and all.

The unseasonably cool breeze had chilled Abby to the bone. The drizzling rain had ruined her red silk skimmers and frizzed her hair. When Philippe offered his room at the lodge as a place for her to dry off and a change of clothes as a substitute for her drenched clothing, she demurely declined in favor of driving home to change and then returning. They would have a bite to eat and go through the property and reports together.

"What say let's meet around seven o'clock?" Abby took her eyes off the road for a moment to assess Philippe's response.

He sighed and said with resignation, "*Bon.*"

Abby sensed that his mood had shifted as she drove toward the lodge. Staring straight ahead through the fan-shaped clearing the wipers left on the windshield, presumably at the wet sidewalks and empty streets, Philippe looked as forlorn as a stalk of corn standing alone in a stripped field.

Tips for Treating a Bee Sting

- If you are allergic to bee stings, seek emergency help immediately. Treat a sting in or on the mouth, nose, or throat as an emergency, because it can result in swelling that interferes with breathing.

- Remove the stinger immediately by scraping the sting site with your fingernail or using tweezers. When the stinger goes into the skin, it releases venom, which can cause a reaction, including localized stinging, burning, itching, swelling, and redness.

- Apply ice to the sting site to reduce the body's inflammatory response.

- Apply hydrocortisone cream to the sting site.

- Take an oral antihistamine, such as diphenhydramine, but always check with a doctor before taking any medication.

Chapter 7

Move chickens and bees at night; when they
awake in the morning, the move is a *fait
accompli.*

—*Henny Penny Farmette Almanac*

Abby understood why Philippe might think it silly that,
when returning him to the lodge, she kept the boxes
of his dead brother's property instead of giving them to
him. For Abby, the choice was clear. Until she could prove
whether or not Jean-Louis had been murdered, she needed
custody of those items.

Waving good-bye to Philippe as he ascended the Las
Flores Lodge steps, she wheeled out of the parking lot and
drove back to her farmette. By the time she was guiding
the Jeep down the gravel driveway, wheels crunching over
the bits of stone, Abby could see a spectacular rainbow
unfolding over her garden, which was located next to the
chicken house. Above the little structure, a pair of red-
tailed hawks circled on the updrafts. Abby hoped Houdini
had alerted the chickens of the danger and had hustled them
into the wire enclosure, instead of adopting what Abby
called "the freeze position," which he often did, looking
like a ridiculous feathered statue standing on one leg.

After locking her car, she went in search of her flock of chickens and found them already inside, on the roost. The little hens huddled against Houdini, who had assumed his usual position on the highest rung. Abby smiled. *Attaboy.* She began counting off the chickens. *A little lady on each side is three, and three on the roost below makes six. A full house. Good night, chickens. Good night, Houdini.*

Abby slid the bolt on the door to the chicken house into place and dashed to the farmhouse. Stripped out of her sopping clothes and wrapped in a towel, she searched her closet for something appropriate to wear for dinner. From a plastic hanger, she pulled a top with a built-in bra and paired it with a simple self-lined lace skirt, both black. Dressing took less than a minute. Now, what could she do with her wild, frizzy hair? Abby decided to hide it in a French twist. With her hair pinned in place, she applied a coat of dark mascara to her lashes, brushed her cheekbones with a dusty-rose blush, and applied her favorite pale fuchsia lipstick and gloss.

From three small perfume bottles sitting on her dresser, she chose Nuit de Noel, a perfume that had made its debut in 1922. Kat, who was as crazy about items from the Jazz Age as she was those from the Victorians, had introduced her to the fragrance. It had become Abby's favorite scent, with its notes of rose, jasmine, ylang-ylang, sandalwood, and oakmoss. One squeeze of the pump distributed just enough. Abby slid her feet into a pair of mules with black-and-white stacked heels and grabbed a pair of beaded chandelier earrings and a white sweater. She gave Sugar a pat on the head, dashed out the door, and climbed in the Jeep.

At the end of the driveway, she braked hard to avoid hitting a tractor pulling a sickle bar mower. It finally inched past as her cell phone chimed. *Patience, Philippe. I'm on my way.* The tractor driver waved. Abby waved back.

"Abby here," she said into the phone, wishing the old man on the tractor would goose it.

"Hey there." It was Kat's voice. "You still have a friend or two in the department, and we have got your back. Check your mailbox."

"As it so happens, I'm next to it. What am I looking for?" Abby asked, hitting the button to lower the window before stretching her hand out to retrieve the mail.

"That report you wanted."

"Oh, really? Chief Bob Allen said I could be waiting awhile for it." Abby grasped the large manila envelope and pulled it into the car.

"Yeah, well, he underestimates Nettie. That woman may be slow on crutches, but she's got the fastest fingers in the department when it comes to computers. Thank her for the report. I had business out your way, so I just delivered it. Enough said. Dispatch is calling. Got to go."

"Thanks, Kat."

Abby guided the Jeep behind the tractor until it was safe to pass. She hit the gas and fairly flew down Farm Hill Road toward town. At seven o'clock, she knocked on the door of Philippe's room.

"Abby, come in," Philippe said after opening the door. Two fingers of his left hand supported a bite-size square of cheese speared on a toothpick. The other hand, now no longer swollen, clasped an empty plastic wineglass. His black brows furrowed. "This cheese is terrible."

Abby quickly assessed him. He was still attired in the crisp white shirt and pleated gray slacks he'd worn for their earlier meeting, but otherwise he appeared as fresh as if he'd just stepped from the shower. She couldn't deny that his vitality and magnetism attracted her, but she was determined to keep her feelings in check. Her heart hadn't yet healed from the abrupt ending with Clay. Surely it would be possible to enjoy Philippe's company without any emotional involvement. She hoped so, but judging from the effect he had on her, limiting their relationship to business only might prove challenging.

"Well, I see the lodge hasn't skimped on the portions," Abby teased. "Let me take you someplace where we can get a decent meal."

"Ah, Abby, you are an angel." Philippe's dark expression melted into a smile.

Abby laughed. "Yeah? Well, I am also an exacting taskmaster. So we'll eat, and then we'll work. What do you say?"

"*Bon.*" Philippe grinned broadly. He dropped the cheese into the wastebasket and plucked his tie and jacket from the back of a chair.

"Take the jacket, in case it gets cool, but you won't need the tie where we're going," Abby advised. "Dress is California casual at Zazi's."

At the bistro, they chose a window seat, where they could watch the sun setting over the mountains to the south of the town. Abby pointed out a rectangle of shimmering light near the top of a peak and explained that the sun was bouncing off a row of windows probably the size of her entire farmhouse.

"Rarified air up there, Philippe," she explained. "Wealthy people who can't live without their twenty-four rooms, swimming pool, tennis court, and maids' quarters. Some of the properties even have their own wineries."

She reached for the wine list and slid her finger halfway down to one of the listings. "For example, this wine comes from the vineyard of the Stanton Brothers. No one really listens to their music anymore, but a generation ago, they were a popular duo who played banjo and guitar." She slid her finger a bit farther along. "And this one is from the personal cellar of a local Olympic tennis player. She donates the proceeds to breast cancer research. Oh, and this one is from the Lennahans' vineyard. Once a year Eva and her husband, Jake, open their home for a wine tasting and food affair to raise money for their favorite charities. Hers happens to be children with incarcerated parents, and his, I'm told, is human rights."

"This is all very intriguing, Abby, but *j'ai faim.*"

"Sorry. I'm starving, too." She placed the wine list aside, picked up the menu, and took a moment to glance over it.

"Do you see something you like?" Philippe asked, almost pleadingly.

"Uh, the white bean soup with organic wilted greens. It's the best. They serve it with an absolutely yummy crostini of melted goat cheese, tomato, and basil."

Philippe nodded approval. "Something else?"

"Then, how about the lamb shanks rubbed with rosemary, garlic, and thyme? It comes with fingerling potatoes and a salad of spring greens spritzed with olive oil and raspberry-infused vinegar."

"A shank of anything sounds good. I place myself in your hands, Abby. My mouth, it waters already. The time is right for a glass of wine also, is it not?"

"Of course. Would you like to try something from a local winery, a Napa Valley offering, or perhaps an import?"

"It doesn't matter. American wines are all terrible. So I am not particular."

Although Abby disagreed with him on that point, she

accepted his right to hold that opinion. She said, "Well, the menu suggests a cabernet, a zinfandel, or even a Ménage à Trois wine—a Napa Valley blend of three reds."

She looked up over the menu to see Philippe gazing intently at her.

Noticing his square jawline and green eyes in the light of the setting sun, Abby felt her cheeks grow warm. Why was he looking at her with such intensity?

Leaning forward with a bemused expression, he announced softly, "I like red. In fact, it is my *favorite* color. . . . And . . . Ménage à Trois . . . hmmm."

She reached for her glass of water and sipped. "Are you saying we should try it?"

"Oh, *mais oui*." A glimmer of amusement lit his eyes.

Abby withheld comment, pretending to study the menu. The awkward moment passed. Her lips trembled as she suppressed a smile. Finally, she quipped, "I'm looking for a good dessert," and she immediately wished she'd kept her mouth shut.

"Ooh la la! The dessert. This is something I desire—a luscious mouth-size berry . . . a silky, warm custard . . . or something sensuous to the lips and tongue, perhaps covered in chocolate. Something we could nibble together."

Abby's cheeks burned. Her palms sweated. She wished for an on/off switch for her hormones. Spotting the petite, dark-haired waitress as she approached, Abby sensed a way to cool down.

The young woman removed a pen and an order pad from the pocket of her white apron and asked, "Ready?"

Abby pushed back her chair and stood up. "Oh, I'd say so. My friend will give you our order. I'll just go and wash my hands. Back in a moment."

Abby bolted from the dining room to the ladies' room,

passing the bistro's kitchen, where the frenzied chatter and the frenetic pace of food preparation became a strong counterpoint to the peace and quiet of the powder room. After locking the door, Abby leaned against it and took stock of the rapid beating of her heart. Her thoughts spun from her giddiness. Her legs felt weak; her pulse thready. Her palms were damp. She turned on the faucet and plunged her hands under the cold water. *Get a grip. He's your client!*

After drying her hands with a paper towel and then tossing it in the receptacle, Abby strolled back to the dinner table. With every step, she reminded herself to stay focused on the business she was hired to do.

Philippe, still sporting a sexy grin, poured the wine and handed her a glass.

Abby was ready. "Let's drink to solving the riddle of Jean-Louis's death." She touched her glass to his.

"*À votre santé,*" he replied. Then in English, he added, "To your health. And bon appétit."

Throughout dinner, she kept the conversation on topic, asking questions about Jean-Louis and his relationships. She asked for details of his personal life, such as his childhood in Montreal and the family art business in New York. She explored how the family came to learn that the young man was gay—a secret he had entrusted to Philippe when he was a teenager, but had revealed to his parents only in a private conversation several years later. Finally, Abby pointedly asked, "Who will profit from Jean-Louis's death?"

To her surprise, Philippe answered, "*Moi.*"

"You? Why is that?"

"He decided to put my name in his will."

Abby rested her fork on her plate. "As sole beneficiary?" She waited a beat to see if Philippe would elaborate.

"Oui." Philippe wiped his mouth on his napkin before laying it back over his lap. "My brother believed in love. Oui, he had many lovers. Sadly, he had not yet found that one special person. I suppose he saw me as the responsible older brother. For him, it made sense to leave his things to me."

"But young people don't usually make wills. At least, not in my experience."

"Well, that may be, but our father and mother wanted to draft their will, and we were together with the lawyer, a family friend, who said he would do it for all of us. I didn't follow through, but Jean-Louis did."

"When was that?"

"Maybe about two years and six months ago—the last time Jean-Louis visited New York. I remember it was Christmas . . . and I had just become engaged."

Abby felt her heart pounding again. *Engaged.* So Kat was right to think he was attached. She took a moment to absorb this new information. "So, did he return for your wedding?"

"No wedding." Philippe stared at her with a curious intensity. "My fiancée . . . it was a big step. For her, too big, too soon."

Abby exhaled a long, even breath. "I'm sorry."

"Life goes on," Philippe said with a shrug of his shoulders.

"So your brother's business, investments, possessions—everything passes to you?"

"He was my family." Philippe's eyes narrowed. His expression hardened. "Oh, Abby, you cannot think that I . . . I. . . ." A sudden chill permeated his words, like frost penetrating pea shoots.

Abby remained still. For a long moment, she assessed him with a cool look.

Philippe swallowed the wine left in his glass, placed the stemware on the table, and pushed it back. Leaning in, his eyes locked on hers, he whispered in a husky voice, "I was three thousand miles away when Jean-Louis died. I worked very late that night because the next day was an important gallery opening for our client. When I was told that my brother had died, I took the earliest flight I could to come here." He sat back and reached for his jacket, which he'd hung on a nearby empty chair.

For a second, Abby wondered if he was going to leave.

"Here," he said, producing a piece of paper from the jacket's inside pocket. "My airline ticket."

She studied the ticket, noting that the dates supported his claim. Flashing a reassuring smile, Abby handed the ticket back. "I never doubted you."

Philippe's expression softened. A disarming smile played at the corners of his mouth. "So then?"

She replied, "So then . . . what?"

Philippe's expression took on a devilish quality. "Dessert?"

Abby tried to suppress a giggle, but when Philippe burst into a deep, warm, raucous laughter, Abby couldn't resist laughing out loud, too.

Hours later and long after the doors of the Las Flores Lodge library were closed and locked, Abby sat at the table in Philippe's suite, poring over the police report Kat had delivered. Nothing stood out. The first page listed the required case number and the section code for the incident, 187 PC—murder. Of course, now the death had been deemed a suicide. The next page was filled with general information about the victim's physical description. Of more interest to Abby were the narratives of the investigating cops and the information gained from interviews of neighbors and owners of businesses in the area. Abby thumbed through the neighborhood check sheets.

Abby stop perusing the documents to reread one entry.

> *A woman sleeping in the upstairs apartment over the architect's unit behind the theater heard a scudding sound around 5:00 a.m., approximately the time the chef died, according to the coroner.*

Maybe something there, she thought.

Abby read through the statement she had given to Kat. She also read Kat's and Otto's narratives. Then she perused for the umpteenth time a two-page form that was broken into sections: investigative activities, physical evidence, victim vulnerability, victim actions, and solvability. Kat had checked the box entitled "significant physical evidence," but as far as Abby could ascertain, the only evidence was the earring, the photos on the pastry shop wall, the worthless surveillance tape, and the box of recipes with the award in it. The boxes for blood and saliva were checked, but there was nothing marked for prints, weapon, clothing, hair, or bodily fluids.

If, as Chief Bob Allen had inferred, Jean-Louis had killed himself, the evidence pointing to that conclusion seemed scanty. She flipped to the report from the coroner's office. No mention of an internal exam or a toxicology screen. The X-rays taken noted the ligature mark above the thyroid cartilage and the Adam's apple, but neither the thyroid cartilage nor the hyoid bone was fractured, another indication that Jean-Louis had died by hanging, instead of from being strangled by a ligature. But no signs of a struggle. If he had been murdered, there would have been a struggle, surely.

Abby's eyes burned with weariness. Her back ached. She locked her fingers behind her head and twisted her spine in one direction and then the other. The stiffness remained. Her tired eyes gazed at Philippe, who was stretched out on the couch, sleeping. He'd rolled the sleeves of his dress shirt to his forearms. His hands still wore the latex gloves she had insisted they use to go through the boxes of Jean-Louis's possessions. With his left hand cradling his head, Philippe's right hand rested over his midsection, rising and falling with each breath. Abby understood grief. The physical and emotional toll of it, the feelings of sadness and deep despair washing over mind and heart like rogue waves. She was sure Philippe needed rest. She'd let him sleep.

Abby searched for a stack of prints—some were crime-scene photos she'd taken of Jean-Louis, and others were pictures of satisfied customers and friends taken down from the pastry shop's corkboard. In one, Jean-Louis stood with a group of people as he sold pastries at the town's annual strawberry festival. Another showed Jean-Louis and waiters catering a political fund-raiser. In yet another, he stood in front of the Black Witch with male friends, all of them holding steins of green beer for what surely must have been a St. Patrick's Day toast.

Meticuously, Abby examined all the photographic images through her magnifying glass. Something caught her attention in one picture of Jean-Louis and a fisherman, but she couldn't quite figure out what was different or unusual about that particular photo. Weariness was compromising her discerning ability. The fisherman held a large swordfish on the deck of boat. Jean-Louis stood smiling at him less than an arm's length away. Both men were bare-chested and were wearing swimming trunks. The tall, thin fisherman also wore a white panama hat. Out beyond the boat's deck, nothing but water stretched to the horizon line. The swordfish was an ocean fish, she thought. Philippe had said his brother had planned a trip to the Caribbean for his birthday. Had he traveled there before? Was the fisherman a friend, foe, lover, or murderer?

With the magnifier, Abby looked intently at Jean-Louis and then again at the fisherman. Her instincts told her something was significant, and even though her eyes and her brain kept searching the image, they weren't latching on to what it was. She lifted her gaze to look over again at the sleeping Philippe. The brothers shared obvious similarities, including the same angular jawline, dark brows, thick hair, and muscular build. Both men were handsome, personable, and in the prime of life. But their differences had set them on different life paths.

Of the two, Philippe seemed more courteous, quicker to smile, less extreme in his mood swings. She had wondered whether Jean-Louis had been using drugs, which might account for his temperamental outbursts. No analysis had been noted. Had the pressures of potentially losing the business and losing his lease, his dissatisfaction in his personal relationships, or something else driven him into a world of drugs? Had he used them with reckless abandon? The tox screen results weren't included. She would check on that. Alternatively, had Jean-Louis crossed paths with someone who shared his short fuse to anger? Whatever it was in his makeup that had compelled him to make different choices than Philippe had made had led to this moment: one brother now slept in restful repose, while the other lay lifeless on a cold slab in the morgue.

Abby reached for a small envelope sealed with red tape. She opened it, and then she pinched the small earring retrieved from the pastry shop and examined it closely. Laying the earring aside momentarily, she thumbed through the police report to look for references to it and to ascertain whether or not there had been a follow-up with a jeweler. She found the report of her own statement about it:

> *She heard a ping while helping to hoist the chef's body onto a gurney, whereupon she and Officer Katerina Petrovsky searched for the source of the sound and located the earring—but only one.*

At the very least, she would take it to the jeweler tomorrow.

As she dropped the earring back into the envelope, the thought occurred to her that it was already tomorrow. The sun would soon be up. Her chickens would be pecking each other, relieving the stress of being locked inside the chicken house, while Houdini was already sounding his gravelly call. The animal world might be waking up, but Abby needed sleep. Two or three hours should be enough. She began packing the items back in the boxes. She'd leave a note for Philippe.

Tips for Planting a Fairy Ring

A fairy ring is a landscape design element featuring a tea rose ringed by several flower beds. You can use a white tea rose and plants with gray-green foliage or choose a red tea rose with pink or purple flowers. The gradation from the

tall tea rose in the center to the shortest plants
of the outermost ring creates a spectacular visual effect.

- Plant a white hybrid tea rose bush, such as an
  Honor, Iceberg, Pascali, or Caroline de Monaco,
  to create an anchor for the surrounding rings of
  plants. The tea rose should be the tallest of all the
  plants in the fairy ring.

- Create concentric flower-bed rings around the
  rosebush using shorter plants, such as white
  bearded irises, white bellflowers, sweet woodruff,
  and dusty miller. The rings should be placed a foot
  apart.

- Finish with a final flower-bed ring of even shorter
  plants with white blooms, such as spirea, baby's
  breath, or ageratum.

Chapter 8

If you enjoy listening to songbirds, it might interest you to know that the male is generally the singer, since he uses song to attract a mate and defend his territory.

—*Henny Penny Farmette Almanac*

Abby steered her Jeep away from the lodge toward Main Street. She had left Philippe a note telling him they would meet at noon. She couldn't remember when she had felt so exhausted, and only hoped she wouldn't fall asleep at the wheel while driving back to the farmette. Even her eyeballs hurt. According to her watch, it was 4:45 a.m., nearly the hour of early morning when Jean-Louis died. Although she was tired, Abby's instincts told her to drive by the back of the pastry shop, see what it looked like at this early hour, determine how well it could be seen in the glow of streetlamps and neighborhood porch lights, and see who might be roaming about.

Pulling the Jeep into a parking space under a dense magnolia tree shading the back side of Lemon Lane, Abby parked, flipped off the headlights, and fought the urge to nod off. She stared at the pastry shop. Nothing obstructed her view of its back door, the theater exit, the Black Witch

Bar's rear entry, and the Dumpster. Since she'd parked in the shadow of the tree, the pale predawn light made it possible for her to see without being seen. The starlight was growing fainter, and only a sliver of moon hung in the sky. The streetlight behind the pastry shop had burned out. The lane was quiet except for crickets chirping and frogs croaking along the creek that ran through the town a few streets away. Overhead, the mockingbirds had awakened and intermittently warbled off a medley of songs: the tweets, trills, *dzeet*s, cheeps, and *peet-a-weet*s of other birds and their own familiar *worky-worky-worky*.

Suddenly, a car approached. Abby's senses went on high alert as the small four-door sedan drove past. The car slowed. Stopped. A man wearing a dark knit cap climbed out. When Abby saw he wore a work apron for collecting coins and carried a bundle, she relaxed. *Newspaper carrier. Delivering newspapers. What time is it? Almost five o'clock.*

Abby watched him drop the bundle and hustle back to his car. Disregarding the marked lanes, the man drove right down the middle of Lemon Lane, tossing papers to the left and the right, over the top of his car when necessary, onto porches and sidewalks. At the end of the lane he didn't even stop at the stop sign, but turned the corner and disappeared.

So, no one has canceled the pastry shop's newspaper subscription. Suppose Philippe will have to do it. Inhaling and exhaling deeply, Abby rested her head against the seat and closed her eyes while her thoughts rambled on. Had a newspaper bundle been delivered on the day Jean-Louis died? Where was that bundle now? Had a newspaper hitting the sidewalk made the scudding sound a neighbor claimed to have heard the morning Jean-Louis died?

With monumental effort, Abby forced her eyes open.

She yawned, straightened her posture, and scanned the lane for other signs of life. After a few minutes, a porch light went on. An elderly, balding man in a bathrobe moseyed out with his cat to retrieve his morning paper. After removing the rubber bands and slipping them into his bathrobe pocket, the man shuffled back to the door, then stopped momentarily to look for the cat, which had disappeared. The lane became quiet. Even the cat was gone. *So the newspaper bundles are tied with twine, but the subscribers' papers are banded.*

Her watch ticked away another few minutes. Listening to the mockingbirds, she fought against the urge to sleep. Then something at the end of the lane moved. Abby peered toward the darkness at the end of Lemon Lane. A figure emerged, pushing a shopping cart bulging with bags, and trudged toward the Dumpster. *Dora. No mistaking you, even in the dark. But this is your routine, isn't it? Waking up and coming to the pastry shop for coffee? What did you see when you came around that morning? What did you do? What did you take?*

Dora shuffled right on down toward the Jeep, then finally stopped at the Dumpster. She hesitated, looked at the back door of the pastry shop, up and down the lane, and then at the Dumpster. She leaned over it, reached in as far as her arm would go. For the next few minutes, Dora riffled through the contents. Abruptly, she stopped, stone still. She peered into the dark shadows, looking straight toward the tree under which Abby was parked. Abby froze.

After a beat, Dora shuffled away from the Dumpster and approached the back door of the pastry shop. She picked up the newspaper bundle, dropped it onto her bags, and left the way she had come. *Now, why would you want a whole bundle of papers? Are you sharing them? Sleeping on them? Using them for blankets?*

I am so going to find out. Abby pulled latex gloves from the box in her glove compartment and put them on. She also grabbed a flashlight. She slid out of the Jeep and walked over to check out the blue Dumpster. Abby used one hand to push aside bags of plastic. Deeper down, she dug through loose flyers, mailers, torn theater tickets, real estate circulars, used drink cups, plastic bottles, and soda cans, and at the bottom, she found newspapers. Plucking them out, she counted fifteen.

With her flashlight, she was able to check the dates and was not surprised when she discovered they all carried the date on which the chef died. So Dora had not taken the papers that day. *Why? Newspaper bundles are always cross-tied and knotted with twine. Where's the twine?* That question stuck with Abby as she drove home with the car windows down to help her stay awake. The acrid scent of smoke drifting south on the wind from three wildfires burning in the wine country made falling asleep at the wheel unlikely. Good for her, bad for the guys working the fire line. Once back at the farmette, however, she drifted off into a dreamless sleep as soon as her head touched the pillow.

It might have been the restorative sleep, the long shower, or the raspberry tea sweetened with honey that filled her with energy. Or maybe it was just the challenge of a new case, but whatever it was, Abby felt energetic and eager to begin working on the investigation again. It was a good thing, too, because it was nearly time to meet Philippe. While making her tea, she'd caught the weather report— hot and expected to get hotter. The rains were over. Watering by hand was a drag, but it was a necessary task to keep the gardens going during the hot Las Flores summers.

A fierce onshore wind blowing from the northeast had gusted for hours, ripping off all but the most tenacious blossoms from the elm tree that stood at the back side of Abby's beehives. The sun had not yet reached its zenith, and already the thermometer on the chicken house wall registered eighty-two degrees Fahrenheit. High winds, high temps, and dry conditions would increase the demand for firefighters from outside the region because of recent cutbacks in funding for emergency police and fire services at the local level.

With Sugar inside the cool farmhouse, Abby sat down in the rocking chair on her patio. With one jeans-clad leg sprawled over a chair arm, Abby sipped her tea, thinking about the afternoon agenda with Philippe. Normally, she wouldn't allow a client to tag along, but he had been so insistent and had promised he would not interfere with her questioning. So, she'd relented.

As she rocked and sipped her tea, she heard an unmistakable high-pitched whine. *Bees! The rallying call of takeoff. Another swarm!* Abby stood and looked high up over the chicken house. A cloud of circling bees ascended into the elm tree, while a few zipped about in ever-widening circles, as if waiting for the scouts to give them the landing location. *You never choose a convenient time for me, do you?* She put down her teacup, dashed into the kitchen, grabbed a stainless-steel pan and a wooden spoon, and laid them on the plywood counter. After taking her cell phone from her jeans' hip pocket, she tapped in Philippe's number.

"It's Abby," she said breathlessly.

"Abby. Are you in the parking lot? I am ready."

"Sorry, Philippe, but my bees are about to take off. I've got to stay here until they land."

"It is all right. Shall I drive to your place? Farm Hill Road, n'est-ce pas?"

"If you are sure you don't mind." Abby grabbed the pan and spoon and dashed outside, closing the slider behind her. The last thing she needed was to have that dog, as curious as she was, underfoot and getting stung. With a little luck and a lot of noise, the bees might become disoriented and take refuge nearby.

Balancing the phone between her ear and shoulder as she made her way to the elm tree, Abby said, "Philippe, you were only here once. Do you remember where I live?"

"Oui, but not exactly."

"Last house, Farm Hill Road. Right side. If you hit the T, you've gone too far. Just look for the chicken on the mailbox."

"Oh, *mon Dieu*. What if it flies off before I arrive?"

"It's not a real chicken, Philippe."

He laughed. "*Très bon.* Nevertheless, for me . . . the chicken . . . it belongs on a plate, not on the box."

Amused, Abby replied, "Now you're teasing me. Seriously, do you think you can find your way here?"

"Do not worry, Abby. My phone, it has the navigation."

Abby watched the bees begin to drift from the tree. She clanged the spoon against the pan bottom. "Great. I won't worry, then." The bees lifted higher, as though suddenly caught in a whirlwind. Abby pounded the pan with such vigor, her arm ached.

"What is that racket, Abby?"

"I'm trying to disorient my bees so they won't take off."

"Is it working?"

"I can't tell yet. Might take a while."

"In that case, Abby, I will find you. I will look for the chicken and listen for the banging. A bientôt."

Abby clicked off the call, dropped her phone into her shirt pocket, and banged the spoon slowly against the pan until the bees coalesced, wrapping themselves in a writhing mass around a limb. *Please, just stay put.*

After racing back to the kitchen, Abby dropped the pan and spoon on the counter. She checked on Sugar, who was chewing on a rawhide bone that, apparently, she had just rediscovered in a hiding place behind the couch. *Just as well you stay put inside, where it's cool. We'll go for a walk later.* Abby darted back to the patio. From an over-size basket, she snatched her elbow-length kidskin leather gloves and her white beekeeper suit. Searching the back-yard, she spotted the ladder lying on its side near the apricot tree from which she'd rescued the last swarm.

With the ladder in hand and her suit and gloves under an arm, Abby lumbered toward the elm. She positioned the ladder as close as possible to the bees' branch. Then she darted into the hive area, where she located the bee box that she'd prepared for the swarming season. In it, she'd placed one frame with a little honey and nine others without. Once the bees were inside that hive, they would have plenty of work to keep them busy, as they would build comb onto those empty frames. She wouldn't have to worry about them taking off again.

Abby suited up, then picked up the bee box, walked back to the elm, and mounted the ladder. Stopping short of the top three rungs, she aligned the bee box directly under the swarm, wedging it between the ladder and her body.

You guys ready? Count of three. One . . . two . . . three. Abby gave the limb a muscular jerk. Thousands of dis-lodged bees vibrating en masse tumbled onto her and into the open box. *What a rush!* Their collective piping sound seemed to Abby like a wild cry of disorientation, but she was confident it soon would return to the happy buzzing of worker bees building a wax honeycomb onto the frames. The honeycomb would hold the colony inside, while sealing out intruders.

Carefully, Abby descended the ladder with the bee box, then positioned it on the ground so that its front opening faced the limb. That way, the bees still flying around the limb, where they apparently still detected the queen bee's pheromones that had communicated the order to swarm, could find their way into their new home.

When, by her estimate, twenty minutes had passed, Abby approached the bee-filled hive and knelt to inspect it. Scout bees were doing the waggle dance around the edges, as if to say, "Calling all bees in our swarm. This is our new home." Abby picked up the hive lid and, after tilting it against the side of the box, painstakingly slid it across the top to avoid crushing any insects. She would leave the hive until after dark before moving it into the bee apiary.

There was no mistaking the sound of a vehicle crunching over the driveway gravel. A horn sounded. *Philippe.* Abby hiked the trouser legs of her beekeeper suit to her ankles to avoid stumbling and dashed to open the gate. She stared in astonishment.

Lucas Crawford eased out of the cab of his old red pickup and strolled toward Abby. He wore a blue- and white-striped cotton shirt, straight-leg denim jeans, and scuffed leather boots.

"Afternoon, Abby."

"Lucas."

"Am I interrupting your work?" He pushed the stained palm-leaf straw cowboy hat back a thumb's length.

"Not at all." Abby tried to sound cool, in spite of the fact that she felt like she was going to have sunstroke inside the beekeeper's suit, and the fact that the butterflies in her stomach were making her feel even more uncomfortable at his unexpected visit. "I was just about to peel off this suit. It's an oven in here."

Lucas looked at everything *but* her.

Abby pinched the fingers of her kidskin gloves and pulled off one and then the other as she waited for him to say something. Reaching behind her neck, she felt for the zipper that secured the net-covered topee. With a tug, the zipper advanced and then stopped, meeting resistance.

"Well, this is embarrassing." Abby struggled to move the zipper. "I think it's caught. Oh, dang. I'm trapped in here. Lucas, could you . . . ?"

"Sure," he drawled.

She turned her back and used her finger to point to the problem. Lucas put his hands against her neck. She felt him tugging, pulling on the net, causing her topee to shift sideways on her head.

"If I pull too hard, it might make a hole a bee could get through, but if I don't, I might not be able to free this net from the zipper track."

"That's okay, Lucas. I can fix the hole."

As his fingers patiently worked the zipper, Abby thought about how any other man might have just yanked the zipper, using brute force in a knee-jerk reaction to her being trapped. She liked the way Lucas weighed the outcome and took his time. *Slow hand, gentle touch. Patience. Such lovely qualities in a man.*

Lucas finally slid the zipper around past her chin and guided her back around to face him before lifting the hat off her head. "Fixed. No damage."

"And I can breathe again." Abby shook loose her hair and ran her fingers through the reddish-gold mass to smooth it. "Much better." Heaving a sigh of relief, she looked up. Her eyes met his gaze. "Thank you, Lucas." She unzipped the suit, let it fall to the ground, and stepped out of it.

He nodded.

"What brings you here?" Abby asked, pulling the hem of her blouse outward from her damp skin, to which it was stuck, and flapping it a bit to circulate some air.

Lucas stood tall and unassuming. His wide shoulders, long legs, and calloused hands gave him the appearance of being all rancher, but his eyes—light brown, the color of sunlit creek water—were the eyes of a poet. He now gazed at her. Abby hoped her own eyes weren't revealing the intense feelings that his presence called forth in her . . . feelings Abby couldn't understand. It was as if she and Lucas shared some ancient connection that defied any kind of logical explanation.

"Passing by. Thought I'd stop."

"Oh?" Abby liked his voice—deep, resonant, and gentle, like a country singer's.

"You got chickens." His tone was matter of fact.

Abby arched a brow. "*Yeah* . . . and?"

"I know that from how much feed and corncob bedding you buy for them."

Cocking her head askance and giving him a "So what's up with that?" look, she asked, "Really?"

"Well, not that I . . . Well . . . I checked to see if you might need me to deliver. . . ." He cleared his throat. "I just thought you might . . ."

Abby smiled sweetly, hoping it would ease his awkwardness.

Lucas changed the subject. "I brought you egg cartons and jars for your honey." He jerked a thumb toward his truck. "I'll get them."

Abby folded her bee suit and waited. *Lucas Crawford dropping by, bearing gifts . . . and driving his little ole red pickup again . . . Now, what's that all about?*

Lucas strolled back and set a cardboard box on the ground at her feet. Abby counted six egg cartons and three jars with metal lids.

"Nice. I'll put them to good use."

"You need anything from my store? I'm headed that way. I could drop it on my way home tonight."

"Can't think of a thing, Lucas." She grinned. "And you already know I've got plenty of chicken feed."

"Yeah." He shrugged and flashed a quick, disarming smile. An awkward moment passed. A sudden seriousness dampened his expression.

"Is there something else, Lucas?"

He lifted his hat and brushed back a shock of curly brown hair before pulling the hat forward again in a single smooth sweep. His jaw tensed. "Heard you're looking into the death of the pastry shop baker."

"Uh-huh." Abby wondered why it mattered. "Who told you?"

"Dispatcher. I called the cops this morning, after I rode the ridge, checking on the fencing in the woods up there. Stumbled upon a marijuana grow plot."

"On *your* land?"

"Yep. Dialed the cops. Took a while, but we took down the field."

"Any idea who owned the plants?"

"Not a clue. Wondering if maybe you heard something, you being an investigator and all."

"I'm only doing investigation part-time. My work here on the farmette keeps me pretty busy and to myself."

"Those grass growers are not going to be happy when

they find out their plants are gone." His brow furrowed. "People like that don't take kindly to losing their cash crop."

Abby couldn't suppress another question. "Who owns the property adjacent to that fence line of yours?"

"Businessman named Dobbs . . . Willie Dobbs."

"Have you called Dobbs to tell him what you found?"

"No." Lucas's angular jaw tensed. "Not too fond of that guy. I've been fighting him over a housing development he wants to build next to my ranch—luxury homes. If he prevails, I won't have a moment of peace, and neither will my cows. Might have to sell, and I don't want to do that."

Abby nodded her head in understanding.

His eyes narrowed. "I like it the way it is. Quiet. Smells like wild thyme and chaparral thickets. Stands of old oaks and buckeye trees. Plenty of pastureland for cattle grazing. Nothing bothers, except for coyotes occasionally making a ruckus. It's pretty peaceful. Know what I mean?"

She smiled.

Letting go a heavy sigh, Lucas said, "Dobbs doesn't care about our farms and ranches. I've heard he's trying to buy the votes of council members to win against me. I wouldn't put it past him getting an ex-con or somebody to plant that grass on my property. Cops haul me to jail . . . well, then, I'm out of the way for a while."

Abby sighed. "Hard to believe. It used to be idyllic here. No crime to speak of in Las Flores, and now a murder and someone starting a marijuana operation on your property . . . like I said, hard to believe."

Lucas looked straight at her, his light eyes softening, almost conveying tenderness. "It got me thinking . . . you living alone and all." He thrust his hands into his pockets and studied his boots, as if he felt vulnerable about sharing his thoughts. An awkward beat passed. "Just do me a favor, Abby. Lock your doors."

"Sure thing, Lucas. And I know you're just on the other side of that there hill." She pointed east.

The corners of his mouth crinkled in amusement.

Abby sensed a longing in Lucas. Like a thistle floating in the air, it was almost imperceptible, but she could see—for a moment, anyway—a tender vulnerability in his eyes.

"Thank you for your concern, Lucas. Means a lot."

He nodded, touched the brim of his hat, and strolled back to his pickup. After sliding onto the seat and slamming the door shut, he leaned an elbow over the window and called out, "Stay alert, Abby. You know as well as I do that bad people can hide in plain sight, and you don't need a reason to call me."

Nodding, Abby waved as Lucas drove off down her driveway. Lucas did not wave back, but his words "You don't need a reason to call me" vibrated through her being. Quiet, serious Lucas, with that deep, resonant voice and unassuming manner, had suddenly and unexpectedly set her heart aflutter.

She stood there, her mind on the man in the truck. Suddenly, Lucas pulled back into view, giving Abby a start. He was backing up his truck to accommodate a car barreling down the drive. It was Philippe, who'd steered his rental car off the blacktop road and onto Abby's driveway, right in Lucas's path. It was either the pickup or the mailbox—unless Philippe yielded the right of way. Which he didn't. So Lucas had to back up.

Abby watched as the Frenchman and the cowboy faced off, and smiled as the two men inched their vehicles past each other in an automotive stare down. Her mailbox was safe—at least for now.

Honey Body Wash

Ingredients:
1 cup oil (sweet almond, sesame, grapeseed, or light
    olive oil)
½ cup honey
½ cup liquid castile soap
10 to 20 drops scented essential oil (lavender, rose-
    geranium, sandalwood, ylang-ylang, or your favorite
    oil)

Directions:
    Pour the oil in a medium-size mixing bowl. Add
the honey, soap, and scented oil and gently mix with
a spoon to blend.
    Pour the body wash into a clean jar with a lid or a
pretty bottle with a stopper.

*Makes enough luxurious scented body wash for four to
five baths*

Chapter 9

The next time you have a hankering for popcorn, try an heirloom, open-pollinated variety and compare the taste of it to movie-theater popcorn.

—Henny Penny Farmette Almanac

The lobby of Cineflicks Theater smelled of hot butter and popcorn. The fresh-faced young woman with the dark hair and hoop earrings at the ticket window inclined slightly toward Abby. "How many?"

"Oh, we're not here for the movie," Abby said. Taking note of the woman's name tag, she asked, "Could we see your manager, Ms. Gonzales?" Abby pushed her business card under the ticket window.

The young woman looked it over, rose, and disappeared from the booth. A moment later, she swung open the theater's glass doors.

"He's in the projection room," the young woman explained. "I'll have to go and get him." A beat passed. She said, "Uh, I'm working the ticket window *and* the concession . . . alone. Don't let anyone in until I get back. Okay?"

Abby nodded.

Laughter erupted from the wings beyond the two heavy doors. Abby looked over at Philippe. His cold expression had not changed since the driveway encounter with Lucas.

"Have you seen this film, *Un virage pour le pire, A Turn for the Worse?*" Abby asked. "The marquee noted it was a French film with English subtitles. Must be a comedy," she said. Abby wondered if he would see through her lame attempt to engage him in banter, perhaps draw him out of his dark mood.

Philippe barked back, "No." His expression remained unchanged.

Changing the subject, Abby pointed to the platters of pastries at the concession stand. "You know, Philippe, the brownies and cookies here are absolutely yummy. They're homemade by the theater staff."

His brow arched dismissively. "How charming."

"And get this," Abby continued. "You can buy a little card for ten movies and go straight inside without waiting in line. They just punch one hole for each film you see. You can buy another card for popcorn and soda. Buy five and get the sixth free. Cool, huh?"

"What can I say, Abby? *Très provincial.*"

Fine. We won't talk. Abby studied the lobby layout. Philippe began to pace. She stole a look at him. He seemed agitated, like he was stewing. Well, she couldn't blame him. The death of a loved one under questionable circumstances was a worrisome affair.

Ms. Gonzales reappeared with her manager. "This is Zachary Peale," she announced before walking behind the concession counter.

Abby sized up Zach. She estimated him to be around six feet tall, maybe 150 pounds, if that. He could be in his late twenties. His stringy blond hair had been pulled into a ponytail. He wore cargo khakis, a tan Hawaiian-print shirt, and black Vans, worn thin over the small toe area. *Probably needs a wider size,* Abby reckoned.

She addressed him in her most courteous voice. "Is there some place private where we can talk?"

"Not really," Zach replied. "Here or outside."

Abby glanced back at the young woman. She was setting up another round of corn in the popper.

"Okay. Would you mind answering a few questions?" Abby asked, pulling a pen from her cream-colored shirt pocket and a notepad from her jeans pocket.

"Well, I'm really not supposed to leave the projection booth. It'll have to be quick." Gesturing toward the young woman, he said, "Just me and her here. We're a person short."

"Duly noted." Abby locked eyes with him. "Did you know Jean-Louis Bonheur?"

"Cake boy?"

Abby glanced at Philippe, who looked tense, as though he felt outraged for Jean-Louis and perhaps for himself, as a silent witness to a conversation that so dishonored his dead brother.

"Yeah, I met him a couple of times," Zach said, raising his voice to be heard over the noise of the corn popping.

"What was the occasion?"

"I smoke. He smokes. There's a Dumpster out back. I take the recyclables and trash out. He takes the recyclables and trash out. So I've seen him."

"We believe his death was a homicide. You know anything about that?"

"Not really, except for people gossiping while they wait in line."

"What have you heard?"

"Good baker, but . . ." Zach stroked his Genghis Khan facial hair, as if doing so would power up his memory.

"But . . . what?"

"Different kind of dude from most."

"How so?"

"Who listens to opera when you've got rock, hip-hop, blues, and bottleneck slide? He did crazy stuff."

"Like what?"

"He put out water and dog biscuits for pooches. Gave coffee and pastries to the homeless. My boss said that if anyone was responsible for the wrong kind of people hanging around, it was the puff pastry next door."

Abby glanced over at Philippe and quickly assessed his emotional response. What she saw concerned her. Philippe had folded his arms across his chest, as if defensively closing himself off to everything. Abby now regretted breaking her own rule about letting clients tag along. Philippe was stewing. She could only hope he would hold it together, because she had to press on.

"We've learned that Chef Jean-Louis and Willie Dobbs, your boss, argued prior to the chef's death. Do you know anything about that confrontation?"

"Yeah, it was all about the lease renewal. My boss said he wouldn't have signed that lease if he'd known the guy was . . . *that way*. The real estate agents set it all up, but once Dobbs realized to whom he'd rented the unit, he immediately regretted it. He wanted the chef gone. No way was he going to renew that lease."

"Did you hear him say that?"

"Yeah, I heard him call the chef a Castro clone and say he wished he could string him up from one of those ceiling hooks that the bike shop owners left there when they moved out."

Philippe dropped his arms and hastily searched his pockets. He retrieved his cigarette case, removed a cigarette from it, and began to tap it frantically against the case.

"No smoking allowed," Zach said.

Philippe's jaw flexed. He stared hard at Zach before putting the cigarette and the case back in his pocket.

Abby directed another question to Zach. "Hearing your boss make derogatory comments about the chef, what did you do?"

"Kept my mouth shut. I need this job. And, if I stay all summer, Mr. Dobbs will loan me the money for film school."

"Do you know where Mr. Dobbs was around five a.m. on the day the chef died?"

"You'd have to ask him."

"Do you have any idea where he is now?" Abby asked.

"I don't know. . . . His office . . . maybe?"

"Would that be the land development office in the old bank building?"

Zach nodded.

"Now think carefully. . . . On the day of the chef's death, when did the last movie let out?"

"Around two o'clock in the morning. We had a midnight showing of *The Rocky Horror Picture Show.*"

Abby knew the film but didn't think much of it, but perhaps it had relevance to the chef's death. "Do you know this movie, Philippe?"

He stood with his hands in his pants pockets, shaking his head.

Abby explained. "I guess you could call it a satire on horror. Fans dress up like ghouls and vampires and participate in the action."

"Dr. Frank N. Furter." Zach said the name, taking care

to enunciate it clearly. "He's the doctor character, a transvestite from Transsexual, Transylvania. We sell a lot of tickets on Halloween for that film."

"Oh yeah?" Abby reckoned the young man's sudden animation was the result of his passion for films.

"My boss doesn't like that movie," Zach explained, "but it brings the theater a wad of cash. The film's darkness is one of the reasons why a lot of disenfranchised teens and young adults relate to it."

Philippe had been staring at his Giorgio Brutini lace-up loafers. He shot a piercing look at Abby.

Abby didn't like the look. One of the common emotions of grief was anger. She'd seen retaliatory anger on the streets. Cornered or not, angry men without appropriate outlets for defusing their anger could attack without warning. She worried that Philippe's temper might have reached a tipping point. No sooner had the thought crossed her mind than Philippe lunged at Zach, grabbing a wad of the young man's shirt in his fist.

"Dobbs murdered Jean-Louis, didn't he? You helped him!"

Abby pushed herself between them. "Stop it!"

"Murder?" Zach's face blanched. "No—"

"Oui, because Jean-Louis was different. And yet you show movies that are about vampires and transsexuals. You and Dobbs are hypocrites." Philippe's hand slapped Zach's shoulder, causing the young man to stumble backward.

Abby lunged between them, planted her feet firmly on the floor, and pushed her backside against Philippe. He was forced to step backward. Abby quickly turned and faced him.

"Philippe, this is not helping."

Zach said, "*The Rocky Horror Picture Show* is fiction—it's satire. The audience pretends to be something they aren't. The chef, however, didn't pretend to be different. He *was* different."

Abby grasped Philippe's arm. "Don't respond to that, Philippe."

Zach looked wide-eyed at Abby. "Dobbs is not a killer. I am not a killer. I have to get back to work."

Abby reached out to shake Zach's hand, but he turned to walk back to the projection room. Following him to the stairwell, safely away from Philippe, Abby said, "Sorry about that, Zach. Mr. Bonheur is still grieving the loss of his brother. We thank you for your time."

Abby left the theater and caught up with Philippe just outside it. They walked in tense silence past the patisserie, with its CLOSED sign on the door.

Philippe started to speak, stopped, and then pulled up short, put his hand on her arm, and looked into her eyes. In a shaky voice, he asked, "Dobbs killed my brother, didn't he?"

"Hard to say, Philippe," Abby answered. She tried to sound reassuring. She reminded herself that the man's dark mood and sudden angry outburst were understandable. His heart was raw. The emotional suffering he had to endure over the loss of his brother could truly be understood only by a professional or someone going through the same thing.

He let go of her arm and walked on.

"According to the police report, Mrs. Dobbs provided an alibi for her husband," Abby said gently. She caught up with him and walked in lockstep. "Dobbs and your brother argued, yes, but that could be a motive to evict someone, not murder him. Dobbs could simply have chosen not to renew the lease, which is what he was doing. We need to find out the truth. When we have the truth, it will all make sense." She touched his arm. "I don't mean to upset you, but I think it might be wise for me to speak to Dobbs alone."

Philippe's lips tightened. He exhaled a heavy breath through his nose. He nodded.

Abby hoped his recent outburst had defused the anger. Zach hadn't made a big deal about the sudden aggression, and he hadn't threatened to press charges. As they turned the corner, Abby thought Philippe seemed more forlorn and desperate than ever.

Shaking his head, he muttered, "*Je suis désolé.*"

"No need to apologize, Philippe. Anger comes after shock. It's the second stage of grief. You just let off a little steam. It's understandable. You want answers. I do, too."

He nodded again. "Mind if I smoke?"

"Not if you can do it while we walk." Abby checked her watch. "I want to question Dobbs and also get over to the jewelry store before it closes, and then I've got to get back to the farmette to see what, if any, trouble Sugar might have gotten into while I was gone." *This is where you offer to take the dog, Philippe. You could use some unconditional love. That's what dogs give.* Abby wondered if she should say aloud to Philippe what she was thinking.

"I'll keep my mouth shut while you talk with Dobbs," Philippe said.

Abby looked at him curiously. Hadn't he heard her say she wanted to talk with Dobbs alone? "What say you hang out for a few minutes at Maisey's, while I do a knock and talk with Dobbs?"

"You think I'll overreact again?"

"No," Abby lied. "It's just that I've got a hunch Dobbs will be more likely to open up to me if you—being the dead man's brother—are not present."

"Oh, I see. So what is Maisey's?"

"A fabulous pie shop, owned and run by an equally fabulous person named Miss Maisey Mack."

Philippe took a long drag from his cigarette and blew the smoke out the side of his mouth, away from Abby. "I cannot think. And these feelings make me crazy."

"Pie will help," Abby told him. "It's a comfort food. Does wonders for me when I'm in a funk." She escorted Philippe through the screen door and into the long, narrow confines of Maisey's, where the tables were small, the space was tight, and the round counter seats were mostly taken by the establishment's loyal customers, the local Rotary Club members, and seniors to whom Maisey provided late lunch–early bird dinner specials. The seductive scent of freshly brewed coffee and hot apple pie wafted through the establishment. Abby fought the urge to join Philippe. Maybe she'd have a cup and a small piece of pie *after* she'd met with Dobbs. For now, she'd introduce Philippe and resist the temptation to sit a spell and chat with Maisey.

Maisey, a large, fiercely independent woman who was always dressed in a frilly white apron and who treated her regular customers and out-of-towners alike as family, took a liking to Philippe right away. That meant Philippe would most likely get his coffee and pie free since it was his first time in the shop, and he would also discover Miss Maisey Mack's incredible storytelling skills. The woman possessed a veritable encyclopedic brain when it came to local history. Assured Philippe would be well cared for, Abby headed off in the direction of the Dobbs Land Development office in the historic bank building.

"Is he expecting you?" The woman inquiring was a statuesque brunette and was wearing a blue summer suit with a matching silk blouse and pearls. She peered at Abby over silver wire-rimmed glasses.

"No." Abby proffered a business card and waited. She took a brochure from the stack on the reception area table and quickly perused it. The land development company not only helped clients find and purchase land but also handled farms and commercial and residential properties. When a man's voice addressed her in one of the friendliest tones she'd ever heard, Abby looked up.

"Well, come on in, little lady. Can I offer you some coffee?"

"No thanks." Abby followed Willie Dobbs into his office and took a seat in the chair reserved for clients.

"What type of land are you looking for?" Dobbs was a heavyset, balding man with puffy cheeks and a rounded chin. He wore gray slacks and a white shirt, forgoing a business tie for a black leather bolo with filigree tips and a large silver eagle clasp.

"I'm not in the market for land, Mr. Dobbs," Abby said, taking note of the length of the bolo and deciding it was too short to hang anything bigger than a box of bird suet.

"That right? Then what can I do for you?" He dropped into the high-backed red leather chair that dominated his smallish office and his antique letter-writing desk.

Abby removed a pen from her shirt pocket and a notepad from her pants pocket. "I am a private investigator, Mr. Dobbs. I just want to ask a couple of questions about your tenant Jean-Louis Bonheur, recently deceased."

Dobbs's eyes narrowed. He crossed his hands over his ample belly, exposing thick fingers, swollen knuckles, and a black and shiny thumbnail.

"I hear he strung himself up."

"That seems to be the gossip going around. His brother has hired me to look into it. He just wants to be sure that nothing has been overlooked by the police, what with our department being so understaffed and all."

Dobbs unclenched his hands and leaned forward, drilling Abby with a severe look. "You got five minutes. That's all the time I intend to give this mess."

"So you didn't like him?"

"No, and I told him so."

"You didn't want to renew his lease?"

"Nope."

"Why?"

"Should be obvious! This town is like a small business, and business is always about economics and image. His kind is not the image we want here."

"When you say 'we,' who do you mean?"

"Mayor, town council members, and the good people who make up our chamber of commerce."

"But isn't it true that Chef Bonheur's business was thriving?"

"I don't believe that for a minute. People lined up to experience the novelty of what he was doing there. There was plenty of talk about that cream puff."

"The talk I've heard is that he was a hard worker, trying to make a go of it," Abby said in a cool tone. She decided to try to bait Dobbs. "It couldn't have been easy for him."

"What do you mean?"

"Like anywhere else, Las Flores has good people. But some folks will never change, you know, people who are bigoted, like rednecks, racists, misogynists, and homophobic folks. You're not one of them, are you, Mr. Dobbs?"

Dobbs blanched. He glared at her in silence.

Abby pressed on. "Sir, on the morning—early morning—

of the day your tenant Chef Jean-Louis Bonheur died, where were you between four and six o'clock in the morning?"

"What are you getting at? You think I killed that fairy?"

"Did you?"

"Wanted to. Didn't."

"Your wife is your alibi, according to what you voluntarily told the police. Is that still your statement?"

"What's your point?"

"Just that I noticed also on the report, your wife mentioned your snoring and sleep apnea."

"So?"

"She said sometimes you use a CPAP machine, in case during sleep you forget to breathe. So you don't sleep in the same room as your wife, do you? I mean, that noise— the machine, your snoring, and all. Your wife cannot say for certain that you were actually home at the hour the chef died, can she?"

Abby watched as little red dots emerged and patterned his forehead and cheeks. Bristling, he lumbered upward, pointed to the door, and said in an icy tone, "You can direct any further questions to my lawyer. Get out."

Abby stood up, put her pen and pad away, and walked out. She heard the door slam behind her. A picture went askew on the wall of the reception area.

Suppose that went as expected. Abby checked the time on her watch and picked up the pace back to Maisey's. Dobbs, as everyone knew, lived in a sprawling gated ranch house on a road that meandered around the other side of the foothills to the east and south of Lucas Crawford's ranch. Maybe there was an alarm system, a gate watchman, or cell phone records she could check to help her nail down Dobbs's alibi. But not now. It was on to the jewelry store by way of Maisey's.

Swinging open wide the pie shop door, Abby spotted Philippe at the counter, hunched over a half-eaten piece of low-country bourbon pecan pie, the house specialty.

"Sit yourself down right there, darlin', next to your handsome friend," Maisey called out in a silky alto voice. "I'll just fetch the pot."

"Oh, thanks, no, Maisey. We've got to get to the jewelry store."

"Are you sure?" Maisey asked.

Abby raised her wrist in front of Philippe and tapped her watch.

"Well, of course you are," Maisey said. "Shopping for something special?" The genteel woman from South Carolina wiped her hands on her apron, waiting for a reply, but Abby pressed her finger and thumb together and traced a line across her lips, indicating they would remain sealed.

"I ain't being nosy. It's just been a while since you been by, Abby. I want to hear what's going on with you and your new life out there on the farmette. We got some catching up to do."

"Yes, but another time, Maisey. We're on a mission and a tight schedule. I'll tell you about it the next time I come in for pie."

"Ooh, sounds good." Maisey flashed a wide grin. "So, off with you two."

After slipping her arm through the crook of Philippe's elbow, Abby gave a gentle tug and felt Philippe resist as he scarfed down one more bite. He stood, wiped his mouth, and stretched out his hand to grasp Maisey's. Philippe pulled her large, long fingers to his lips. "The pie, Madame Maisey . . . it is the best I have ever eaten."

Abby stood silent. *Boy, somebody's mood has changed.*

"How about a box? I can wrap it for you," Maisey offered.

"No, no, merci. We will return, won't we, Abby?" Philippe announced, grinning broadly.

"Yes, we must." Abby winked at Maisey and led Philippe from the pie shop.

"Didn't I tell you pie would help?"

Maisey's Low-Country Bourbon Pecan Pie

Ingredients:
4 tablespoons (½ stick) unsalted butter
1 cup packed brown sugar
3 large eggs, beaten
½ cup dark corn syrup
3 tablespoons bourbon (for that extra brown sugar, caramel, and vanilla flavor)
½ teaspoon salt
1½ cups toasted whole pecans, plus 1 cup, coarsely chopped
One unbaked 9-inch pie crust (either your own recipe or store-bought)

Directions:
Preheat the oven to 350°F.

Melt the butter in a medium saucepan over low heat. Whisk in the brown sugar, eggs, corn syrup, bourbon, and salt until well combined. Remove the saucepan from the heat. Fold in the whole pecans.

Pour the filling into the prepared pie crust. Sprinkle the chopped pecans over the filling and bake for 50 to 60 minutes on the middle rack of the oven. After 15 minutes, cover the pie with foil to prevent the crust and nuts from burning. Test for doneness by pushing a toothpick into the center to make sure the filling is set in the middle. Remove the pie from the oven and let it cool before serving.

Serves 4 to 6

Chapter 10

Boxed and jug wine are fine as long as you
never drink or cook with a flawed wine.

—*Henny Penny Farmette Almanac*

Tucking the evidence envelope containing the earring
found near Jean-Louis's body into a pocket of her pea-
green cropped pants, Abby held it there as she dashed
across Main and darted into Village Rings & Things.
Philippe walked briskly beside her, keeping pace despite
the humongous piece of pie he'd just devoured. The afternoon sun streamed in through the windows of the store,
glancing off the surfaces of glass cabinets, shimmering dis-
plays of gemstone jewelry, and shiny mirrors. The pleasing
scent of cedarwood and citrus permeated the interior. On
any other day, Abby would stroll straight to her favorite
area, the marcasite display case . . . but not today. She
wanted to interview owner Lidia Vittorio about that earring . . . and her timing seemed near perfect; there were no
customers inside the store.

Lidia, emerging from behind a beaded curtain that only
partially hid the back room where her husband, Oliver,
did the cleaning and repair work, called out sweetly, "May

I help you?" Standing next to the curtain and stroking the beads into stillness, she stared at Abby for a moment. "Why, Abigail Mackenzie, is it really you, dear? We've missed having you patrol our premises."

Abby smiled. "I've missed seeing you."

Lidia smoothed an imagined wrinkle from the black crepe dress enshrouding her petite frame. Her silver hair was swooped up tightly in a bun. She walked with the uprightness of a young tree, despite the osteoporosis that had forged a dowager's hump over her upper back. After embracing Abby warmly, Lidia held her at arm's length. "You look so healthy. I take it the police work is keeping you fit."

"Well, I'm no longer with the police, although occasionally I do a little investigative work for the DA."

"So that explains why you're not in uniform."

"True. I bought a farmette outside of town. It's the farmwork that keeps me fit."

"Well, nothing beats a homegrown tomato, dear." With a sly wink at Philippe, Lidia touched the cuff of Abby's shirt and added, "I've got a pair of Australian opal earrings with green pinfire streaks that would go beautifully with the color you are wearing."

Abby chuckled. "I'm sure you do."

Lidia turned her attention to Philippe. "You know, young man, I haven't seen you around town lately, either." She extended her hand to Philippe, who took her long, tapered fingers in his and bowed ever so slightly, evoking from Lidia a pale-lipped smile.

"Philippe Bonheur," he said politely. "From New York. I am just visiting."

Abby explained, "Philippe's brother was the chef down the street who recently passed away."

"Oh, dear. I'm so sorry for your loss." Lidia's tissue-thin, blue-veined hands inched upward to the diamond-studded cameo at her neck. After years of visiting the store, Abby had learned why the old lady wore that cameo every day, regardless of her attire. The piece had belonged to Lidia's maternal great-aunt, the family's matriarch. As a preadolescent girl whose mother had already passed, Lidia had been fascinated by the carved face of the jewelry and had often touched it while sitting embraced by her great-aunt's arms. The irony, Lidia had pointed out to Abby, was that surrounded as she was in the shop by exquisite jewels, the only piece she truly cared about was that cameo. Lidia believed it carried the same soothing vibration that her great-aunt had possessed.

Abby discounted the idea that a piece of jewelry could manifest a vibe but didn't doubt the sentimental connection Lidia felt to the piece. But Abby hadn't come to discuss Australian opals or Italian cameos. She wanted Lidia's expert opinion about the earring she had found in the pastry shop, near the body.

"Philippe and I are looking into the circumstances of his brother's death. You knew Chef Jean-Louis Bonheur, didn't you, Lidia?"

"No, I don't think we ever met. Bonheur, that's French, isn't it?"

Philippe's expression warmed at the interest Lidia expressed in his family name. "We're French Canadians."

Before the conversation could veer off too much into the origins of names, Abby asked, "Is there any chance your husband might have known Philippe's brother?"

"Not really, dear. When we are not here in the shop, Oliver and I keep pretty much to ourselves. Well, except for my quilting club on Tuesday evenings. And, of course, there's Oliver's investment group, which meets the last Wednesday of the month, after their power breakfast at the pancake house."

Abby smiled and exchanged a quick look with Philippe. She pulled the earring from the police evidence envelope. "What about this? Have you seen this earring before?"

Lidia took the earring and turned it in every direction to scrutinize it.

"I'm not sure. . . . Something about it seems familiar." She reached for the nearby velvet-covered board on the glass countertop and picked up her loupe. Holding the earring just above the black fabric, she peered through the loupe. "The facets are sharp, not rolled. The girdle is frosty. Oh, dear, the stone has a small crack."

Philippe arched a brow, as if intrigued, and Abby shrugged. "What does all that mean?" she asked.

Putting down the loupe, Lidia gripped the earring post between a long, bony forefinger and thumb. "Meaning, dear, your diamond is real. With the fakes, you don't get the carbon, cracks, or tiny pinpoints of mineral that Mother Nature includes in her stones."

"And that . . . uh . . . girdle part?"

"It's here," Lidia said. Using the nail of her little finger, she indicated the area of the stone below the crown that rested in the setting. "It's just another sign that it's a real diamond."

"Is there more to tell about it?" Philippe asked.

Lidia picked up the loupe and stared through it at the earring once again. "Might be fourteen-karat white gold, but I would have to do an acid test to be sure. Based on the clarity and the style of the filigree, I would say this is an old European-cut diamond earring dating to the early part of the last century. There's a fracture in the filigree, but it's still quite lovely." She turned the earring around slowly, methodically, peering at it from every direction. Suddenly, she gasped. "Oh, my goodness, I remember something."

Abby, who had been leaning against the counter and staring at the earring almost as closely as Lidia, looked at Philippe. He had been leaning forward, too, but now stood erect, his eyes shining.

"What do you remember, Lidia?" Abby asked.

"This isn't an item we carry, dear, but I'm certain it came in for repair—a broken piece of filigree in the scroll-work around the square cushion. It also had a loose mounting prong." Lidia put down the loupe.

"And you remember this because . . . ?" Abby asked.

"Because it's an antique, Oliver showed it to me right away. He said no one does this kind of work anymore." Lidia picked up the loupe and put it over the side of the mount. "My memory isn't what it used to be, but I couldn't forget this one."

Abby felt her stomach flutter. "Please tell me, Lidia, that you remember the name of the person who brought this earring in."

"Well, let me think." Lidia put down the earring. She placed both hands on the edge of the counter, long fingers splayed across the top. Thus steadied, she closed her eyes.

Abby looked at Philippe and put a finger to her lips. If Lidia needed to shut out the visual world to conjure up a clearer memory, Abby figured some silence couldn't hurt, either. What she didn't want was to break the spell.

A moment later, Lidia opened her eyes. "It was last September," she said. "Students from the high school had started coming in with their backpacks. That's always a problem. You've got to keep such a close eye on those young ones. They tend to pilfer, you know."

"Yes . . . and so, last September, as you were saying?" Abby asked.

"A man came in. I'd wager he might have been in his

early forties. Our cleaning lady's husband is about that age. I remember the man's clothing seemed too nice for a sweaty hike up to the reservoir. Said he went up there with a friend. But what I remember most about him is that he wore a Yacht-Master II. Who wears a Rolex on a rugged hike into the foothills?" She smiled at Philippe. "Oh, you might see a yachtsman wearing such a piece in the Old Port of Marseille, but not at the reservoir in Las Flores! Of course, that was the day our air-conditioning broke down. It was hot as blazes out, even hotter here in the shop. Every store in town was running its AC. Triple-digit temps that week and—"

"Yes," Abby interrupted. "I remember that sweltering heat. The county rationed water, and most of my heirloom corn roasted on the stalk."

Philippe took a turn at guiding Lidia back on topic. "The earring, it was broken, and your customer wanted you to fix it?"

"Yes," Lidia said. "The man gave my husband the earring to fix."

"Do you remember anything else?" Abby asked.

"He hadn't been in here before, but he said that his wife had. The earrings were for her. I gather they had been in his family and had been passed down. The man said he needed something to placate his wife for a recent misdeed."

Philippe had stepped away to stare beneath the glass at a pair of Edwardian-style gold cuff links in a spiral shape. But at hearing "misdeed," he looked at Abby with a lifted brow. He seemed to be fully attentive again to what else Lidia might remember.

Abby watched as Lidia, seemingly annoyed that a silver strand of hair had fallen over her shoulder, expertly twisted the strand back where it belonged. "You know, we had to get rid of that AC unit. I guess it must have lasted us three decades." Chuckling softly, she added, "Not nearly as long as my husband and I have been married."

"So," Abby asked, "any chance you recall the man's name?"

"Oh, no, I don't think. . . . No, sorry." She frowned as though her attempt to remember was not without a great deal of effort. "We might have a repair ticket in our files. We always write the customer's name on the ticket and match it with the jewelry by the ticket number. I'll ask my husband if he remembers that man or the earring. In old age, two heads really are better than one." She chuckled. "He's six months younger."

Abby was suddenly aware of the bright twinkle in those aging eyes. That and Lidia's sweet temperament endeared her to everyone in town.

The storefront door chimed as a young woman pushing a baby stroller entered with two women friends.

"Be right with you," Lidia called out.

Abby stood, thoughtfully chewing her lower lip. She wanted to ask Lidia a few more questions, but she'd prefer to do it out of earshot of any customers. Then she had an idea. "Any chance that adorable husband of yours is working in the back?"

"Oh, no, dear. Oliver is recovering from hip surgery. He's grumbling away in the nursing home next to the county hospital."

The shop door chimed as five teens walked in. Some held containers of super soda with large red straws; others carried cups of frozen yogurt, all bearing the logo of the ice cream shop several storefronts away.

A withering expression crept across Lidia's face. After

handing the earring to Abby, Lidia marched from behind the display case to address the teens. "We don't allow food or drink in here. You're welcome to take your treats outside and come back in when you've finished. Now, go on with you." Lidia pointed an authoritative finger toward the door.

After the last teenager was outside, Lidia whispered, "I tell them repeatedly. Still, they come with the drinks. There's a sign just next to the door there. I wish I could change the wording to read 'Teens, small children, and pets are not allowed,' but I can't very well do that, can I?"

Abby shook her head. Her heart went out to Lidia—the grand old lady was past retirement age but was still working, and now she was working without Oliver. *Must be difficult.*

Lidia was watching the customer with the sleeping infant in the baby stroller. The young woman, with dreadlocks tied back in a red bandanna, had removed several pairs of earrings and was holding each pair up to her ears for feedback from her girlfriends before tossing the pair aside and reaching for another.

"Oh, dear Lord!" Lidia exclaimed. "One pair at a time. That's our policy." She lowered her voice to a whisper. "When the earrings are all laid out willy-nilly, it's so easy for them to disappear." She glanced up at the wall clock. "I'm sorry, Abby. I need to help that girl make her selection. I also have to close shop and drive to the nursing home to sit with Oliver while he has his dinner. He grumbles when he has to eat alone. Would it be possible for you to return tomorrow, dear? I'll see if I can find that receipt for you."

Sensing Lidia's utter distress, Abby nodded and returned the earring to the evidence envelope in her pocket.

"Would you like for Philippe and me to flip over the OPEN/CLOSED sign as we leave?"

"Oh, yes, dear, if you would. I'll lock the door behind you."

Abby plucked a business card from her pocket and handed it to Lidia. "Call me if you or Oliver remembers anything else or you locate the receipt. It's important."

"Of course, dear."

Abby squeezed the old woman's hand. "Thanks."

From the jewelry store, Abby walked alongside Philippe as they took the shortcut through the alley from Main Street and then headed up to the church school yard where their cars were parked.

At the cars, Philippe started to say something but was interrupted by the bell at the Church of the Holy Names as it began chiming in harmonic sequence five times. He stared into space, waiting until the echo of the last chime died away. Finally, he looked into Abby's eyes. "I hope your Lidia Vittorio finds the receipt, Abby. I think this is an important clue, n'est-ce pas?"

"Might be," Abby replied. "If it reveals the man's identity, we can talk with him. I want to know what misdeed he did and what the wife knows. What act could have been so egregious as to compel him to give her those earrings? Adultery? Abuse? Murder?"

Philippe smiled broadly. "Fascinating. You are the most interesting detective. I like how you detect."

Abby looked at him curiously. *Where are you going with that?* She felt relieved when Kat pulled up and parked alongside them. Exiting her cruiser, Kat said, "You've got to clear your messages, girlfriend. Your cell is going straight to voice mail. Again. What's up with that?"

Abby reached for her cell in her pocket.

Philippe extended his hand to Kat. "Officer Petrovsky."

Abby watched Philippe appraising Kat. His voice sounded sexier than it had all day. For a split second, she felt a twinge of envy, but she quickly reminded herself for the umpteenth time that Philippe was a paying client. She couldn't let herself feel *that* way about him.

"Right back at you, Mr. Bonheur," Kat said.

Abby knew Kat loved to flirt but never in the line of duty. Turning her attention back to her smartphone, Abby exclaimed, "You called four times! Sorry! I must not have turned the ringer back on after shutting down the phone when I got home at dawn."

"Dawn?" Kat seemed surprised. "So your chickens and bees had to do without you for a night? I hope you can see what this means." Kat eyed Philippe but directed the question to Abby. "Can you say *social life?*"

Abby sighed. "I'm working on it."

"How's the case going?" Kat asked.

Abby opted for the shortest reply she could think of. "Still looking for a major break."

"Well, I come with a tidbit," said Kat.

"Spill it."

"So, here's the setup. I have to work the park tonight. *A Midsummer Night's Dream.*"

"Sheesh . . . Is it that time of year already?" Abby asked. To Philippe, Abby explained, "It's a major fund-raiser for our local acting troupe and for the park. It also raises the profile of our town."

Kat looked directly at Philippe. "Your brother got rave reviews for his beautiful dessert creations at the festival last year." To Abby, she said, "But with Jean-Louis gone, organizers had to pick someone else to make the world-class desserts this year. Guess who?"

Before Abby could say anything, Kat remarked, "Stephen

B. Flanders, now at the Baker's Dozen. Still goes by the name Jean-Louis gave him, Etienne."

"I'm not surprised," Abby said. "He wanted more money, and going to a competitor, giving away Jean-Louis's secrets, could be his ticket."

"Well, we all want more money," Kat said.

Abby broke into a wide grin and said, "Must have thought his dough would rise higher somewhere else."

"Oh, *please*." Kat rolled her eyes. "Seriously, look into Etienne's alibi. In his sworn statement, he said he texted a friend in the middle of the night from his friend's apartment in San Francisco. However, his car was seen in Las Flores at four thirty in the morning."

Abby raised a brow, fully aware of the quizzical expression that must have taken over her face.

"Vanity plates," Kat replied. "Etienne has vanity plates." Kat filled Abby in on the details.

"Ah." Abby gazed at Philippe. "You know, suddenly I have an insatiable urge for a pastry."

Kat pushed her thumbs into her duty belt. "I thought you might."

Abby reached over and laid her hand on Philippe's arm. "Feel like taking in a performance of Shakespeare in the park?"

He did not hesitate in his reply. "Park . . . two beautiful women. *Bien sûr.*"

Inside the downtown park, Abby led the way along the paved walkway to the wooden theater set near the gazebo and arboretum. A temporary cyclone fence had been erected to keep out park visitors without tickets. Philippe chose front-row seating and promised to save Abby a seat while she went to get her pastry.

The food court was situated where it usually was, in the stand of old oak trees. Abby spied Etienne working in the Baker's Dozen tent and watched him awhile before approaching him. He expertly sliced a tall triple-layer white cake with a fruit filling. Using squirt bottles, one raspberry colored and one a dark shade of chocolate, he swiftly created a pattern on each white plastic plate set out on the table before placing slices of cake upon the pattern. He had dressed the part of an expert baker—a toque blanche and a shirt with a double row of snaps, trousers with black-and-white stripes, clogs, and a wide name tag, on which the name Jean-Louis had given him, Etienne, had been written in cursive.

When Abby heard the announcer asking for applause for the festival sponsors before the actors took the stage for act 1, she approached Etienne with her questions about the death of his former employer.

"Like I told the police," the young chef explained, "I went up to San Francisco for the night. I stayed over at a friend's place. I didn't even hear about the death until I got home around noon the next day."

"Your friend got a name?" Abby asked.

"Wayne Wu. Call him."

"Well, the police did call him. Wu, your flight attendant friend, says that you come and go and that he didn't even see you that night, because he was at the airport, waiting to take off from SFO and fly to Denver."

"Like I said, he lets me use it when I'm in the city . . . North Beach neighborhood. I sent him a text at midnight. I remember hearing the foghorn sound just as I sent it. Check it out."

"Okay. What did you do after you sent the text?"

Etienne didn't answer, so Abby pressed on.

"Didn't you drive back to Las Flores? Weren't you here

in town by five in the morning on the day Jean-Louis died?"

The young chef set aside the bottles of raspberry puree and chocolate and picked up a paper towel. He wiped icing from a serrated knife and set it aside.

"Look, I went to see Jean-Louis that night, around ten. He was working. I asked him for money. He said no. End of story."

"Why do you need money?"

"Why does anybody need money? It's not like I was asking for a gift. He owed me. Anyway, I made him an investment offer."

"What kind of investment?"

Etienne seemed to be thinking through his story as he tossed the paper towel into the nearby trash can and retrieved another from the roll on the table, which he used to wipe his hands.

Abby waited. Still no reply, so she decided to take a different approach.

"Etienne, I'm not working for the police or the county sheriff. I don't care what nefarious activity you are into. I am only interested in who killed Jean-Louis Bonheur. His family members are devastated and want answers. Talk to me, and I go away. Keep silent, and you are going under a microscope."

Etienne tossed the paper towel and reached for a long box of plastic wrap. He methodically covered each cake piece on its plate. "Chef fired me and never gave me another cent. An opportunity came along. I took it."

"Opportunity? What kind of opportunity?"

He looked up and narrowed his eyes. "A plant-based business."

Abby arched a brow. "Well, I can understand using edible plants and herbs in pastries, but I suspect those are not the kind of plants you mean, are they? I mean, we're not talking sugar-dusted rose petals or crystallized violets here, are we?"

Etienne stopped what he was doing to stare at her. His tone grew more sarcastic. "You're not the police. I don't have to tell you anything."

Abby responded in a steely-edged voice. "True, but I have contacts at all levels of law enforcement. With one phone call, your life radically changes. The sooner you talk to me, the sooner I go away."

Etienne frowned. "Whatever!" He lined up several more plates of cake to wrap in plastic. He seemed to be thinking about her threat. His tone shifted. "I asked Jean-Louis for money to pay for a place to dry some plants."

"So you need a drying shed. Not talking about herbs, are you?"

He shook his head. "I think you know exactly what I mean. . . . I found a place . . . more like a shack, but no way to grab it."

Abby rubbed the lobe of her ear as she thought about how to phrase the next question. "So you and your friends, you wanted to actually rent the place, instead of just moving into this drying shed?"

Etienne looked at her dismissively. "And have the owner call the cops? Get real."

"Okay . . . so, what kind of money are we talking about?"

"Seven hundred rent, fifteen hundred up front for that shack."

"Where is the shack?"

"Wouldn't you like to know?" He leaned over and retrieved a new roll of plastic wrap from a box of supplies and continued cutting sheets of it to wrap the plates.

For a moment, the thought of Lucas digging up the marijuana field he'd found crossed Abby's mind, but she said nothing. While she didn't appreciate Etienne copping an attitude, as long as she got some answers from him, she would push him for more.

"Did Jean-Louis give you the money?"

"Nope."

"So what did you do?"

"Said a few choice words . . . initiated my backup plan."

"Which was . . . ?"

"Give me money or kiss your reputation good-bye. Folks around here fear what they don't understand . . . and they wouldn't understand their town's illustrious pastry chef stealing recipes from other chefs and elbowing others aside to win a competition."

"Well, that's creative. Did he really do that?" Abby asked.

"It doesn't matter if he did or not, if people believe it. He had so many in this town looking up to him, I had to make sure his ivory tower came crashing down."

"And you had a plan, didn't you?"

"I would say so," Etienne said. Then he added, "I knew where he kept all his recipes. I just took a few. I knew he'd want them back, and maybe he would even pay for them. Hopefully, it would change his mind about ponying up some cash."

"But from what I hear, Chef Jean-Louis was cash-strapped."

"That's what he said. But I didn't buy it."

Abby watched as Etienne wiped his forehead with a towel. She wondered if Etienne sweated because he was feeling cornered. As a cop, she'd seen plenty of guys sweat under questioning; some had even cried like babies after they were caught. "Then what did you do?"

"Had a Baileys at the Black Witch. But I got madder. The more I drank, the angrier I got. You know what they say about alcohol releasing inhibitions. Guess I started spreading it on thick."

"About the chef stealing from other chefs?"

"Yeah."

"So, who'd you tell?' Abby asked, trying not to sound disgusted.

"The bartender . . . the guy on the stool next to me . . . I dunno. What does it matter now? The chef is dead."

"It matters."

"Okay, so I chatted up a few people, had a drink, drove up to the city."

"Your car was spotted in Las Flores around four thirty a.m."

Etienne stared at Abby in an intense silence.

Oh, you're angry, aren't you?

"You're not pinning his death on me."

"You ran a stop sign at the end of the exit ramp from the highway into town."

"Big deal. So what?"

"You careened past the newspaper carrier delivering his route. He wrote down your vanity plate. LFCHEF, isn't it? So I ask again, at five o'clock on the morning the chef died, where were you?"

"Watching reruns on The Food Channel with a friend. We didn't get out of bed until lunchtime." Etienne glared at her and then pulled out his phone and scrolled through his contacts. "There. Name. Photo. Number. Now, can I go back to work?"

Abby jotted the info on her notepad. Looking up at last, she said as a parting shot, "Listen up. Drugs. Blackmail. You might want to come clean with the cops, or you'll be playing patty-cake behind bars, Mr. Stephen B. Flanders, aka Chef Etienne." She spun around and swiftly walked back to the fenced-in enclosure.

Philippe was on his feet, enthusiastically cheering the actors along with the rest of the crowd.

"You look like you are enjoying it," she said.

Nodding, he said, "You missed the opening."

"Oh, if you only knew how many times I've sat through that."

"Find out anything from Etienne?" Apparently, Philippe was so eager to learn about any new development, he took hold of Abby's elbow and guided her toward the exit.

"Perhaps," Abby said as they walked to a quieter part of the park. "He's changed his story again, but my gut tells me he didn't take your brother's life." She caught a whiff of something, which reminded her that she hadn't eaten since breakfast. "Oh my! Do you smell that? Butter, parmesan cheese . . . barbecued oysters! Are you hungry?"

"*Un peu.*"

"Only a little? I'm famished. Let's grab a glass of vino and let our noses lead us to those oysters."

Philippe's mood seemed to have lightened, and they strolled like young lovers past tents housing offerings from local wineries. As they walked, they spotted many varietals and blends. While some wineries provided engraved commemorative glasses, others poured their vino into plastic stemware. Abby thought about stopping at the pouring station for High Ridge Wines, but seeing the long line of park visitors there, she opted to walk on to view Casa Lennahan's offerings.

"Shall we taste their cabernet?" she asked Philippe.

"*Avec plaisir.*" Philippe stepped into the short line at the pouring table and soon returned with two Casa Lennahan etched glasses filled with a dark ruby liquid.

Abby touched her glass lightly to Philippe's and sipped. Licking her lips, she pretended to be a master sommelier.

"Black fruit, olive, a hint of anise . . . smidgen of mineral, and a touch of oak. Lovely."

Philippe sniffed the wine twice, once with his mouth slightly open to allow the vapors to cross his palate, and then took a real sip, which he held in his mouth before finally swallowing. "For me," he said, "not so good. Too astringent. Not enough oak. Just average."

"But it's aged for mellowness. It says so there on the sign."

"Average wine aged remains average. It is simply older." Philippe sniffed the wine again, putting his nose very close to the rim of the glass.

Abby took another sip. "Well, I kind of like it, although I confess I really don't know much about wine. But isn't it true that California wines have been giving French wines stiff competition and even winning some major awards for quite a long time now?"

Philippe sipped, swished the liquid around in his mouth, swallowed, and shook his head. "No, this is really not good. West of Toulon, my father's brother owns a small farm. The soil, it is limestone. It is where the Mourvèdre grapes thrive. From those grapes, he makes a wine that is *magnifique*. It is corked and aged for ten years. You and I, Abby, we must go to Toulon and taste that wine together."

Abby looked at him, batted her eyes, and smiled. "And where in Canada is Toulon?"

"Oh, no, no, no. Toulon, it is not in Canada. It is in southeastern France. In Provence, to be exact," he said with a quick wink.

Oh, like it's just down the road and round the bend. Abby lifted her glass and nodded.

Smiling, he strolled off and picked his way through the crowd to the Shakespeare in the Park fund-raiser table.

Abby gazed at the swaying branches of the dark pines and oaks, illuminated by the peach-colored glow of sunset. For a moment, she imagined sipping wine with Philippe under a Mediterranean sky while the sea breeze tousled her hair and that light, so beloved by the Impressionists, cast its magic spell. Absorbed in her reverie, she nearly missed seeing Eva Lennahan's signature white-blond hair as the councilwoman strode past. With her spell broken, Abby hurried to Philippe's side and pressed her glass into his hand. Catching his questioning look, she jerked her head toward the politician and then fished in her pocket for a business card.

Philippe seemed to be getting used to her sudden actions. He nodded and stepped to the side of the walkway.

When the councilwoman stopped to sign a program for one of her supporters, Abby interjected herself. "Excuse me, Councilwoman. I'm Abigail Mackenzie. This is Philippe Bonheur," she said, gesturing to Philippe and pressing her business card into Eva Lennahan's hand. "Such a tragedy . . . the death of Chef Jean-Louis Bonheur, isn't it? You knew him, didn't you?"

The councilwoman slipped Abby's card into the left waist pocket of her cream-colored suit. Her gaze switched quickly from Abby to Philippe. She apparently liked what she saw and flashed an engaging smile, suggesting interest, which he returned. Ignoring Abby's question, she said, "I see you've got our winery's commemorative glasses. . . . Philippe, right? Enjoying our wine?"

Philippe smiled and raised the two glasses, but said nothing.

"It defies expectations," Abby said. Before the councilwoman could so much as bat another fake eyelash at Philippe, Abby continued. "The chef defied expectations, too, didn't he? I mean, in a good way, and you must have known that. Didn't I read that you used him exclusively to cater desserts for your political fund-raisers?"

Eva Lennahan curled the long fuchsia nail of her forefinger against her thumb and flicked an imaginary speck from her suit lapel. "Yes, a rising star, that chef . . . sadly no more." She again made eye contact with Philippe. "My condolences."

Abby pressed on. "Didn't I also read that you are using the Baker's Dozen for catering now?"

"Oh . . . did that bit of news make the paper? I didn't know. What section?"

"Business," Abby replied.

Eva Lennahan sighed contentedly. "Well, of course, everyone knows I support local businesses, and the sudden demise of Chef Bonheur left me in such a lurch." She cast a come-hither look at Philippe. "The people around me, well, I require them to be not only good at what they do, but also trustworthy and dependable. . . . It's an election year, for goodness' sake. One can't be too careful."

Abby wasted no time in getting to the heart of her line of questioning. "You signed a contract with the Baker's Dozen one week before Jean-Louis died . . . almost as if you had a sixth sense about his fate."

Eva Lennahan raised a perfectly plucked brow. "Good grief. Reporters do make the silliest linkages."

Abby eyed her more closely. "Did something happen to make you want to stop working with him?"

Eva's mouth molded itself into a syrupy smile. "Which media did you say you work for?"

"Oh, I'm not a journalist," Abby replied.

Eva Lennahan slipped two fingertips into the left waist pocket of her stylish suit and retrieved Abby's card. As she looked at it, her expression hardened. "I do wish we could continue this chat, but I'm just here to show support for the Shakespeare troupe. Sorry to have to end our little discussion, but my husband awaits." She looked at Philippe, who, supporting an etched wineglass by the stem in each hand, was obviously unable to shake her hand. Eva plucked away one of the glasses and held it against her chest while she extended the other hand toward Philippe.

The ensuing handshake was long enough to give Abby a full view of the rings Eva wore, especially the diamond engagement ring, with its filigree work.

"Pleasure to meet you, Philippe. . . . Ms. Mackenzie," Eva said in a dismissive tone. In less than a heartbeat, the platinum-haired politician returned the glass to Philippe and pivoted away. As she strolled back down the walkway, she tossed Abby's card into the nearest spit bucket. At the end of the paved walkway, a dark-haired man joined her. Together they disappeared into the packed parking lot.

Motioning to Philippe to come along, Abby followed Eva's footsteps, peering into the sea of cars. Finally, she spotted a black sedan pulling away. Taking her glass from Philippe, she asked offhandedly, "Was it something I said?"

Philippe snorted. "You are asking me? I find . . . sometimes . . . American women difficult to comprehend. They smile too easily. They look you right in the eyes. This says to a man, 'I want to have sex with you.'"

"No, it doesn't. Surely not. Is that what you really think?" Abby didn't try to hide her surprise.

"Oui. Is this not accurate?" Philippe stared at her, a baffled expression on his face.

"Well, that notion is certainly fodder for a long discussion, which we'll have at another time," Abby replied with a chuckle.

"This woman, is she a suspect?" Philippe asked, seemingly perplexed.

"I'm not sure," Abby answered. "Murder suspects generally have a motive. I can't fathom what hers might be. But I don't think she welcomes any questions about your brother. Now, that arouses my curiosity."

"Let me tell you what is aroused in me," Philippe said. "It is *l'appétit*. The oysters . . . We are on a quest, n'est-ce pas?"

"Oh, my goodness, yes," Abby replied. "Let's go this way." She took his free hand in hers and pulled him into a short line that ended at a roped-off area where two cooks slaved away over a smoking grill. When it was finally their turn for oysters, the apologetic expression on the cooks' faces said what their words affirmed. "We just ran out."

Wine Country Grilled Oysters with Garlic Butter

Ingredients:
1 stick unsalted butter
2 teaspoons finely minced garlic
12 fresh oysters on the half shell
1 cup freshly grated Parmesan cheese
2 teaspoons finely minced fresh parsley

Directions:
Heat a barbecue grill.

Meanwhile, place the butter in a small saucepan and bring it to a simmer (but not to a roiling boil) over medium-low heat. Clarify it by spooning off any foam that forms, and then reduce the heat to low. Add the garlic and cook for 2 minutes, stirring frequently. Remove the garlic butter from the heat and set aside.

Arrange the oysters in their half shells on a large plate. Sprinkle some Parmesan cheese and parsley on each oyster. Transfer the oysters to the prepared barbecue grill and cook for 3 to 5 minutes, or until the cheese darkens.

Drizzle the oysters with the reserved garlic butter and cook for another minute. Remove the cooked oysters from the grill to a clean plate. Add more Parmesan cheese if desired and serve at once.

Serves 3 to 4

Chapter 11

Use a dab of raw honey or bee propolis (the resinous material bees collect and use to seal their hives) to treat a peck wound on a chicken, since honey and propolis have antiseptic, antibacterial properties.

—Henny Penny Farmette Almanac

They had to get Jean-Louis into the ground . . . and fast. An uptick in gang violence on the county's east side had left seven dead in stabbings and retaliatory shootings. Space was filling up at the morgue.

Abby learned about this latest news after attempting to hoist a hefty bag of chicken crumbles over the feeder. Lifting the bag was one thing, but pouring the poultry feed into the hanging metal chicken feeder while answering her cell phone proved impossible. She dropped the bag to take Philippe's call. It soon became apparent that he was feeling overwhelmed and more distraught than usual. He talked nonstop, frantically flipping between French and English, attempting to explain how the situation with Jean-Louis had gone from *très terrible* to *absurde*.

"Slow down, Philippe. Breathe. Now tell me slowly in English, please."

"We must bury Jean-Louis and soon."

Abby failed to see the issue. "So what's the problem? The funeral home can pick him up from the county facility. It's easy enough to transport the body back to the East Coast for burial."

"The problem . . . the problem," he said, his volume rising a decibel, "it is that I have yet to make arrangements."

"Oh?" Abby eyed the poop floating in the chickens' watering canister. *Why can't you ladies just drink without climbing up and pooping into your water?*

"This whole affair has been most difficult." Philippe rambled away from her question and complained about the morning news show he'd watched in the lodge's dining room and, explaining how it had ruined his breakfast muffin and coffee, wondered why American hotels had to have televisions in every room, anyway, showing clips of violence when people might be eating.

"But let's back up a minute. Have you called Shadyside Funeral Home? Or visited the priest at Holy Names? The church is right there by the pastry shop, less than ten blocks from the Las Flores Lodge, where you are staying."

"Non." His tone sounded sullen now. "I haven't been inside a church in years."

"Jean-Louis's body has been in the morgue for several days now. Do you need help making these arrangements?"

"Oui. I thought I could deal with this tragedy . . . for my mother, for my father . . . but I did not know it would affect me the way it has."

Abby sighed heavily. The weight of grief she understood from her experience with victims, their families, fellow cops, her folks. Death was something you had to deal with when working the streets and when you had aging relatives. Everyone died. But thinking about death philosophically and intellectually was much different than personally experiencing the death of a loved one.

"The ruling of suicide is *très terrible*. It occurs in a moment of insanity, and surely anyone who takes such action is out of his mind, n'est-ce pas? But someone snuffed out Jean-Louis's life. I had hoped you would find out who did this. Then I could take care of Jean-Louis. But you haven't. I haven't. Now we must."

"Oh, Lord." Abby latched the henhouse door and sank onto a bale of straw, her thoughts swirling. Of course, morgue space would be needed for the incoming. Now Abby understood the urgency Philippe had expressed about proving Jean-Louis death was *not* a suicide. He couldn't face putting his brother's body in the ground if people were thinking his brother had taken his own life. It was already day six. The body was going to have to be buried somewhere . . . and soon. But another thought loomed— once the body was buried, if murder was proven, it just might have to be exhumed and reinterred. There was the whole issue of embalming.

Abby sat on the bale, elbows on her knees, cell phone to her ear, listening as Philippe rambled. She knew that a buried body took its secrets with it. Murder victims required an in-depth external and internal exam, but had Jean-Louis's body received that kind of scrutiny? From what Abby remembered from the coroner's report of their limited investigation, an external examination had been done, and blood and tissue samples taken for toxicology— usual for homicides but getting those results could take up to two weeks. The ruling of suicide meant Chief Bob Allen could close the case, which he did because all indicators pointed to suicide. That conclusion would save the cash-strapped county money. Chief Bob Allen might be a pain in the rear end, but he did everything by the book. Furthermore, the coroner's office could make the call to do an autopsy with an internal examination, or not. Abby realized she would have to take another look at the report and work the case even faster to get at the truth *before* Jean-Louis was laid to rest.

Henrietta, the small speckled Mediterranean hen, began a series of trilling purrs as she took her dust bath, squirming, scratching, and tossing herself sideways. Her sister hovered on the nesting box. Houdini eyed Mystery, a large black Cochin, whose feathers never got ruffled over anything, as if to say, "Hey, baby, come perch with me." Reminding herself that her chickens seemed to respect the rooster to make decisions for the entire flock in times of distress, Abby asked Philippe, "What is your father's advice?"

Philippe's voice dropped slightly, as if the edginess he'd felt over the problem had somehow dissipated by talking it over with Abby. "My father says perhaps it would be best to bury Jean-Louis here. My mother is in the hospital— complications from her late-stage Parkinson's disease." He hesitated and then added, "My father doesn't want to leave her. What if something happened to her while he is here? Abby, he isn't in the best health, either. This overwhelms me. I need your help."

"Of course. You have it, Philippe." Abby hurriedly created a mental checklist. *Contact Shadyside, the local funeral home. Choose a burial site. Plan a wake. Or consider a graveside service. Find out if videotaping is permitted.* How else could Philippe's parents witness their youngest son's final send-off?

Staring at a pile of freshly deposited chicken droppings, Abby heard herself say with more optimism than she felt, "Don't worry, Philippe. We'll work this out."

When Abby had finished cleaning and refilling the chicken

watering canister, she gathered the eggs and, deep in thought, walked back down the gravel path to her farm kitchen. On any other day, she would check the ripeness of the apricots and peaches, count the number of fruits on her White Genoa fig tree, and note the swelling and striping of the Fuji apples, espaliered against a wooden trellis. But the state of her orchard seemed less important than the state of mind Philippe had worked himself into as a result of inaction.

Inside the kitchen, Abby fed Sugar and sank onto a high stool next to her unfinished cup of coffee. She would at least allow herself time to drink the rest of the coffee, though she wished she had a linzer cookie—her favorite— to go with it. Then she needed to make some calls to the local funeral home, check on Etienne's new alibi details, see if she could plug the hole in Willie Dobbs's alibi, and then hook up with Philippe to search his brother's apartment for anything of relevance to the case. But no two ways about it, Sugar needed a bath. The dog stank. Sensing she would regret it, Abby resolved to let the doggy bath wait.

Her first call was to the morgue to make sure that Philippe had his facts straight and that he could take the body. He could. The next call was to Shadyside Funeral Home, a full-service facility that offered everything from picking up the body to preparing it for viewing and burial and conducting chapel services. Several funeral services were already scheduled for that week at Shadyside, and the facility's director told Abby that staffing-wise, they were stretched thin. But they would try to accommodate Abby and Philippe's needs. The director offered an option: a viewing of the body at 2:00 p.m. and a graveside service at 4:00 p.m. at the small Catholic cemetery next to the

Church of the Pines, which was about a mile out of town, up the mountain. There were no cemeteries in town, except for the historical one, because of local zoning laws and also concerns over flooding. Part of the town, where the creek ran through, was a designated floodplain. No one wanted buried caskets to rise up and float during seasonal floods.

Abby called Philippe. Would he and his parents object to a wake at the funeral home and a graveside service at the Church of the Pines? She figured Philippe would at least want to see the location first. Her call went to voice mail, so Abby left a message. While she waited for him to return her call, Abby dialed Kat to ask about rendezvousing at Dobbs's estate.

"But it's my day off," Kat protested.

"I know," Abby replied, "but Dobbs and I have already had a run-in. If he's there, he might call the cops. If I bring my own cop friend, maybe he'll be a little more helpful and a little less aggressive. And you know I'll make it up to you."

"How? I already have a year's supply of honey."

"Okay, no honey. What else?"

"Stand in for me on a dinner date with Bernie."

"Now, why in the world would I do that?" Abby felt a sinking feeling in the pit of her stomach.

"He doesn't do favors for nothing. Remember all that evidence bagged and tagged at the pastry shop? You know that evidence is supposed to be logged in by the investigating officer. So, Bernie helped me out. I was drowning in paperwork and had to write my report. I owe him dinner." Kat was beginning to sound a little whiny.

"Arghhh. You told him you would take him to dinner?"

"It's what he wanted! Abby . . . girlfriend! Just tease him. Tell him you're skipping dinner and going straight to dessert. Then take him for a scoop of ice cream and use that stupid line he uses on women. 'I'm here for a good time, not a long time.'" Kat chuckled. "It might work."

"Not funny," Abby said. "It's *you* he wants to go out with, not me."

"Do I have to remind you that we are talking about Bernie here, a guy who would go out with a Saint Bernard if it wore a bustier?"

Resigned that this was an argument she couldn't win, Abby asked, "If I agree to that date with Bernie, will you meet me at Dobbs's place in twenty-five minutes?"

"No problem."

"Okay. Let's rendezvous in front of the guard gate."

"I won't be in uniform," Kat reminded her.

"It doesn't matter. Dobbs knows you."

Before dressing, Abby brushed pearlescent finishing powder and a softly colored peach blush on her face, then dabbed a bit of gloss on her lips. She chose a conservative black skimmer dress and a black summer sweater with white piping at mid-elbow, a black headband, and black flats—simple attire, but appropriate for pinning down Dobbs's alibi and then calling on the priest and the funeral director.

A half hour later, she wheeled the Jeep in front of the Dobbses' electric wrought-iron gate with the ostentatious D emblem. Kat's silver Datsun roadster, restored with a new engine, was parked along the stone wall that was part of the guardhouse. The guard was standing outside and was already talking with Kat, who looked like a teenager in her blue-green print sundress, which hit her at mid-thigh, exposing lean, muscled legs from daily runs.

Seeing Abby drive in, Kat hurried over to greet her. Running her fingers through her blond tresses, which had been cut in an edgy style and moussed, Kat said, "You dressed up for a knock and talk?"

"No, I dressed for a visit to check out a cemetery with Philippe."

"Oh, gotcha," Kat said. "Well, you look . . . solemn." She changed the subject. "Dobbs isn't here. I've already explained to the guard that this is an informal investigation. I asked for a little of his time and promised him we would be brief."

"I appreciate that. Thanks," Abby said. She followed Kat to meet the six-foot uniformed security guard, who was cleanly shaven and wore his brown hair in a crew cut. He stood as straight as a hoe handle.

"What can I do for you, ma'am?" the guard asked politely.

"Well, first of all, thank you for your time." Abby handed him her card. "Five days ago, between three and six in the morning, Chef Jean-Louis Bonheur died in his pastry shop. He and your boss, according to some eyewitnesses, argued prior to the chef's death. Do you know where your boss, Mr. Dobbs, was during those early morning hours?"

The guard studied her card, looked up, and replied, "Most likely, he was asleep up at the big house." He walked into the guardhouse and slipped her card into a drawer.

"Is there any way to prove it?" Abby asked, motioning Kat to follow her and the guard into the narrow room equipped with surveillance monitors.

The guard sighed. "Not sure. I don't get here most mornings until seven, and I go home around seven at night. But Mr. Dobbs, when not away on business, is always here at night. He prides himself on being a real family-type man."

"Is there a night guard on duty?" asked Abby.

"No, ma'am. For night security, we rely on the gate and house alarms and surveillance equipment."

"So, are there cameras inside the house?"

"Yes, ma'am. Inside and out."

"In the vicinity of the owners' bedrooms?"

"Yes . . . at each end of the hallway."

"Any chance," Abby asked hopefully, "that I could take a look at what your surveillance shows? I'd like to verify where Dobbs was when the chef died."

"No, ma'am, I couldn't let you do that. It's against the rules."

Abby didn't want to start off on the wrong foot with the guard, but how to tactfully persuade him?

"What if you looked the other way?" Abby asked. "Or what if you stepped outside to smoke? I mean, with your back to me, how you could be expected to know what I could or could not see?"

"I don't smoke, ma'am. It's a nasty habit that shortens your life. As for what you want to see from the surveillance, it's irrelevant, since I can't show it to you without my boss's permission. And I have to log in your visit here. He pays me to keep track of who has been on the premises."

"Well, it's your boss that concerns me. I want to clear him as a suspect in this murder investigation. I bet he would appreciate your help in doing that."

"He might. But Mr. Dobbs has never mentioned anything about being a suspect. As far as I know, the police haven't come calling, so unless one of you has a badge, I'm afraid you'll have to leave."

A tense silence ensued as the guard did a stare down with them. Abby steadied herself against the side of the desk, her gaze sweeping the room as she tried to come up with another approach. Finally, she said to the guard, "I guess this is where I open my purse and flash my badge. Except I don't have one."

The guard, who stood with his back to Kat, pivoted stiffly and swept his hand toward the door. Kat reached into her purse and took out her badge. She held her shield on its leather holder in the guard's face. He looked at it closely.

"So this *is* police business," said the guard.

"Well . . . ," Kat began.

Abby spoke before Kat could characterize the visit as unofficial. "Why else would we be here?"

The guard relaxed. "Why not show me your badge right off?"

A quick smile flitted across Kat's lips. "Some guys are intimidated by lady cops. But I can see you aren't one of them."

The corners of the guard's mouth twitched into a smile. "Of course not."

"Well, it's clear," Abby noted when they had finished looking through the images, "that the maid has brought a glass of milk or something on a tray to Mr. Dobbs."

"Maybe he couldn't sleep," Kat said and then pointed to the screen. "But check out that smile when he opens that door. Time stamp says four forty-six a.m."

"Well, dang it, that nails his alibi. When the chef died, Dobbs was with the maid. Dobbs could have just told me as much." Abby sighed.

"You might say something to the missus," Kat said.

The guard piped up. "She's new. Mrs. Dobbs brought her on staff three weeks ago."

Kat smiled. "I'll bet she warms the mister's milk just the way he likes it."

The guard cleared his throat and, avoiding eye contact with both of them, loosened his tie.

Abby looked at them with amused bafflement. When the guard again gestured toward the door, she followed Kat out of the guardhouse.

Kat said, "You'd think the missus might worry about that pretty little chicklet in the house, visiting hubby's room before dawn. If I were married," she said, emphasizing the word *were*. She paused. "I'd never hire household help that looked better than me in a uniform." She flashed a flirty smile at the guard.

He cracked a smile, too, but then grew serious. Addressing Abby, he said, "The maid doesn't leave the room until five forty-five a.m. That suggests they were in there together for about an hour."

Abby asked, "Is the maid working today?"

The guard shook his head. "Day off."

"You have my card. Ask her to call me," Abby said, extending her hand. "Thanks."

Walking Abby back to the Jeep, Kat asked, "With Dobbs out of the lineup, who else are you looking at?"

"It's a short list, growing shorter, without prospects. I'll be checking out the bar's regulars, like Sweeney and the bartender. I've got questions for Dora, since she may have seen something, but you guys didn't get much from her in the way of information, so I'm not too optimistic. She could have seen something she's not telling us about."

Kat scratched her head. "Maybe Chief Bob Allen is right, Philippe is wrong, and it's a suicide, plain and simple."

"Well, I don't agree with that, either," said Abby. "Etienne verified he was blackmailing the chef. And he started that vicious rumor. And, as you know, in a small town, gossip spreads like wildfire." Abby sighed heavily. "I'm just going to keep digging. Philippe and I are going through his brother's apartment later today. Maybe we'll turn up something there." Abby unlocked the Jeep. She touched Kat's arm.

"Before I go . . . what can you tell me about Eva Lennahan's work with prisoners?"

"Not much," Kat replied. "She's well respected. I think she heads a nonprofit that videotapes prisoners addressing their families. You know, they talk about their hopes, fears, and dreams, tell stories for their kids, even sing sometimes. The organization gives the tapes to the family. Seems like meaningful work. She has a lot of contacts in and outside of prisons and a huge fan base."

"And her husband?"

"Jake Lennahan, businessman, spends a lot of time traveling. He financially backs lots of ventures. I think I heard he's aligning with some backers to fund a resort of some kind. Don't think he's too involved with his wife's political career or her nonprofit work. Keeps a pretty low profile."

"Well, thanks, Kat. I appreciate your help."

"My pleasure . . . especially since it got me a date for the Friday night movies."

Abby had opened the car door but stopped short of climbing in. She stared at Kat in surprise. "The guard? He doesn't seem your type."

"You never know. . . . He has a wicked sense of humor, likes garage sales and weight lifting."

"You found out all that while waiting for me for what? Five minutes?" Abby said in amazement. She sucked in a deep breath and let it go. "It occurs to me that you got something nice out of my invitation to come here, so how about letting me off the hook for that date with Bernie?"

"Not negotiable."

"You want me to suffer, don't you? For something so slight, I can't even imagine what it is. I thought I was your best friend."

"You are. But you are my best friend who needs favors . . . often."

Abby sighed. "When you're right, you're right. But I can't tell you how much I hate the thought of having to suck it up and deal with it. Anyway, Philippe is waiting for me, so I'd better be on my way."

After a quick wave good-bye, Kat strolled back. Abby watched her return to the guardhouse—chest out, boobs high, and a light swing to her hips, all, no doubt, to titillate the guard.

Glancing in the rearview mirror as she made the turn onto the blacktop, Abby caught a glimpse of Kat and the guard laughing. Abby admired how easily Kat formed relationships with people, especially guys. When a love affair didn't work out, Kat wasted no time getting right back into the game, looking for someone new. Her well-meaning advice to Abby after Clay had left was to move on. "You've got a blind spot where it concerns Clay Calhoun. Wake up, girlfriend. That hound dog is hunting again."

For the longest time, Abby had tried to shut out thoughts of Clay, but her memories of him, like water from a deep hidden spring, would surface and ripple outward into myriad what-ifs. What if he didn't like the new job? What if he walked back into the farmhouse like he'd never left? What if he still loved her with the intensity he'd expressed that day in the kitchen, when he'd knelt before her, taking her hands in his? She had believed that day that his profession of love was the beginning of a proposal of marriage—one she would have accepted—but he'd been interrupted by a phone call, and for whatever reason, Clay never got around to finishing what he'd started.

A week later, Clay had hugged and kissed her in front of the farmhouse, as though he would be back in time for dinner. He'd called ten times that day—at least once for every state he passed through. But when the calls stopped after a week, she called him. By then, she was angry at the man whose abrupt departure had left her feeling like a jilted lover. Her first call and all the subsequent ones went to voice mail. It made no sense. But in retrospect, she had learned something—her inner urge to be rooted and to nest was not his need. He suffered from a wanderlust that would ever urge him to seek out new and changing landscapes in the world.

Tips for Drying Mint

- Gather mint from your garden. Use shears to clip the stems close to the ground, as they will grow back.

- Wash the mint, place it on a large absorbent bath towel, and gently dry it.

- Gather the mint into bunches and tie the stems, cover each bunch with a small paper bag, and then hang the paper bags with cord, twine, or rubber bands in a well-ventilated place so that the mint air-dries.

- Store dried mint in an airtight container in a cool, dark place.

- Make tea using the dried mint leaves, or crumble some dried mint leaves between your palms and then sprinkle them on salad to season it.

Chapter 12

Each nostril of a dog's highly sensitive nose can track separate scents, proving useful in helping humans find illegal drugs, locate dead bodies, and even detect cancer.

—*Henny Penny Farmette Almanac*

Abby expertly guided the Jeep along the switchbacks, easily negotiating the curves of the two-lane highway from Las Flores to the forested summit of the coastal mountains. She stole a quick look at Philippe, whose face during the past few minutes had turned as white as a parsnip in April.

"You don't look so good. Do I need to pull over?"

Cars had been whizzing past them in succession during the eight-minute trip from town to the summit. The shoulder on the right had eroded in places from mud slides during the recent rainy season. Pulling off the road wouldn't be that easy, but Abby didn't want poor Philippe upchucking his breakfast muffin on his charcoal linen dress pants. She flipped on the turn signal and prepared to turn.

Philippe swallowed hard. He hung on to his seat belt with a white-knuckled grip. "Much farther?"

"Half a mile more."

Apparently planning for the worst but hoping for the best, Philippe pressed a white monogrammed handkerchief against his mouth and loosened his raspberry silk tie. By the time Abby had turned off the highway and had traveled a mile or so down a two-lane ribbon of asphalt, some color had returned to Philippe's cheeks.

They searched for signs along the road for the Church of the Pines, built during the last century. Abby couldn't use the navigation app on her phone, because it had lost its signal. She braked and searched harder for signs for the church. It was a pretty drive through towering redwoods interspersed with fields. The houses were few and far between, but there were signs of a thriving community—bicycles and trikes in a driveway, a plot of tomatoes growing out front, and chickens and ducks roaming about. The mountain had its own way of linking families through its rugged environment. People had to depend on each other when misfortune or bad weather struck.

As she drove, Abby's thoughts drifted to Philippe's family. She wondered how the conversation might have gone between Philippe and his dad about where to bury Jean-Louis. All Philippe had told her was that he had talked with his father by phone and they had decided as a family that a quick burial made the most sense, especially since Abby's private investigation was ongoing and the health of Philippe's mother was deteriorating. Nevertheless, Abby decided to broach the subject of Sugar.

"Philippe, could you take Sugar when you return home to New York? I mean, the dog is thirty-five pounds of pure love. And since she belonged to Jean-Louis, isn't there a chance your mom and dad would also welcome her into their lives? She just needs a bit of training, but she's smart. Really smart."

Philippe looked at Abby with an incredulous expression. "I am sorry, Abby. I know you think I should take her. But this dog, I cannot take. I am not a dog person. I do not want the responsibility. And my parents are not able to take the dog, either. My father has his hands full, and my mother, she cannot care for herself. A dog would be too much for them."

Philippe pressed his white monogrammed handkerchief against his mouth.

"No, you are right. It wouldn't be good for Sugar, either."

"There!" Philippe pointed to a narrow dirt road that twisted away from the heat-shimmering asphalt several hundred feet ahead. The weather-beaten gate on the split-rail fence had been flung open wide, as if in permanent welcome to visitors. The church building itself appeared in harmony with a landscape that included many dark and deep canyons; the Las Flores River, which dried to a trickle in the summer but swelled in the winter to fill the local reservoir; and towering coast redwoods, pines, and oaks, which swayed year-round in an ancient dance orchestrated by forceful winds sweeping up the western side of the mountains from the Pacific.

The church's dark exterior suggested to Abby repeated applications of redwood paint and annual coats of stain, a feature characteristic of buildings in the harsh microclimate of the mountains. A single wooden step rose from the thin soil to the black-handled doors of the sanctuary. From the roof overhang above the entrance, a solitary porch light hung inside a squat metal frame. As Abby studied it before stepping inside, she doubted a single bulb would cast much illumination, but any light, however dim, would facilitate finding the door during moonless nights or during the dark, stormy days of winter, when the fog wafted by in sheets so thick that you couldn't make out the person standing next to you.

"During our brief phone call," Abby told Philippe, "the priest said to push the button by the literature table." She walked straight to it and pressed her thumb against it. "I guess it rings in his cottage behind the church, so he'll know when we've arrived."

While they waited for the priest to show, Philippe strolled up the center aisle, hands outstretched, briefly touching each carved pew. His steps ceased before the altar, a simple wooden table with four straight legs and draped in a cloth of white lace. The weekly bulletin had been placed on the table, next to a vase of wildflowers and a white pillar candle. Philippe bowed his head slightly and made the sign of the cross so quickly that it almost seemed like a circle. Perhaps it was an old habit, learned in childhood but not practiced so much in adulthood. He walked back to the rear wall, where a religious painting caught his attention. Darkened possibly by candle smoke and exposure to the elements, the painting required close examination to make out the figures. Abby stepped aside so Philippe might peer closely at the images.

He murmured, "This is old . . . beautiful. It needs cleaning." He stood with fingers interlocked behind his back. "To her, the Samaritan woman, He revealed himself."

"Yes," Abby, replied, not sure what to say. She, too, looked intently at the painting, trying to discern the images of Jesus and the Samaritan woman at Jacob's well, a Bible story she actually knew. The Samaritan woman was neither Jewish nor chaste, having had five husbands and living with another. Even she was surprised when Jesus asked her, a woman shunned by her own people, for a drink of well water, knowing that it would necessitate Jesus—a

Jew—to use her utensil, and that doing so would make him ritually unclean. But he spoke of living water and revealed himself as the Messiah. Philippe was right. Jesus had revealed Himself to her and on many other occasions had demonstrated His inclusiveness of women and men whom society had marginalized.

Philippe heaved a heavy sigh. "God willing, my brother's soul can rest in peace now." He stared at the painting, then finally turned and retreated to a pew, where he slid onto the ages-old, worn wooden seat. Hunched over, eyes closed, Philippe fell silent.

Abby strolled quietly and slowly toward him. She marveled at how the clerestory window light bathed the interior and splayed across Philippe's dark hair, highlighting strands and creating shimmering undertones of color. Shut out of his interior world, she imagined he was thinking about the site they were about to see and perhaps wondering what criteria to use in deciding if it would be the right place for Jean-Louis. Or maybe Philippe was reacquainting himself with interior prayer.

She strolled to where he sat. As she gazed down at his bowed head and perfectly proportioned hands folded in his lap, her heart swelled with the desire to throw her arms around him and to whisper words of comfort. Wasn't that what he needed? What everyone needed when they felt bereft and alone? But Abby stopped herself—as she always did—with thoughts of how such spontaneity could muddy the boundaries of their relationship. Maybe if she were entirely truthful, it was she who needed the warmth and the words of comfort. She quickly moved past the thought, turning her attention to the church's sparse design and interior furnishings.

With its lovely simplicity, the small sanctuary could be

appreciated not in terms of what it had, but in terms of what it didn't have. It had no fancy architecture, no stained-glass windows, and no statuary in niches. Rather, the small church offered a cool refuge against the heat of the mountains, a quiet place to sit, and nothing to detract from prayer. The room smelled woodsy, earthy, as if the wooden surfaces had been anointed with oil of cedar, sage, and camphor.

Absorbed in her observations, Abby was surprised to hear Philippe whisper her name. His hand reached for hers. Taking it and responding to his gentle tug as he scooted over, Abby permitted him to pull her gently down into the pew.

Philippe whispered hoarsely, "Who could have imagined such an ending for someone on purpose with his life? He was destined for better things. I can't make sense of it."

Abby shook her head. She was aware only of the gentleness of his hand wrapped around hers, the warmth of his fingers.

"I wrestle with what is not possible to know. Did he die quickly"—Philippe's voice faltered—"or did he know in his final moments that he was leaving?" He fell silent for a beat. "Has his spirit ascended some great distance or to a place unknowable except in death?"

Abby tried to think of something consoling to say. "Some say we can feel those who love us around even after they are gone."

"I cannot feel him. And I know not about an afterlife, although my faith tells me there is one." Philippe stared at the altar.

Struggling with her own feelings of sadness, Abby remained quiet. His dark despair might seem unbearable to him now, but she knew it would eventually lift. She would do whatever was needed to help him through this period—be the caring friend, a warm body sitting close, fully present to his pain.

His voice cracked as he spoke again. "But I am thankful for you. . . . *Vous êtes ma lumière.*"

She swallowed and looked away. There were times when she wished she could allow herself to express her feelings at the moment she felt them. Referring to her as his light was such a tender thing to say. It deserved a response. But which? A hug, a kiss, a thank-you . . . ? Abby briefly tightened her fingers against his but said nothing. More moments passed, during which she was acutely aware that not only were their hands touching, but so, too, were their thighs.

Abby felt the tension dissipate as the priest walked into the back of the church. She quickly pulled her hand from Philippe's to swivel in the pew. Philippe lifted his head in alertness as he, too, turned to look at the man of the cloth. The priest looked like an elf. He was short, standing maybe five feet, plus an inch or two. He had a head of thick reddish-brown hair and a short cropped beard. He wore slacks and a dark shirt with a cleric's collar.

"I see you found the way." The priest smiled and set aside his walking stick to shake their hands warmly, putting them at ease with a genuine friendliness, which Abby hadn't quite expected. In truth, she hadn't known what to expect. But her heart felt lighter, for she thought that perhaps this man of God could help Philippe in his darkest hour.

Abby stared at the walking stick, remembering the story her grandfather had told her about the Glastonbury hawthorn tree that supposedly grew from the walking stick that had belonged to Joseph of Arimathea. After Joseph had journeyed to Glastonbury, in England, he'd plunged the walking stick into the ground, where it rooted. He bequeathed the tree to Glastonbury, but the Puritans came along and destroyed it. But leave it to the monks to have taken cuttings and therefore to have ensured the tree's survival. After hearing that tale as a six-year-old, Abby had stuck every kind of stick into the ground, hoping for roots, but to no avail.

They followed the priest out of the sanctuary and along a stone path up the steep hill in back of his house behind the church. Alongside the path, chaparral, sagebrush, yarrow, and lupine grew in wild abandon. Abby pointed to the top of the hill, where she could see several moss-covered headstones leaning sideways, as if destined to collapse before another century on the mountain had passed.

"If you would follow me," the priest said, running his finger around his white neck band. His damp face glistened with sweat from the exertion. Beneath bushy brows, his dark eyes shined. "I have a site in mind. Just over here."

He led them to a sheltered area under the largest live oak that Abby had ever seen. The girth of the trunk seemed in excess of a couple of yards. The lower limbs curled outward, like ancient gnarled arms of a wise old woman welcoming all to take shelter. When Abby heard the nasal *yank-yank* from the top of the oak, she smiled in recognition of the red-breasted nuthatch. For a moment, she considered how it might have pleased Jean-Louis to have a feathered friend who, too, flitted between America and Canada.

When Abby climbed a few more steps up from the oak and saw the view, she instantly forgot the bird. Her smile widened and her breath caught in her throat. She could hardly get out the words, "Hurry, Philippe. The fog is rolling back in. You can see across every mountain ridge . . . all the way out to the Pacific. Oh, my . . . it feels like we are next door to heaven."

Philippe picked his way up to her, the wind whipping at his trouser legs and shirtsleeves. When he finally caught up to her, he was out of breath. He stood quietly, closed his eyes, and seemed to be fully present and anchored. Perhaps he wanted to listen to the birdsong and the wailing wind. Finally, he opened his eyes to take in the 180-degree view. Abby gazed with him. In the foreground were blue-green ridges, like waves on the sea, which towered on a north-to-south axis. The ridges were punctuated with plunging, green forested valleys. More ridges jutted upward as one's gaze moved farther out, before finally resting on a slip of white coastline and, beyond, a gray fog bank that merged with the sky. In the coastal waters near the beach, the shimmering blue sea was dotted with the white triangles of sailboats, their crews apparently sharing an optimism that the sun would hold and the afternoon sailing would be smooth.

A sudden gust tugged at Philippe's trouser legs, ruffled his curly hair, and nearly knocked him off balance, causing him to reach out to Abby. "Magnifique," he whispered. Eyes shining, sounding almost joyful, he practically shouted to Abby, to the priest, to anyone within earshot, "C'est magnifique!" He stepped forward, turned his gaze to the sky, and threw his arms out wide. "Brother, do you not love this place?"

"I take it this spot will do?" the priest asked.

"Certainly seems so," Abby replied, grinning at Philippe's exuberance.

Philippe reached out and vigorously shook the man's hand. "Yes, indeed. This is the place."

The smiling priest fixed his eyes on Abby. "On the phone, you suggested a short graveside service, right?"

Abby sobered and looked to Philippe for a response.

"*Oui, très simple.*"

The priest nodded. "Very well, then."

Stealing a final long look out over the vista, Abby felt a sense of accomplishment. This tiny mountain cemetery might not be the right choice for everyone, but it seemed to have pleased Philippe, and therefore, it was perfect, although the headstones and slabs in the sunny areas were losing the battle with sticktight weeds, sweet broom, and wild onion, and those in the shade had moss creeping over them.

"The area could use a little weeding," Abby opined on the way back.

"Yes, that work is done by our volunteers, but the work parties are only scheduled the last weekend of the month. No worries. I'll get a parishioner up here today to whack the weeds so it'll look nice for tomorrow." He stopped to catch his breath. "Our community up here is small. It's made up of independent-minded folks who help one another. It's not easy in the winter, what with the frequent power outages, fallen trees, and washed-out roads. Old folks want the certainties of retirement living, which includes access to medical care, so a lot of them move back into Las Flores."

The priest gestured toward the path. Leading the way back down, he explained the burial arrangements as he walked.

"You'll have to sign some papers, Mr. Bonheur. I'll need a copy of the death certificate. I ask for a donation only for the graveside service. However, your donation is separate from the plot and the fees for the diggers."

After nearly slipping, the priest stepped off the path, then dragged a tissue across his forehead to sop up beads of perspiration. With a self-deprecating chuckle, he placed a large boot-clad foot forward a little more carefully.

Nearing the bottom end of the path, the priest raised another concern. "Shadyside Funeral Home will transport the body up here, but do you want a closed casket or a viewing at the grave site?"

Abby looked to Philippe for the answer.

Philippe hesitated, chewed his lip, as if measuring the pros and cons. He ran his hand through his hair. "We'll have open viewing at Shadyside's chapel, but perhaps for a moment or two, I might like to see his face one last time at the grave."

"So that's settled." The priest mopped his face again. "Shall I contact some of our flock to serve as pallbearers?" The diminutive man of the cloth chuckled as he verbalized his thought. "Barring heavenly intervention, I can't see another way to get the casket up the incline."

Abby's wide-eyed gaze met Philippe's. "We must have them," she said.

The priest cleared his throat. "Surely the deceased had friends who would want to bring the body up here."

"Oh, that's a problem." Philippe's face took on a stricken expression.

Abby replied as diplomatically as she could. "We would welcome volunteers."

"I'll make some calls," the priest said. "We'll gather at the church at four o'clock tomorrow."

During the car trip back to town, Philippe sat in silence, hands folded, head only slightly moving in gentle rhythm with the radio music. Abby navigated the switchbacks more slowly on the descent, expecting Philippe to get carsick again, but he seemed kind of peaceful, with no signs of feeling ill.

"In about a minute, Philippe, we're going to take the exit ramp right down Main Street on the way to Jean-Louis's apartment. What do you think about posting a notice in the window of the pastry shop?"

"Burial notice?"

"Yes. I realize how painful all this is for you, but there might be customers, friends, or acquaintances of Jean-Louis who would want to be there, you know, to honor his life, to say their final good-byes."

"I do not know his friends. And the notice, it would be too late, n'est-ce pas?"

"Perhaps. But remember, we have his cell phone in the box of materials from the police. We can call the numbers stored in the cell phone contact list. Those phone numbers belong to people that Jean-Louis surely considered important in his life."

"You have another reason for wanting to do this, I think."

"Well, I suppose *not* to do it would be to miss an opportunity."

"Opportunity for what?"

Abby thought about how to say it as simply as possible without sounding callous.

Philippe looked at her, his expression alert and serious.

"The burial might bring together people who knew him, customers, friends, and . . ." She stopped herself from saying the words "the killer," quickly adding instead, "A lover." But she did not want to begin a discourse about how a lover—jealous, controlling, or in an affair that ended badly—could be the same person as the killer.

Spotting the pastry shop on the left, Abby drove past it

and made a U-turn. After parking in front, she asked Philippe to unearth the small box of supplies she kept in the car for her farmers' market events, when a sign for something might have to be quickly drafted. Using a purple marker on white paper, she printed the details of the graveside service and invited all who had known the chef to attend.

Philippe took the marker from between her fingers, added a quick sketch of a toque blanche, and wrote his brother's birth and death dates just below it. Satisfied that there was nothing more to say, they taped the notice to the pastry shop's plate-glass window.

"Let's stop by the DIY center for some boxes and head over to your brother's apartment, grabbing sandwiches on the way," Abby suggested in a cheerful voice once they were back in the car.

Philippe nodded and buckled up. As Abby steered the Jeep away from the pastry shop, he lamented, "My heart feels as heavy as stone. I don't know what called Jean-Louis to this place, but I do know he loved it here."

"Really?" Abby said, popping a mint into her mouth.

"Yes, really. He said the climate was quite like the Mediterranean. He loved the farmers' markets, where the ingredients are the freshest—farm-fresh eggs, organic fruits and nuts, especially the almonds, and the local honey. He raved about your honey. His favorite, you know." He touched her hand where it rested on the console. "And I've yet to taste it."

Abby's stomach tightened. *Is that a couched desire expressing itself?* She looked over at him, but Philippe's attention had already turned to the spectacle outside his window. Abby recognized the bicyclist with the two dogs before and behind him on the bike seat The trio disappeared down the asphalt path leading away from Main in the direction of the park. Abby felt her temperature rising. "I'm so going to report that guy."

Tips for Making Lavender Flower Essence

Flower essences carry a light scent, one that is not as potent as that of essential oils, but they can still be used in aromatherapy to reduce stress and restore a sense of calm. To make a flower essence, you'll need sterilized bottles with stoppers or caps, tweezers, a glass bowl to hold the petals, sterile water, and brandy (as a preservative). Wear nitrile gloves, because touching the utensils and ingredients with your hands can potentially contaminate them.

1. Pluck one half to one cup of lavender buds, using tweezers, if necessary.

2. Put the buds petals in a glass bowl.

3. Cover the buds with sterile water.

4. Leave the lavender water in direct sunlight for three hours.

5. Fill the sterile bottles half full of brandy.

6. Strain the lavender water and pour it over the brandy to fill the bottles.

7. Insert the stoppers in the bottles or twist on the caps.

8. Label the bottles LAVENDER FLOWER ESSENCE and include the date.

Chapter 13

Red wine remains drinkable for decades
because the tannins in it act as a natural
preservative; however, the wine must be
properly bottled and stored.

—Henny Penny Farmette Almanac

Abby removed the flatbread wraps from the paper bag, while Philippe located glasses in the upper cabinet of Jean-Louis's small galley kitchen. Philippe had insisted on having their meal while sitting at a table, not in the car, a habit of Americans he found barbaric. After removing the fistful of napkins thrown in the bag at the Las Hermanas Healthy Food drive-through, Abby peeled back the wax paper on one of the steaming hot chicken wraps and inhaled the scent of the chipotle chilies, black beans, avocado, sweet corn, and tomatoes stuffed in with the grilled chicken, as if sniffing alone could quell her growling stomach.

Philippe seemed in no hurry to eat, taking an inordinate amount of time to select the perfect wine to pair with the wraps. And even before choosing the wine, he had sought appropriate music, even asking Abby for a suggestion.

She had deadpanned, "You could try a little rap."

He had frowned.

"Or hip-hop."

When he apparently didn't get her humor, she confessed to not liking either style. "Why not surprise me?"

Philippe had fanned through Jean-Louis's CD collection and had popped into the player one of Maria Callas singing Puccini arias. When they'd first entered the kitchen, Abby had sensed a cold emptiness in the room, despite it being furnished and well stocked. But with the music, Abby felt an almost palpable energy shift.

She hadn't eaten all day, and for that reason, actually consuming the meal, for her, far outweighed Philippe's desire for music, wine, and table settings. While Maria sang and Philippe perused his brother's wine collection, Abby took the fragrant flatbread wrap—which already had her salivating—into Jean-Louis's bedroom. With a gusto that would have embarrassed her were Philippe or anyone else there to see, Abby bit into the wrap without any concern about contaminating the scene. She felt confident that the police had already removed from the room anything that might have relevance, and, anyway, such items had been returned in the evidence boxes they gave to her and Philippe once the death was ruled a suicide.

Feverishly munching, Abby studied the bedroom, hoping to notice something that would benefit her own investigation. Jean-Louis had painted his room a latte color, with bright white on the wood trim around the windows, on the crown molding, and on the closet doors. On the wall above a black-hued, Mandarin-style altar table—which stretched out long and low opposite the bed—hung a tasteful collection of framed black-and-white prints of some of Albrecht Dürer's woodcuts. She remembered studying that artist in a high school art class. *Ooh, I am liking this room, Jean-Louis. You definitely inherited that art gene. Everything you touched turned golden.*

Abby's gaze move from the art to the bed, which was covered with a white cotton duvet with black piping, large black throw pillows, and smaller red silk ones that looked like giant roses. Next to the bed, on a white country French chest onto which had been stenciled a black paisley design with occasional dabs of red, perhaps to resonate with the silk pillows, stood a mahogany frame containing a photograph of a man with an engaging smile, large brown eyes, and thick, wavy hair. *Now, where have I seen you before?*

"Philippe, can you come here? I want to show you something," she called out.

"I am searching for the corkscrew." Philippe's answer was punctuated by the banging of drawers as he opened and slammed them closed. "Ah, here it is."

Abby heard a pop.

Philippe called out, "I found a fabulous French import. My brother had good taste. Not one bottle of American wine."

When he entered the bedroom, Abby pointed to the picture and asked him, "Do you know this man?"

"Non. Must be a friend of Jean-Louis," Philippe suggested.

"Oh, I'd wager he was more than a friend. Who puts a friend's picture in such a romantic frame and keeps it at the bedside?" She pulled the wax paper up over her flatbread wrap to protect it and handed it to Philippe. Then she carefully removed the picture from its frame and turned it over. On the back, in cursive, was written, *Love, J.*

Philippe pointed to the writing. "Jean-Louis never signed with a single *J.* It was always *J-L.* Nor did he ever mention a friend . . . or, for that matter, a lover whose name began with *J.*" Where Abby had pulled the wax paper up over the wrap, Philippe peeled it back down again, exposing a chunk of chicken.

Abby studied the photo. "This man is very attractive, wouldn't you say? His hair is crisply cut just above his shirt collar, like yours, only a little longer. Tailored black suit. White shirt with cuff links, no exposed buttons."

Philippe observed, "The red silk pocket square and the tie add just the right amount of color."

"So, he's a power dresser. What else does this picture tell you?"

Philippe peered closely at the image. "The background tells me nothing. Probably it is the sort of background screen a professional photographer uses. He looks posed. This is not a candid image. It is not art."

"Might it be a publicity photo?" Abby asked. "That's what it looks like to me."

"For a company profile or a charity event . . . That would make sense," Philippe said. He turned his attention to the wrap he was holding and slowly lifted it to his lips, as if to take a bite.

"Hey, that's mine." Abby hurriedly laid the photo and the frame on the bed and reached for the wrap.

Philippe, grinning, lifted it out of her reach. "Ah, but you gave it to me, n'est-ce pas?"

"You have your own. In the kitchen."

"Yes, but we are in the bedroom, and now I no longer wish to return to the kitchen." His expression remained mischievous as he watched her reaction.

Abby's eyes narrowed, and a devilish look came into them. "Philippe. You are messing with me!"

"Is it that obvious?" he asked with a laugh, handing Abby the wrap. "Your wine, mademoiselle, has breathed enough. The table, it is set. We need only the stimulating conversation. Shall I regale you with stories of my youthful indiscretions?"

Abby cocked her head to one side. Lifted a brow. "I wouldn't miss that for the world." She followed him to the kitchen, aware of her heartbeat quickening. What was it about this man that made her feel like a piece of malleable putty whenever he turned on that seductive charm? He could be so disarming and yet, at other times, tortured, distant, and confused.

Although tempted to submit to the attraction, Abby always stuck to her ethical high ground. There were questions to be answered. He had paid her to ferret out the truth. She had the habit of always asking herself the worst-case scenario for what-ifs. What if she succumbed to the attraction and ended up having an affair with Philippe? If things did not work out between them, the worst-case scenario would not be two broken hearts; the worst-case scenario would be that a tangled personal relationship would alter Abby's perception of the truth. Still, she reasoned that drinking a glass of wine while listening to Philippe's stories might be just the thing to relieve the pressure of the past few days. And Philippe, for sure, needed a break.

Philippe loosened his tie and removed his jacket as soon as they finished eating. They talked easily as they cleaned up the kitchen and threw away the garbage. Leaning against the sink, he removed his cigarettes and a lighter from his pants pocket and handed them to her.

"I've decided to quit. You're a good influence," he said, grinning broadly.

Abby tried to sound nonchalant, placing the items on the table. "Was it something I said?"

He shot her an enigmatic look. "Not exactly."

"Then what?" Abby replied, with a puzzled expression.

"I don't know. Cigarettes are, for me, something to share

with a woman after dinner, after a walk, after making love. But if you do not like smoking, then I must give it up." Philippe's eyes met hers.

"No, you don't," Abby shot back defiantly. "Maybe I don't smoke. But you do. Friends allow friends to decide for themselves."

"Is that what we are, Abby? Friends?"

"I suppose so, yes."

"For the Frenchman, there is none of this silly friends stuff like you have in that Harry and Sally movie. When a man with the French blood takes a woman to dinner, she must understand the signal he sends."

"What signal is that?" Abby asked.

"*La romance.* What else?"

Abby felt a warm flush creep across her face, burning her cheeks.

"Oh, now I have embarrassed you," Philippe said, waving his hands in the air. Apparently realizing that the timing was not right for that discussion, he said, "I will tell you about the first time I smoked. It was also the first time I kissed a girl."

Although hockey had been his favorite sport, Philippe said, he also had played middle school football, as a second-string quarterback. After the starting quarterback injured his throwing arm in an on-field crush during one game, Philippe had taken the field and thrown a game-winning touchdown. It happened only once, but the girls looked at him differently after that. One, especially, took notice.

"Olivia," Philippe said, "was a risk taker. She dressed provocatively in short skirts, tight sweaters, and lots of fishnet. She smoked. At a party with some friends, she led me outside and lit up. I tried it, too. I inhaled and held the smoke in my mouth and lungs, against the urge to cough. Olivia must have thought I was sexy, because she suddenly pushed against me and kissed me with her tongue in my mouth. When I exhaled and coughed violently, she asked what kind of French I was if I did not know how to French kiss."

Abby laughed.

As Philippe spoke of the adventures he'd shared with Jean-Louis while growing up in Canada and immigrating to upstate New York, Abby listened attentively. His younger brother, he said, had always been the better looking and more creative of the two. As children, they were very close, but in high school Philippe's love of hockey consumed most of his free time, while Jean-Louis's early interest in cooking developed into a full-blown passion for baking. Philippe stayed on a course plotted out for him through high school and college to take on the family business of art acquisitions and sales. During his college years, he studied art and business by day and worked in his parents' gallery in the evenings and on weekends. Despite his early propensity for cooking, Jean-Louis surprised the family when he decided to immerse himself in the culinary world, eventually settling on pastry as a specialty.

By the time Abby's cell phone rang, playing the theme song to the TV series *Cops*—the ringtone that told her Kat was calling—she and Philippe had moved to the brown and cream quatrefoil-patterned couch. It was a little weird, making themselves at home in Jean-Louis's apartment, but Abby soon acclimated, especially after Philippe had replenished their wine. Kat's phone call interrupted Philippe's story about when he was a teenager and was babysitting his ten-year-old brother while their parents went on an errand to the gallery. The boys wanted muffins and decided to make them. The batter was delicious, and the muffins would have been, too, had the oven not caught fire. The blaze singed Philippe's eyebrows and caught the pot holders on fire before the boys managed to call for help. Although no serious damage was done, the kitchen smelled like burnt rags for weeks afterward.

"That's when I realized I could appreciate food without cooking it," Philippe said with a smile. "It traumatized me." He sucked in a mouthful of red liquid and held it in his mouth a long moment before swallowing.

Giggling, Abby answered the incoming call.

"What's up, Kat?" Abby raised her wineglass and held it poised in position for a sip.

"News flash, girlfriend. Our illustrious leader has been in an accident."

"Oh, no! Chief Bob Allen?" Abby asked. Gone were the giggles. Her expression grew serious. The chief had a tendency to be a bit of a hypochondriac, complaining about every ache, sniffle, or hangnail to anyone within earshot. Everyone knew that. Nobody cared. And to complain about a wart was just plain silly, given the serious nature of police work. But an accident, that was different. Rising from the couch, Abby asked, "Is he okay?"

"Oh, good Lord, yes." Kat chuckled. "He has been calling Nettie every five minutes from his hospital bed, with mostly complaints, a few orders. Ever the micromanager, he insisted on a police scanner at his bedside. Just can't let go, even when it's in his best interest."

"How did the accident happen?" Abby asked, giving Philippe a thumbs-up sign to indicate that the chief was okay.

"You could say he got picked off at the pass by a fire truck." Kat's tone suggested she was into telling the story her way.

"Be serious."

"I am. Dispatch got word of a fender bender up at Turkey Pass. Then a grass fire broke out. Oh, the chief was all over that. Jumped into his Tahoe to head up there. Never one to miss a photo op, and you know reporters listen to our scanners. He inched his car around some rubberneckers who had pulled off the road, but fire engine three—the pumper—came flying along. While trying to pass, the pumper hit the rear corner of Chief Bob Allen's SUV. Over he went—twice—before coming to a halt in a ditch."

"Break any bones?"

"One . . . a small one. Don't laugh. His tailbone."

"Ooh, not good."

"Now we can legitimately use the words 'chief' and 'pain in the ass' in the same sentence." Kat's giggle erupted into laughter. "It's how we all see him, anyway." Her pitch rose several degrees as she talked through her laughter. "Can you imagine the one-liners going around the department?"

Abby tightened her lips over her teeth, trying not to laugh.

Philippe stared at her, a bemused expression on his face.

Kat went on. "He has to sit on a doughnut for six months."

Abby doubled over in peals of laughter.

Watching her lose control, a smiling Philippe shook his head, got up, and rescued the wineglass from her.

Abby dropped onto the couch, in stitches. When she could talk again, she panted, "I'll bet he can't even see the irony in being such a pain in the butt . . . with all that pain in his butt."

"Doubt it. Pushed out of a photo op by our engine three pumper, that's gotta be a first," Kat replied drolly. And they both lost it again. Gasping, Kat said, "That, my friend, is karma."

"We shouldn't be laughing at the poor guy. I mean, a broken bone."

"Oh, you can bet he'll be whining ad nauseum to any-body who'll listen for the next year or two. Anyway, gotta go. Cruiser is coming out."

"Where are you?"

"Down at the car wash. Chief says we got to have the cruiser cleaned, tank filled, and our shotguns and Tasers locked in the armory every night at the end of shift. Come on. Now, don't tell me you've been gone so long, you don't remember all his rules?"

"How could I forget?" Abby got up and walked over to the window, opened the blinds, and peeked out at the gar-den in the courtyard. "Hey, if you aren't working tomor-row afternoon, Kat, join us for Jean-Louis's graveside service . . . around four o'clock . . . Church of the Pines, off the road at the summit."

"Yeah, I'll see if I can get off."

Abby clicked off the phone and stared into the small manicured garden beyond the apartment window. Light shimmered on the grass. A blue-tile pool looked so re-freshing, it was hard to believe no one was using it. Next to the pool a patch of roses and two wooden benches cre-ated an inviting place to contemplate the meaning of life and how quickly it could be taken away. A staid white-haired lady sat on one of the benches, reading a paper-back, her small poodle on a leash sunning at her side. A man strolled by, pushing a bike, his loose trouser bottoms tucked into his socks. Absent were the sounds of children laughing as they played. Children were not allowed in this quiet adults-only complex on a cul-de-sac, several blocks uphill from the main section of town. This was where Jean-Louis had chosen to live. It made perfect sense for someone who worked nights and slept during the day.

Abby turned away from the window to look for Philippe, and she found him sitting on his brother's bed, head in hands. Sinking onto the bed beside him, she spoke in a tone that conveyed a settled calmness. "Hey, partner. You okay? What happened?"

Philippe shook his head, heaved an audible sigh. "Jean-Louis and I used to laugh like that. . . ." His voice trailed off.

Abby nodded, ready to listen if he wanted to talk. But he didn't. She sat with him for a few minutes, looking over at the bookcase. Hardbound classics filled the top shelf. Below, oversize art books occupied the two lower shelves. Cookbooks and two shrinking green jade plants in clay pots and saucers filled the rest of the bookcase. Next to one of the plants, Abby spotted a phone charger.

"He had a terrific sense of humor. It put people at ease. But Jean-Louis, he was quick to anger. I never understood his emotional swings."

"I know," Abby said. "I once felt the wrath of his anger."

After a moment, she got up and unplugged the charger. "But he had friends. How could he not? Shall we call them?" She dangled the charger in front of him. "We have his cell, and now its charger."

Philippe's expression brightened. He stood up, walked over to her, and cupped her chin in his hand. "Thank you."

"There's nothing to thank me for, Philippe."

Abby took the charger to the kitchen. She went out to the car and returned with Jean-Louis's cell phone. For the next two hours, Abby sat with Philippe at the kitchen table, scrolling through Jean-Louis's phone directory, reading aloud the names and phone numbers while Philippe wrote them down on a piece of paper. Finally, they had compiled a master list from which they could start calling people.

"Those are all the numbers Jean-Louis saved in the various directories," said Abby. "But there's a starred number. Looks like one entry with a name spelled v-i-e-i-l-l-a-r-d. You mentioned this French name before?"

Philippe's eyes met hers. "Abby, this must be the Vieillard that Jean-Louis mentioned to me on the phone—someone Jean-Louis said he had strong feelings for."

"And how do you feel about speaking to this Vieillard?" Abby laid the phone on the table and pushed it toward Philippe.

"What do I say?"

"Tell him who you are. Invite him to the burial." Abby thought through possible scenarios. If Jean-Louis was romantically involved with Vieillard, the man might know something that no one else knew, some piece of information that could shed light on the senseless death.

Philippe dialed the number, listened for a moment, apparently to a message, and then began to speak. "Bonjour. It is I, Philippe. . . ." Suddenly, Philippe's eyes locked with Abby's. His expression went as flat as a fallow field and was just as unreadable. He laid the phone on the table, pushed back his chair, and scurried out of the room.

Abby snapped the phone to her ear in time to hear the beep signaling the end of the allotted time to leave a message. She heard Philippe bang something against a hard surface in the bedroom. Abby knew that men who were grieving often behaved differently than women. They sometimes dealt with their pain through anger. But what had set him off? It probably had been a bad idea to ask Philippe to make the call in the first place.

Philippe ambled back into the kitchen. "Everything in this room, this apartment, it screams Jean-Louis. Look there." He pointed to the large wall calendar that displayed several months at a glance. "See the red circle? Jean-Louis's birthday. See the red line with the word *départ* over the top? He was going away. Don't you remember me telling you about his plans to go to the Caribbean for his birthday?"

"Of course I do," Abby said. "The calendar date goes to your argument that his death was not due to suicide, since, clearly, he was planning something for the future. When we take the case back to the police, we will include that information. But we are not there yet. We have to deal with the burial service. Calling his friends seems unnecessarily hard on you, so how about I make the calls and you look for pictures, letters, trip itineraries, and tickets of any kind—personal stuff that could establish your brother's relationships with others? If you feel up to it . . ."

He nodded. "I am angry that Jean-Louis is gone. I am angry that he will never celebrate another birthday. And I am angry that his murderer is still free."

Abby redialed Vieillard, but there was no pickup and no greeting, just a beep. She called the other individuals on the master list. The majority of them offered excuses for why they couldn't make the wake or the burial, some saying that it was too far, especially for those in San Francisco or Napa; that it was too late in the day; or that traffic on the mountain would be intolerable, as it always was on weekends, when inland-valley residents headed over the mountain to the beach towns. Others confessed that they had heard the rumor about the chef and expressed worry that further association in any way could compromise them. In the end, a loyal group of three said they would try to make it to the graveside service.

At a minute before eight that evening, the phone rang while it was still in Abby's hand. She looked at the name that had popped up on the screen—Vieillard. Her heartbeat quickened. Philippe was beside her, sorting photos he'd found in a book about Caribbean cooking. Abby held the phone out so he could read the name.

Philippe dropped the pictures. He snatched the phone from her hand.

"Bonsoir. Philippe speaking." Locking eyes with Abby, he listened and then raised his hand, palm out, as if to say, "The caller is not speaking."

Twirling an open hand, Abby tried to get him to engage the caller in conversation.

"*Allô,*" he said. "It may seem strange that I answered Jean-Louis's phone, but, you see, I am his brother, Philippe. I was calling you on his behalf."

Abby stood up and stepped next to Philippe. She tapped the speaker button on the phone. The caller, although silent, remained on the line.

"You must know by now that my brother . . . recently died." Philippe paused, drew a breath. "Sorry. As you can hear, I am quite emotional, and I apologize for delivering the news—if you did not know—and the invitation by telephone. But we bury Jean-Louis tomorrow, and it is my hope that you will join us for the farewell service."

A deep masculine voice softly replied, "My condolences. Where is the service to be held?"

Philippe's eyes grew large. When he shook his head in desperation, Abby thought, *Surely he hasn't forgotten the name of the church?* She jotted the location and the time on a piece of paper and twirled it around so he could read it.

Philippe spoke haltingly into the phone. "The Church of the Pines in Las Flores . . . four o'clock tomorrow afternoon."

Abby sat back down and spun her forefinger in repetitive circles, encouraging Philippe to keep talking while she wrote another note.

Philippe's hand trembled as he held the phone to his ear. "Although I do not know you personally, your presence, I am sure, would have meant a lot to Jean-Louis. You were his close friend, n'est-ce pas?"

The man sniffed in that heavy masculine way and cleared his throat.

Philippe added, "The viewing will begin at two o'clock at Shadyside Funeral Home."

Abby held up her note. She'd written, *Ask his name.*

"Sir, if I may ask, what is your name?"

The phone clicked off.

Philippe laid the phone on the table, turned his head away from her.

Abby stared at the chiseled lines of his profile, saw his jaw grow tense. She reached over and gave Philippe a reassuring pat on the shoulder. "You delivered the message. Hopefully, he will show up."

Philippe ran his fingers through his thick black hair, leaned forward, and grabbed the large full-color Caribbean cookbook from the top of the stack on the table. He held it above the table and opened it, and pieces of folded paper, scribbled notes, recipes, and cards fell out. Philippe riffled through them, peering closely at those with any writing on them.

"Abby, look," he said. "Everything written on these paper notes was written by Jean-Louis, except this address of a hotel in Santo Domingo." He dumped two postcards out of a small paper bag, along with a receipt.

Abby examined the postcards. Each depicted an idyllic beach scene, and although they were purchased in an island shop in Santo Domingo, they were blank, never written upon or mailed.

"Abby, look at this," Philippe said, animated again. He held up three photos, placing them side by side. They each showed Jean-Louis and the man whose photo stood in the ornate frame at Jean-Louis's bedside. One image revealed the man and Jean-Louis on striped beach chairs on a private dock next to a wide swath of sandy beach dotted with palms. There appeared to be a large estate house behind them. The second image showed the two aboard a yacht, sipping from champagne flutes. The third image was darker than the other two and was similar to the one Abby had previously seen in the police files. It showed the two men on the deck of a boat in the open sea.

"There are eleven photos in all," Philippe told her.

Abby dug through her handbag and took out a small magnifier. She looked at a fourth photo. It showed Jean-Louis and the mystery man fishing, naked to the waist and wearing flip-flops. It was the exposed biceps on both men that warranted a closer examination.

"Well, well," she said. She touched Philippe's hand and pointed to the picture.

"What? I see nothing out of the ordinary."

"Look at the mystery man's bicep." Abby handed him the magnifying glass. "His tattoo looks like a six-nine or a nine-six on its side, depending on what angle you view it from. That is the astrological sign of Cancer. Jean-Louis was a Cancer. Would his friend get the same tattoo?"

"Perhaps he was a Cancer, too, and they got those tattoos together."

"What if they became lovers on that trip? People get inked for all sorts of reasons. Maybe their identical tattoos pledged them to each other," said Abby.

"C'est possible." Philippe ran his hand through the curls at the back of his neck. "Good work, Abby." He reached over and patted her on the shoulder, allowing his hand to linger momentarily before pulling away.

"Okay, I've got an idea," Abby said. "I'm going to take a picture of this man's face with my smartphone and text it to Kat to see if she knows or can find out who this guy is."

"You think he's from Las Flores?" Philippe looked at her with excitement in his eyes.

"Maybe. I don't know if he's local or not. I mean, I don't know everybody in town. Used to when I worked my daily beat as a cop, but I pretty much stick to myself these days. As for this guy with Jean-Louis . . . I have a hunch that they were on vacation together. Those postcards and the photos suggest the Caribbean. This man J. could shed some light, I think, on that trip and maybe tell us where to find Vieillard."

Philippe frowned. "Do you think Vieillard is responsible for Jean-Louis's death?"

"Not wise to speculate on that yet. But Vieillard is a missing piece of this puzzle. I need to find out who he is and what his connection is to Jean-Louis's life narrative." Abby pressed the camera app on her phone and attached the picture to a text to Kat. The reply came back within minutes.

"Philippe, we got it!" Abby exclaimed. "The man in the picture with Jean-Louis is Jake Lennahan . . . Eva Lennahan's husband." Abby leaned back into the chair. "You didn't put away the wine, did you? I think I need a refill," she said, reaching for the pictures of the two men and the postcards.

"I've got to look at this from every possible angle," Abby said. Then she added, "If Eva Lennahan and her husband, Jake, took Jean-Louis on vacation, why didn't she mention that when she met you and offered her condolences yesterday at the Shakespeare Festival? Another thing . . . Why do you think there is no image of her anywhere in all those pictures of that tropical vacation? To me, that's just weird."

"Couldn't there be a logical explanation?" Philippe asked, arching his brows.

"Well, yes, I suppose Jake could have invited Jean-Louis as his guest as a thank-you for all the work he'd done on Eva's political fundraisers. Or maybe the trip involved guy-only activities, and Eva opted out, knowing she wouldn't be welcome. Or maybe she did go, but with other people to other functions."

"All are possible." Philippe's eyes were fixated on Abby.

"What I find curious is that Jean-Louis did not post any of these photographs on his social networking page. Did you see any of these or other images of this man on Jean-Louis's laptop?"

"Non. Not that I recall."

Abby's cell phone vibrated on the table. She answered it and smiled when she heard Lidia's voice. She was most likely calling back about the man who had brought in the earrings for repair.

"Abby, dear, I located that receipt. The handwriting is a little difficult to decipher, but it looks like Lemadan or Lenadan."

"Could it be Lennahan?" Abby asked, pulse racing.

"Well, I suppose it could be, dear."

"Lidia, if the rest of the name is there, would you please read it to me?"

"Oh, there's no rest of the name, dear. Just the initial J. and a phone number."

Chipotle Chili Chicken Wraps

These simple, quick wraps are best when made with vegetables fresh from the garden and with grilled or rotisserie chicken. Place the fresh ingredients in bowls to make it easy to assemble the wraps.

Ingredients:
¾ cup chipotle chilies in adobo sauce, mashed
3 tablespoons honey mustard (or to taste)
2 flatbreads
1 warm rotisserie or grilled chicken, shredded or cubed
½ cup warm black beans
½ cup warm cooked sweet corn
½ cup diced fresh garden tomatoes
½ cup diced red onion
Several sprigs of fresh cilantro, minced

Directions:
Combine the chipotle chilies and the honey mustard in a small bowl and mix well. Toast the flatbreads. Spread some of the chipotle-mustard mixture on each flatbread.

Layer some of the chicken, black beans, and corn atop each flatbread. Garnish each with tomatoes, onions, and cilantro. Roll up the flatbreads and serve at once.

Serves 2

Chapter 14

If you want to lower your cholesterol, decrease
your stress level, and improve your blood
pressure, adopt a dog.

—*Henny Penny Farmette Almanac*

Abby awoke hours before dawn. In the dark, she lay
unmoving . . . listening. It was hot, stiflingly so. A
sound had awakened her—a long creak. Then a thud.
Someone or something was on her roof.

Even groggy, Abby remembered the ladder that she had
propped against the south side of her house, where she
had torn out a paper-wasp nest a week ago. She had left
the ladder there, intending to pick the ripe figs and then
cut the branch overhanging the roof. The last thing she
needed was a colony of roof rats. But she had never gotten
around to finishing, and the ladder was still there, waiting.

She eased off the mattress, feeling chilled in her short
cotton gown, and searched for her flashlight on the bedside table. Her fingers soon touched the grooved metal.
Leaving the flashlight turned off so it wouldn't signal to
the intruders that she was on to them, Abby felt her way in
the dark along the hallway wall and over to the kitchen
sliding-glass door. Sugar was not to be left behind. She

bounded off the foot of the bed and shot past Abby to the door, her strong tail rhythmically smacking the wall.

"You stay here. Guard the inside. I'll be right back."

Sugar was having none of that. She squeezed right through the door, between Abby's legs. *Whatever!* Abby slipped outside, then limped, barefoot, along the gravel path to the ladder. She climbed up it until her fingers felt the edge of the roof. Sugar had bounded off into the black night, whining and sniffing. Suddenly Abby brought the light beam up and shined it across the roof. The blinding light exposed the black, banded eyes, the white-tipped ears, and the ringed tail of a raccoon on a predawn raid with her three youngsters. The mother coon was standing on her hind legs, reaching upward for the figs and knocking some down in the process. Abby swore under her breath and backed away down the ladder. It was never a good idea to get between a wild coon and her cubs, especially when they were dining on their favorite food. Abby didn't mind sharing, but she could have done without the startling fear that a dangerous man might be on her roof.

"Sugar, come here." Abby flashed the light around the yard. She spied Sugar at the back gate, where the raccoons must have come onto Abby's property. "Sugar! Come here, girl. Come." *Oh, good grief, dog. Tune me out, as you always do.*

Abby returned to the kitchen and fished some doggy biscuits from a canister. *Maybe one of these babies will bring you back.* Abby found her shoes, slipped her feet into them, and walked toward the back fence, where Sugar stood on her hind legs, pawing at the fence. She leaped backward. Barked. Pawed some more.

"Look. Look what I have here," Abby said as she walked toward the back fence. "Doggy biscuits. Come get 'em."

Sugar took a flying leap at the fence, knocking over a pottery saucer filled with water. Now the poor animal had drenched herself. Abby shined the light at the back of the gate and saw another raccoon cowering in a half-turned position, as if ready to run. It would not be good for either Abby or the half-pint-sized dog to be trapped between two groups of coons. Abby dropped the biscuits, lunged, grabbed Sugar, and carried the wriggling, wet, yapping dog to the safety of the farmhouse.

Back inside, Abby flipped on the light and looked at the clock. It read 5:30 a.m. The raccoons would leave before sunup—they were shy creatures who foraged at night. Most likely, their den was close by, probably on the deserted property in back of the farmette. Abby had noticed lately that the fresh water she put in the birdbath each day would go muddy overnight—a sure sign of raccoons on the prowl. They liked washing up.

Sugar was now dripping on the clean kitchen floor. When Abby grabbed a towel to dry the dog, Sugar darted from Abby's arms and made a mad dash for the couch pillows, where she threw her body upside down and sideways, wiggling in delight. Next, she dried her ears and head, rubbing her wet fur against Abby's new throw rug, and when Abby lunged to capture her, Sugar flew to the bedroom and dried her dirty paws on Abby's white sheet and hand-embroidered quilt.

"Dang it, Sugar. If there was the slightest chance I might have gone back to bed, it's not possible now! Thanks to you the bedding has to be washed. And just FYI, that is my grandmother's quilt."

Sugar cocked her head to look at Abby.

Like you care. "Arghh!"

Abby pulled the sheets from the bed and the pillowcases off the pillows and threw them into the washer. At least an early start meant she could get some chores done before the funeral. She made a pot of coffee, dressed in work clothes, and pulled her copper-colored hair into a ponytail. Coffee cup in hand, she headed to the back part of the property to pluck some squash for dinner and the last of the spring peas—vines and pods—to throw to the chickens.

At the chicken house, she spotted Henrietta already on the nest. The bantam rooster Houdini was in a mood and jumped on the back of Henrietta's sister—who was too quick for his advances—before settling on one of the brown hens, who was larger, slower, and more submissive. The hen shrieked her objections in ear-piercing squawks as Houdini mounted her, and then she wriggled out from under him after he had had his way with her. The proud Houdini pranced around the pen, his chest out and his iridescent blue-green tail feathers flicking. The poor hen ruffled her feathers, squawked for a while, and proceeded to find a quiet corner where she could scratch and peck in peace.

Abby watched Houdini strut the cock walk. "You think you are such hot stuff, but here's a news flash, Mr. Dandy in Short Pants. Fertilizing eggs produces roosters as well as hens. Trust me, you don't want more roosters in the henhouse. You remember Frank, don't you? After a rooster half his age almost did him in, we had to find him a new henhouse with some ladies who were, let's just say, getting up there in years."

Houdini defiantly flew up to a fence post and let go a gravelly cock-a-doodle-doo, which sounded to Abby a lot like "Not listening to you-ooo."

When the chicken chores were finished, Abby walked past the open-pollinated corn patch. The ears were filling out nicely, but some were covered in ants. The ants had to have a food source, a fact that worried Abby and prompted a closer look. Colonies of corn leaf aphids had formed, their numbers no doubt amplified by the extreme heat and the dry soil, and the ants were feeding on the sticky honeydew produced by the aphids. She spotted a couple of ladybugs and hoped for lacewings, the natural predator of the aphids. Their presence suggested there was potentially an eco-balance in place, but she still might have to mix up a quantity of insecticidal soap. What she didn't want was a major infestation that she couldn't control. But harsh chemicals and poisons would harm her bees. She'd deep soak the corn patch with water and keep a close eye on the pest problem.

Her next stop was the garden. The eggplants were plump and had turned from white to shiny dark purple, almost matching the Ananas Noire heirloom tomatoes. Abby plucked the biggest tomato she could find. Back in the farmhouse, she washed and cut the tomato, then tossed it into a bowl, along with slices of Armenian cucumber, red onion, baby spinach, pine nuts, and feta cheese, which she spritzed with basil-infused olive oil and vinegar. Perched on a bar stool at the kitchen counter, she bit into the crisp Greek salad. Two bites later, her cell phone rang. Philippe was calling to tell her not to pick him up. He'd meet her at the funeral home.

"Afterward, shall we take one car up the mountain, Abby?"

"Why not?" she replied, trying to crunch a piece of crisp, cold cucumber quietly.

"Then would you mind driving? I find those switchbacks daunting."

"Uh-huh." She swallowed the mouthful of salad and held the phone away from her mouth as she chugged some iced green tea to wash down the lump.

There was a pause.

Philippe said, "A staff member of Shadyside Funeral

Home called and asked me to meet her earlier today. She wanted to know Jean-Louis's favorite music. She also wanted pictures of him for an audiovisual tribute to Jean-Louis. This idea, it made me crazy at first. But then I searched for images of my brother on my laptop. I took Jean-Louis's phone to her. She removed the pictures. Wait until you see what we've made."

"Philippe, it sounds lovely. I can't wait to see it."

"It is beautiful."

"So, see you there." Abby understood that many things could facilitate coping and healing. Working on something that celebrated his younger brother's life—even against a time constraint—might help Philippe begin to heal his grief. And a memorial in the form of an audiovisual tribute might help him gain closure. She liked the idea that Philippe would have emotional support, and found herself actually looking forward to the closure the ceremony would provide.

Abby showered and changed. In fact, she was in such a good mood, she decided to take the last of the salad to the chickens and check to make sure all the gates were shut so Sugar could romp out back while Abby was gone. Turning the corner past the flowering purple wisteria and the blooming Iceland roses, Abby looked around for the dog. She soon spotted Sugar digging like crazy, dirt flying high behind her long white legs, in the very patch where Abby had newly planted the beans.

Abby dropped the plastic container of salad remnants, rushed to the bean patch, and found it totally destroyed. She soon spotted a long ridge in the dirt and volcano mounds of freshly dug soil. A mole. It had to be a mole; gopher mounds were crescent shaped. Abby stared at the dog. "I don't know who upsets me more—you or the mole." She looked around for the beans, which were now scattered on top of the dirt. "Ooh, you little brat."

She pulled the dog away from the mounds and carried her back to the house.

"You're in big trouble, little girl." She pulled the patio door ajar so that Sugar could come and go as she pleased. "Just don't take down the rest of the farm while I'm gone," she admonished.

Abby pulled up to Shadyside Funeral Home at 1:30 p.m. Finding a parking space proved difficult. After three times around the lot, she gave up and parked on the street. Shadyside's director had warned her that the funeral home had two funerals scheduled that afternoon, so she shouldn't have been surprised that the lot was so full. She made her way into the chapel area.

Sprays of white lilies, roses, and gardenias were positioned on either side of the doorway. As Abby stepped inside, she was shocked to see how many more arrangements lined the interior walls, creating a lush floral backdrop for the casket. Pristine white orchids with a startling reddish-purple hue staining the inner edges of the blooms rested in pots atop faux marble columns at the head and the foot of the casket. Who had sent such an abundance of beautiful flowers? And where was Philippe? she thought.

Abby walked over to the casket. A peaceful-looking Jean-Louis was visible from the head to just below the waist. The bottom half of the casket was covered by a massive spray of white lilies. Philippe had dressed his brother in a tropical-print shirt of muted colors, which made Abby smile. Jean-Louis looked like a carefree young man napping on his favorite beach on the island of Hispaniola.

"Chef Jean-Louis," Abby whispered, leaning in. "Just so you know, I was on time for the last honey delivery." Unexpectedly, a shiver shot up her spine. Abby tensed as she stared at the corpse. His features, once so expressive, seemed intensely somber now, as if holding a secret. She swallowed hard against the lump forming in her throat. "I hated finding you like that." The back of her eyes burned as she stifled the cry building within. "I haven't been able to bring myself to tell the bees about your passing. I'll have to tell them, although I guess I'm more of a bee whisperer than a talker." Abby's lip quivered. "You know, they sometimes"—her voice cracked—"sometimes sing to me." She swallowed a sob and sniffed hard.

"My grandfather, may God rest his soul, now, he was a bee talker," she explained. "He was the one who told me that when someone close to the bees dies, the bees know. They sometimes fly away with the spirit of the dead. Listen, Chef, I don't want to lose my bees, so if they fly off with you, please tell them to come home to the farmette."

The tears that had welled now trickled over her cheeks. Abby dabbed them away with the backs of her hands. "Once we get you tucked in, I'll open the hives, I promise, and whisper what they surely already sense. You know they liked having you visit them. I'm going to find out who did this to you, Jean-Louis. I promise."

"Abby," Philippe's voice called out softly.

Abby quickly wiped the tears and turned to greet him.

Philippe took her in his arms and held her close.

Abby felt her heart aching, her stomach knotting. Even as she told herself to hold it all in, a sob erupted. *Pull yourself together.* From Philippe's warm and sheltering embrace, she began to draw strength and calmness.

"Philippe, he's so beautiful, so peaceful," she said when

they parted. "And the flowers are exquisite. Your doing?" She made a sweeping gesture with her hand.

"Non. They have been delivered with cards, all but this one." He reached out and touched the spray of white lilies tied with ribbon that lay atop the casket. "The staff told me a thin man in a dark suit and sunglasses brought these. There are also two roses just there, where the casket lid comes down. He laid them in a way, it seems, to suggest that Jean-Louis carry them into the afterlife." Abby knelt down to see the two roses for herself and then stood up again, facing Philippe.

"Do you know who that man might be?"

"Non. He requested time alone with Jean-Louis. The staff told me that he sobbed so hard, they brought to him tissues and a glass of water."

"Did he tell them his name?"

Philippe shook his head. "He stayed a short time. That is all."

At that moment, a lithe, petite woman in a navy shirt-waist dress and pearls walked through the chapel door. As she approached, Philippe introduced her as Brenda, the coordinator he had been working with.

"We have some business to complete," he explained.

Abby excused herself and walked to the back of the room, set her phone to video record mode, and waited to see who else would show up. When Brenda left, Philippe sank into the chair nearest the casket to receive the condolences of those attending the viewing. He'd told Abby that if no one showed, the two of them would watch the tribute and drive up the mountain for the burial, then share a simple meal afterward to celebrate Jean-Louis's life.

From somewhere beyond the chapel, a clock sounded two chimes. At five past the hour, the mayor and the city manager filed in, followed by Nettie, who spotted Abby and nodded. Nettie would not be there except by order of Chief Bob Allen, and Abby knew that Nettie would be watching and listening and reporting back to the chief any relevant information that the police chief should know about. The three spoke to Philippe, waved to Abby, and filed by the coffin before taking a seat. Word traveled fast in a small town, but Abby hadn't realized just how fast and what the impact would be. Others came. Many others. Abby recognized customers, pastry shop workers, suppliers, and business associates among them, but there were also people she didn't know, presumably from the art and culinary worlds of San Francisco.

Abby was not surprised that mayoral candidate Eva Lennahan—who once had called Jean-Louis "the most talented pastry chef in town"—was a no-show. Hopeful that the man in the dark suit, the bearer of white lilies, might return, Abby kept a watchful eye on the door as the lights dimmed for the audiovisual tribute.

The soft strains of "Vissi d'arte" from Puccini's *Tosca,* coincided with an on-screen close-up of Jean-Louis. His large light brown eyes and dark brows dominated his angular face, made more so by a straight nose sans a bump or excessive fleshiness and his smiling Cupid's-bow lips. The camera loved the handsome French Canadian immigrant who'd made Las Flores his final home. On film, he exuded vitality and a commanding presence. Abby marveled at Philippe's selection of music. Of course, Jean-Louis would have loved hearing this aria again. Its opening line, "I lived for art, I lived for love," encapsulated the narrative of his life. And as Chef Jean-Louis had once exclaimed, no one could sing *Tosca* like the incomparable Maria Callas.

The sniffles and muffled cries Abby heard from where she stood at the back of the room tugged at her heart. There were moments during the twenty-two-minute tribute when she had to pinch her nose and squeeze her eyes shut against the tears that were welling. The sequence of shots depicting Jean-Louis at work in the pastry shop kitchen proved the most difficult for Abby to watch. The close-up of his fingers holding scallop-shell pans filled with freshly baked honey-almond madeleines brought new tears. And there, on the counter next to him, was his familiar vermeil teapot and a jar of Abby's honey, with its unmistakable label, which captured the beauty of Henrietta, her favorite little Mediterranean hen.

Other images depicted Jean-Louis and Philippe in a school yard, as adolescents, arms around each other, their school backpack straps draped over their shoulders. In a picture of the boys at an art show with their father, Abby could see the family resemblance. Yet another showed a teenage Jean-Louis outside a Parisian-style patisserie, studying the offerings through the glass window. There was an image of him with Sugar, the mini English pointer–whippet–beagle mutt, whom Jean-Louis had acquired after moving to Las Flores.

The voices of Bocelli and Dion sang "The Prayer" as the last image lingered—a grinning Jean-Louis in his tropical-print shirt and hiking shorts, hands outstretched to heaven, standing atop the spillway of the Las Flores Reservoir. Jean-Louis's tall, thin friend—perhaps less adventurous—stood nearby, as if ready to catch Jean-Louis in the event that he slipped. The haunting and unmistakable image of that friend—one Jake Lennahan—stuck with Abby like no other.

As the lights went back on, a priest by the name of Father Joseph entered the room. He gently placed his hand on Philippe's shoulder and asked if anyone wanted to share stories about Jean-Louis with those in attendance.

Philippe rose and spoke endearingly about how the loss would affect him and his family. "My mother, especially, doted on him. He was born late in her life, and she always called Jean-Louis her late season surprise." Philippe talked about how Jean-Louis had a guiding principle, which was always to put people before material possessions. "He lived as if tomorrow might never come," Philippe said. Choking up, he added, "He believed it was how we all are meant to live."

When Philippe finished talking, there seemed to be a collective reluctance by everyone else to speak, but finally Tallulah stood. She spoke of using her empathic powers when she first interviewed for a job with the chef, and described how she sensed a deep vulnerability, which he would not discuss. "He told me once that prison takes many forms, that to be an artist is to be a pilgrim ever haunted by the thing that desires to be created."

A prayer followed and then the blessing of the body. During it all, Abby thought about Jake Lennahan, who was clearly the friend who had seemed ready to protect Jean-Louis, whatever the price. And now she was beginning to wonder whether the relationship Jake shared with Jean-Louis might have had a dark side.

The Jeep radio was tuned to the weather report as Abby and Philippe drove to the Church of the Pines. The afternoon had become warm and muggy, and winds were kicking up. According to the local weather report, the easterly onshore breeze that served as California's air conditioner had combined with a low pressure at the coast, causing the wind to gust up to forty-plus miles per hour at the crests of high hills and mountain peaks. A heavy fog would set in along the coast later that night, but inland areas, like Las Flores, would remain clear enough to view the full moon.

At the grave site, the winds were already howling. Abby held on to the billowing overskirt of her black, cap-sleeved mourning dress and said to Philippe, "It's ironic and sad that so many showed for the wake, but just you and I are here to see him off."

"Oui," Philippe replied. "It's better this way, no? We two care the most about what happened to him. We two will lay him to his rest."

Abby nodded in agreement. She watched as the six pall-bearers, faces glistening with sweat, walked slowly and with solemnity, holding the casket by its handles. When she and Philippe had reached the mountain summit, she'd set her cell phone to vibrate so it would not ring during the short service. And now it was vibrating. Abby checked the screen, then took the call.

"Say it quick, Kat. . . . My phone doesn't have much battery power left."

"Thought you'd want to know, girlfriend . . . the bicycle guy you reported, with the two dogs . . . just took him in for a hit-and-run."

"Oh yeah?"

"There's more. He collided with Dora."

"Is she okay?"

"Hospital staff says she's lucky. Nine lives, that one. Has a fractured hip and a broken right wrist. Malnourished, of course, so they're keeping her long enough to build up her stamina."

"So, our colorful Dora will have hot meals and a roof over her head for a while."

"Yep. At the taxpayers' expense."

"What about those poor dogs?"

"They're being checked over by a vet at the animal rescue."

"Dare I ask about the bags in Dora's shopping cart?"

"Well, unfortunately, some were ripped."

"Meaning stuff spilled out, and you didn't need that pesky little search warrant to find it." Abby's adrenaline kicked in.

"Why, yes, it did, and we couldn't help noticing the bag contained Chef Jean-Louis's apron."

"*No.* Really?"

"And that's not all. Dora has a thing for string. We found a bag full of the nasty stuff—all sorts, used for God knows what. There was a long piece of twine in there, too, with a slipknot, cut at one end."

"Ha! So she had the twine from the chef's neck all along." Abby's heart leaped. "Ooh, I'd love to talk about this more, but we're up here at the grave site. I've got to go. The priest is walking toward us. We'll talk later."

As if fearing a powerful wind gust would topple him, the priest held on to a walking stick and clutched his Bible, its purple ribbon hanging loosely from the frayed edges, as he picked his way from the stone pathway over to the gaping hole in the ground, where freshly dug dirt had been heaped into a black pile. The casket was positioned atop the wide straps laid out so that the pallbearers could easily take hold and lower Jean-Louis into the ground. They stood ready.

The priest took a moment to put down his walking stick and look into the eyes of each person before commencing the service, and then he began to speak, projecting his voice over the howling wind and making the sign of the cross. "In the name of the Father, the Son, and the Holy Spirit. We meet on this solemn occasion to honor the life and the passing of Jean-Louis Bonheur, a beloved son and a much-loved brother. With reverence, we lovingly place his body into this sacred dwelling place, as a sign of our respect for Jean-Louis, who lived among us for a time. We commend his spirit to the heart of the Lord. And we comfort one another in our grief."

Opening his Bible with the ribbon, the priest spoke again. "For it is written in Psalm forty-six, God is our refuge and strength." He read on and then paused, as if trying to think of some other words of comfort. Finally, he closed his Bible. "Let us pray. Look upon us, O Lord, with compassion, as you did when Jesus cried at the grave of his friend Lazarus. Give us hope. Strengthen us with faith. Safeguard the friends and family of those who must now carry on without their beloved in their midst. Amen."

The priest asked Philippe if he wanted to open the casket one last time before it was lowered into the ground. Philippe nodded. Abby had slipped a small vial of rose geranium water into her purse and had told Philippe he might use it to anoint his brother's forehead. Philippe now looked at her, as if needing her support and strength. His eyes, gray-green now, turned misty as he took the vial from her.

The pallbearers pulled the casket cover back to reveal the face of the deceased. Philippe knelt in the dirt to draw the sign of the cross over his brother's forehead. He tilted the vial against his thumb and middle finger just as a heavy wind gust pushed him forward and sent the vial flying from his fingers. Simultaneously, a paper wafted upward from the casket and drifted on the wind. Abby didn't care about the vial, and she was pretty sure Philippe was all right, but her instincts screamed for her to chase after that paper as the wind lifted and dropped it on an erratic path. She breathed a sigh of relief when it snagged on the base of a bush several yards away.

The priest helped Philippe to his feet and carried on. "Although your hearts grieve"—the priest motioned for the men to take their positions and lower the casket into the earth—"you can take solace in the words faithfully recorded in the Gospel of John. The Lord says, 'I will not leave you comfortless. I will come to you.' "

Leaning down to place his Bible next to his walking stick, the priest picked up a handful of dirt. He motioned for Philippe and Abby to do likewise. As they did, the clergyman intoned, "We have committed our beloved's spirit to your eternal keeping, Father. We now commit his body to the ground. Earth to earth, ashes to ashes, dust to dust. Merciful God, we do this with the belief and absolute hope in the resurrection to eternal life. . . ."

Abby didn't hear the last words. The wind wasn't just gusting. It howled now. She held her breath in hopes that the paper didn't cast off again. As soon as she heard "Amen," she backed away from the burial site and swiftly marched toward the bush where the paper waved still. Leaning down, Abby plucked the piece of paper from its entrapment. The paper was actually a small colored photograph of Jean-Louis and Jake Lennahan. The image showed them clowning around, both displaying unmistakably happy smiles. Jean-Louis wore his chef's toque and double-breasted shirt. Jake wore a sandwich sign with straps over his shoulders. A multilayered, frosted cake had been painted on the sign. On the back of the photograph, in cursive, was written, *Happy Birthday, Jean-Louis. My grief is unbearable. You are my heart. I never believed she would make good on her threat, but now she has taken from me everything, even my reason for living. I curse the day I married her. May she burn in hell! —J.*

Abby tucked the photo in her purse, steeled herself against the gusting wind, and returned to the grave, where the priest was shaking hands with the pallbearers. The diggers had already begun filling the grave. Abby joined Philippe and the priest as they picked their way back to the stone path. Shadows had already lengthened on the mountain. Abby touched Philippe's arm and pointed to the blazing orange ball of a sun sliding down into the now gunmetal-gray Pacific.

He dropped back a step to create space between himself and the priest. "Abby, what was on that paper?"

"Just a missing puzzle piece. For a bowl of white bean soup, I'll tell you all about it. What do you say?" Abby asked, trying to assuage his sadness and quell the singing of her heart at their stroke of good fortune. She was certain that Jake was the distraught man who had delivered the lilies and those two roses, and that, while alone with the body, he had secretly tucked the photo inside the coffin.

"Sounds good," Philippe replied, taking her arm to help her negotiate the stone pathway.

She stopped. "And pie at Maisey's."

"I would never say no to that."

Abby grinned and grabbed him with both hands to steady herself as a wind gust tugged hard at her balance. "And maybe a drink at the Black Witch after dinner?"

He arched his brows. A quizzical look crossed his face. "Maybe even two. And stiff ones at that. Should I read something more into this?"

"It's up to you. I'll explain while we fill our tummies with comfort food," said Abby.

"Bean soup is comfort food? Americans!"

White Bean Soup

Ingredients:
1 cup dried Hutterite small soup beans or other white
   beans
3 medium celery stalks, diced
2 large carrots, peeled and cut into 1-inch pieces
1 large smoked ham hock
1 medium yellow onion, peeled and diced
½ cup torn fresh spinach leaves
1 packet Lipton Golden Onion Recipe Soup & Dip Mix
6 cups chicken stock
2 to 3 medium bok choy leaves, torn into small pieces

Directions:
   Combine the beans, celery, carrots, ham hock,
onions, spinach, and Lipton mix in a Crock-Pot. Pour
in the chicken stock. Cook, adding water as needed,
until the beans are tender, about 5 to 6 hours. Add the
bok choy during the last 5 minutes of cooking.

   Serve the soup with slices of warm homemade bread,
a chunk of Manchego (or another sharp cheese), and a
crisp, chilled salad.

   Option: You can make this dish vegetarian by omit-
ting the ham hock and using vegetable stock in place
of chicken broth.

Serves 4

Chapter 15

Pacific oysters can engage in annual sex
reversals—male one year, female the next—
one of nature's many surprises.

—*Henny Penny Farmette Almanac*

Philippe pointed to Zazi's chalkboard sign right inside
the restaurant's entrance and exclaimed with exuberance, "Oh, mon Dieu! The grilled oysters, we must have
them to start . . . and champagne!"

"Sounds good," said Abby, recalling how crestfallen his
expression had been at the Shakespeare Festival, when the
concession stand had run out of oysters. "Would you mind
ordering while I give a quick call back to Kat? It's not the
kind of conversation I want to have in public. I'd like to
make it from the car. Okay?"

"Ah, oui." His brows knitted. He looked puzzled. "You
won't be long?"

"I promise. I'll be back before the oysters are served."
She put her hand on his arm and said softly, "There are at
least two people who know the truth about what happened to poor Jean-Louis . . . three, if you count an accomplice. It's high time the truth comes out, but I'm
thinking things have to be set in motion first."

She reached for the bar across the door to open it but re-linquished it when Philippe placed his palm against it and pushed the door open. He followed her outside into the fading light of early evening. The wind unrelentingly whipped his trouser legs and lifted the sheer flounces above the hem of Abby's black mourning dress.

"You must enlighten me," he said, "as soon as you return. I do not like suspense."

Abby nodded. The wind gusted and tugged at her hair, loosening the comb anchoring her thick mane, which she'd twisted into a loose braid at the nape of her neck. Instinctively, her hand flew back to catch the comb, but she was a millisecond too late. As the comb slipped from her hair and the unrestrained locks tumbled over her shoulders, Abby pivoted away from Philippe and darted after the comb. It somersaulted down the street, lifted and tossed by the airstream. Giving up hope of ever catching it, she turned back to Philippe. He stared at her, his gray-green eyes sparkling with intensity.

"What?" Abby asked, shaking out her hair and reaching to pull a lock of it from her eyes.

Gazing intently at her hair, he murmured, "Alexa Wilding."

"Huh?" Abby was sure her face had a stupid expression on it, but what was he talking about?

"Your hair. Your face. This light."

"Reminds you of another woman?" Abby asked incredulously.

"Oui. An English girl named Alexa Wilding."

Abby wasn't expecting him to tell her the truth about his intimate relationships. But Philippe, she'd learned, was full of surprises.

"She was a working-class girl who posed for Dante Gabriel Rossetti."

"Oh." Abby sighed in relief. "You mean that Pre-Raphaelite artist? I've heard of him, but not her. So tell me, Mr. Art Dealer, what was so special about Alexa Wilding?" Abby wasn't too sure where this conversation might go, but she would play along. Maybe she would learn something.

"Rossetti had already completed *Lady Lilith,* one of his most famous paintings. Then he saw Alexa Wilding. His usual model did not possess delicate features. To reflect an image of refined beauty, Rosetti reworked the painting to capture Alexa Wilding's face."

Philippe moved a half step closer and clasped a strand of Abby's long, curly hair in his hand for a closer look. "Alexa Wilding's hair was the color of grain. But I can imagine that painting with your gold-red hue with undertones of burnished copper." Releasing her hair to cup her chin in his hand, he gently studied one side of her face and then the other. "Extraordinary, *ma chérie.*"

"The painting?"

"You." Philippe's eyes locked with hers.

Abby's heart hammered. His nearness felt as palpable and luscious as the first time she had held an exquisitely ripe summer pear to her mouth, sinking lips and teeth and tongue into it. *Oh, my . . . is he going to kiss me? Right here, in front of Zazi's Bistro?* But when Philippe flashed a flirtatious smile and stepped back, Abby quickly regained her composure, smiled weakly, and murmured, "Thank you for the compliment." She paused to take a short, deep breath. "I just need to make that phone call. Give me two minutes, and I'll be back before the appetizers are served."

Philippe watched her cross the street to her Jeep. Abby looked back and waved.

In the car, Abby paused before tapping Kat's number on her phone. She needed to settle her thoughts and calm the crazy drumming of her heart. Had he just compared her to the Pre-Raphaelite romantic ideal of beauty? It seemed so. When the mere touch of his skin sent a shiver racing through her, Abby couldn't help wondering what it really would feel like to kiss him. *I can't think about that now. Focus.*

When Kat picked up, Abby said, "I think I know who killed Jean-Louis, and, Kat, I need a favor."

"Only one?" Kat replied.

"Who is acting chief of police now that Bob Allen is in the hospital, recovering?"

"Otto."

"Great," Abby said. "Do you think you could convince him to reopen the case?"

"He'll want a strong theory and the evidence to support it."

"Well, I've got a handwritten note that practically spells out that the chef was murdered and even suggests who the killer is. Are you hanging on to your handcuffs? That note blew out of Jean-Louis's coffin just before it was lowered into the ground."

"You're not joking, are you?"

"I never joke about murder," Abby said.

"So, who killed our chef?"

"Eva Lennahan looks good for it." Abby checked her face in the rearview mirror and decided she could quickly freshen her makeup while explaining everything to Kat. If she was to represent beauty idealized, a bit of blush couldn't hurt and a touch of lipstick seemed in order. She glanced away from the mirror to look through the windshield. She could see Philippe inside, chatting with the waitress; undoubtedly, he was ordering their champagne. "I tell you, Kat, it was like divine intervention," Abby said, opening her purse. "And the photo with the handwriting on the back nearly blew away before I could snag it. Anyway, here's my theory.

"Jean-Louis and Jake Lennahan got together in the Caribbean. Could have been any number of reasons why they met, including a business trip, a guys-only outing, or even an accidental run-in. But their mutual attraction was stronger than their power to resist." Abby took out her mascara and touched up her lashes.

"While they were there, they each got identical tattoos of the astrological sign Cancer. Philippe told me that Jean-Louis didn't have that tattoo before he went to the Caribbean. Both men were born in the month of July, making them Cancers. Jean-Louis loved the sea. Jake had access to a yacht in the Dominican Republic. They were about to celebrate their birthdays again in a few weeks. It's a verifiable fact that Jean-Louis was planning to return to the Caribbean—most likely with Jake, further solidifying their relationship."

"Illicit relationship," Kat chimed in. "As we both know, Jake is married to a woman with unstoppable political ambition."

"And there's your motive for murder—Eva couldn't afford a scandal. She had connections within the prison system that could fix her problem. After all, she had met a lot of inmates, wardens, and corrections officers through her charity work with families of the incarcerated. Guys on the inside know how to get a favor done by their buddies on the outside." Glancing up at the mirror again, Abby noticed a speck of mascara on her cheek. She fished a tissue from her purse and brushed it off.

"But why not kill the husband, instead of his lover? Or, better still, just get a divorce, like everyone else does?" Kat asked.

"Stop the money flow and there ends her lifestyle and her ambitious dreams. I'll bet she has wheedled a small fortune from Jake, including his family heirlooms. I saw her wedding ring setting when we ran into her at the park. It's a perfect match to the earring Jake had repaired at Lidia's jewelry shop. I'd say it is pretty nice bling for someone who once worked as a convenience store clerk. Well, that's what I've learned, anyway, from perusing back issues of the *Weekly*. Apparently, Jake used to go into the Stone Bridge Road convenience store on Sunday mornings for coffee and a newspaper, since his place up in the hills is outside of the news delivery area but near the store. According to one story, that's where she met him."

"I gotta say, girlfriend, you have certainly done your homework. Do you think the earring just fell off during the murder?"

"Maybe there was a struggle."

"Plausible. Proof would be nice."

"Well, maybe her campaign manager or someone else saw her wearing those earrings that night. I mean, think about it. What reason would Jake or anyone else have for bringing them . . . ever . . . to the pastry shop?"

"She could have dropped it while visiting the chef on another occasion."

"True, but my instincts tell me different." Popping a mint into her mouth, Abby said, "This is where Otto could be effective in unearthing her whereabouts in the wee hours of the morning, what she was doing, and what she was wearing when Jean-Louis died. I'm thinking she got a call from someone who thought they could solve her problem by making it seem that the chef had become deeply depressed, depressed enough to hang himself."

Kat said, "Makes sense, but who would make that call

or even know how to reach her in the middle of the night?"

"Whoever it was most likely accompanied Eva to the pastry shop. We know she needed muscles to lynch him."

"Ah," Kat said, "so the chef would see Eva's face and open the door to her."

"Exactly," Abby said, checking out Philippe, who was staring back at her.

"Probably," said Kat. "So she went there to convince the chef *not* to go to the Caribbean with her husband, and when he wouldn't agree, she murdered him?"

"Oh, this is where it gets muddy for me," Abby said. "Maybe Otto could grill Jake, see if he'll turn on Eva . . . or maybe he could call Eva in, insinuate that he knows about Jake and the chef's little affair, and make her think we are hot on her trail. She's too calculating to spill, but if she doesn't lawyer up, we might get her to reveal something or keep her talking long enough to analyze her behavior. Of course, we could hope for a confession," said Abby. "We know her marriage to Jake gave her access to power, privilege, politics, and all sorts of people. All that access would change, and a scandal would ensue, if Jake revealed his secret."

"So if Eva knocked off the chef, who was her accomplice?" Kat asked.

"My guess . . . she called in a favor from a local biker, an ex-felon, or a gangbanger—someone who knows how to get things done, inside or out. I suppose it could also have been a hit for hire. Either way, I think she was there with an accomplice."

"She'd have her pick of thugs hanging out at the Black Witch, right next door to the pastry shop," said Kat.

"Yes, and I'd love to know if the killer's epithelials are on the twine. You did say the twine you found in Dora's bag was a long piece with a knot. I've seen those newspaper bundles with a double length of string," Abby said.

"Yes, but multiple people would have touched it—surely the killer, but also the newspaper carrier, and let's not forget Dora."

"No, maybe not Dora. Well, yes, she would have touched it, but she almost always wears those ridiculous white gloves from the last century. The news guy's skin cells certainly would be found. But the killer's cells are likely there, too, unless he wore gloves," Abby stated. "As for the newspaper carrier, he is not really a person of interest, because we know from a pastry shop neighbor on the back side of Lemon Lane that a thump was heard around five a.m., possibly the newspaper hitting the sidewalk. We also know from the call the newspaper carrier made to dispatch that his car was nearly hit by Etienne, who ran that stop sign around four thirty a.m. So, although the deliveryman would have touched the twine to tie the bundle, his alibi of running a route is airtight, and he has no motive for murdering the chef."

"All good points. But what about that Vieillard fellow?" Kat seemed to be anticipating Otto's skepticism, since Otto was the acting chief now, working directly under Chief Bob Allen's authority.

"Since you asked, Vieillard is really Jake Lennahan. It is a name that Jean-Louis used as a term of endearment to keep the identity of his secret lover private. You know how Jean-Louis was about giving other people pet names. Jake was older, but only by five years and two days, and he was still in the closet, so to speak."

"The possibility has crossed my mind that Jake might have framed his wife," Kat said. "How would you refute that?"

Abby laughed. "He couldn't have known that his note would fly out of the coffin. A handwriting sample will prove Jake wrote that note. His wife killed his lover. We have to find out who helped her do it."

"Yeah, so I'll bring her in for an interview. But before I go, I need to tell you that there's talk concerning you."

"What kind of talk?"

"I guess the questions you've been asking are beginning to make some low-life types nervous."

"Yeah? Who?"

"To start with, associates of Dora from the encampment under the creek bridge. Word has got around that you've been looking for the murderer among our citizens, and you know how paranoid the winos down there can get. They think one of them will be wrongly fingered for it. Then there's the buzz at the Black Witch, among the bikers."

"They got a problem with me trying to figure out what happened to Chef Jean-Louis?"

"It doesn't take much to get them riled. I'm told Sweeney didn't like the cold shoulder you gave him the night he was mouthing off in the bar. He told his drinking buddies that if he ever gets you alone, he's going to teach you a lesson. Plus, you're a former cop, and you've been meddling in his business."

"What business?"

"Drugs, blackmail, flavor of the month."

"Well, that just tells me that Etienne is a rat. He's the only one I've asked any questions about drugs. Etienne was the blackmailer. I'm surprised that Sweeney, as homophobic as he is, would have any association with Etienne."

"Just watch your step. And keep me on speed dial."

"Sure. And thanks, Kat, for the heads-up."

Abby looked through the windshield. "Oh, before I go, I think Jean-Louis was drugged. You agree?"

"Well, something kept him from fighting off his killer."

"We still have the cup from the ivy shelf of the baker's rack." Abby straightened in the seat. "Maybe it has a print on it. Or traces of what was in it."

Kat sighed heavily. "I'll get with Otto, pressure him to reopen the case and bring in Eva and Jake for questioning. Meanwhile, I'll get started on that twine and the cup. You'll need to bring back the evidence boxes."

"Right. So, I'll let you get started. Philippe is waving a glass of champagne at me. We're at Zazi's for a quick dinner, and then I've got to get back to the farmette to check on the dog and my chickens."

"OMG, Abby! You are with a gorgeous man, and all you can think about is your chickens? I seriously don't understand you," Kat chided. "I'd be more interested in that lovely French Canadian rooster showing me his wattle and spurs than in trotting home to Henrietta, Heloise, and Houdini on the roost."

Abby grinned. "You've got a point there. Catch you later."

Despite Kat telling her to keep her phone handy, Abby tucked it into the glove compartment. She didn't want phone calls or other interruptions as she methodically laid out her theory for Philippe during dinner.

Crossing the street, Abby caught sight of Philippe waving to her and pushing back his chair. Suddenly, to her right, an engine revved. Abby watched as Philippe walked to the glass door and pushed it open. Wheels squealed, and a car shot past in a blur. Alarm bells sounded as Abby lost her footing and fell between the cars parked parallel in front of Zazi's. In milliseconds, Philippe was at her side, his strong arms lifting and supporting her until she was able to stand on her own.

"That idiot almost killed you! Are you hurt?"

Abby shook her head. "It's broad daylight. . . . Probably just a teen driver with a lead foot," she said reassuringly. But Kat's warning popped into her mind. If someone was delivering a message, Abby had certainly gotten it.

When they were seated, Philippe handed her a glass of chilled bubbly. Reaching for his own glass and lifting it, he said, "To Jean-Louis. He was—"

The petite, dark-haired waitress arrived, bearing a white scallop-patterned plate with steaming oysters. She set the plate before them and offered freshly cracked pepper, which neither Philippe nor Abby wanted. With the cheerful command "Enjoy," she left them.

Abby waited for Philippe to finish his toast to his brother, but he now focused all his attention on the steaming oysters.

"To Jean-Louis, who touched us all with his joie de vivre!" Abby said, lifting her glass.

"Oui," said Philippe, clinking his glass gently against hers. He sucked in a mouthful of champagne, then picked up Abby's plate to serve her a large-size grilled oyster on the half shell.

Abby poked her small fork into the sizzling mollusk and carried the bite to her mouth. It was succulent. "Delicious," she said. "I can't think of anything so absolutely scrumptious and sensuous, can you?"

Philippe finished his bite, wiped his mouth with his napkin, and leaned forward until he was eye to eye with her. He whispered seductively, "Ah, oui. I can imagine. It remains an experience for us to share, n'est-ce pas?"

Abby's second forkful froze in midair. What *should* she say? Fanning herself with her napkin, she reached for her glass of champagne. "Is it hot in here?"

"But of course," he replied. He riveted his gaze on her, eased back in his chair, and dropped his napkin over his lap. His grin deepened, accentuating the chiseled angle of his jaw. Apparently, he was enjoying his ability to fluster her.

It was too late to take the question back. Abby wished she had a mask handy to hide behind—one that covered the whole face, like Carnival dancers wore. It was work to keep tamping down the currents of desire this French Canadian kept igniting in her. The sheer animal magnetism he generated when he turned on the charm was becoming almost impossible to resist.

Abby reminded herself of the boundaries she had set. But as her will weakened, she wondered if holding firm was still necessary. He'd hired her to prove his brother's death was a murder, and she'd pretty much figured out who killed Jean-Louis. There were still loose ends, of course, but she was confident that she'd have all the details figured out in short order. Philippe would be on a plane in a day or two. She'd most likely never see him again. So . . . was it still necessary to honor the boundaries between client and investigator?

As they dined on creamy bean soup, Abby recounted her theory. Philippe listened thoughtfully.

"When will you know for sure?" he asked when she was finished.

"Soon," Abby said. "I hope very soon."

After Zazi's, they walked slowly past the storefronts along Main Street, looking into the windows of each one. Passing a display table in front of Horace's New and Used Books, Abby stopped to thumb through a couple of cookbooks, taking particular notice of a copy of Julia Child's first book, *Mastering the Art of French Cooking*. It bore evidence of heavy use—food stains, underlining, and erasure marks. But given the closeout price of one dollar, Abby took out her wallet. Philippe shook his head and took the book from her, then paid for it, along with a back issue of *American Art Review* magazine that had caught his attention. Carrying their purchases in his left hand, Philippe put his free hand on the small of Abby's back and guided her to an antique store window that displayed an Arts and Crafts–style chest with Van Gogh's sunflowers painted across all four drawers.

"Ooh, I love it," Abby said, pressing a finger against the window. "You know, sunflowers are the honeybees' favorite food."

Philippe smiled.

Crossing Oakwood Way with the light, Abby slipped her arm into Philippe's and remained on high alert for speeding cars. Within minutes, they walked into the pie shop, just as Maisey was emptying a pot of stale coffee.

The apron-bedecked Maisey, looking like a full-figured southern belle with not a white hair out of place, ambled over to the counter. "Well, hello, you two. What can I get you?" Before either Abby or Philippe could answer, Maisey said, "I know you love my bourbon pecan pie, Philippe, but I served up my last piece an hour ago. Could I interest you in a dish of rhubarb fool or maybe a serving of date crumble?"

Philippe looked perplexed. "I regret I do not know what fool or crumble is. . . . Perhaps you have something chocolate?"

"Why yes, I do. A piece of flourless chocolate cake coming right up. I'll just plate it for you."

Philippe nodded.

"I'm not too hungry, Philippe," Abby said. "Shall we split it?"

"Oui. Good idea." Philippe led her to the counter. Abby assumed he preferred the counter since they could include Maisey Mack in their conversation while she finished her chores.

After Maisey served them, Philippe took one bite of the flourless chocolate cake and declared, "Oh, how I love a woman who knows her way around a kitchen." He directed his remark at Maisey but winked at Abby. "It is amazing, n'est-ce pas, how cooks create sensuality with food and capture a man's heart? He eats, and his mind, it spins, and his heart, it pounds." He sighed. "His waistline, alas," he lamented, "it grows."

Abby and Maisey laughed.

Philippe continued. "Women and witches cast spells with food."

"Why, Philippe," Maisey asked, smiling, "are you saying someone has cast a spell on you?"

Philippe's eyes locked with Abby's. With a pronounced exaggeration, he said, "Oui, this must be what has happened."

"Then I'll have the rest of that chocolate cake," Abby said, playfully reaching for the dessert plate.

Philippe let go a boyish laugh and pulled the plate closer to his chest, apparently to protect it from further incursions by Abby's fork.

Abby raised her fork, as if ready to do battle. "Sir, you play with fire."

Philippe shot Abby a seductive look before lowering his gaze from her eyes to her lips and then farther down to her décolletage, where her dress suggested ample curves. "I can take the heat," he said.

Abby glanced up at Maisey, who raised a finely arched brow. Looking back at Philippe, Abby positioned her fork on a napkin, cocked her head, and replied, "Oh, yeah?"

"I'll just bet you can take the heat," said Maisey, inter-vening. "But this little lady is known to *pack* the heat."

The three burst into laughter.

As soon as the laughter had subsided and Philippe had enjoyed the last bite of cake, Maisey reached for the dessert plate and forks. "It's on the house," she said. "Now, scoot on outta here, because I've got to open early tomorrow. The Optimist Club is having their meeting at seven thirty in the morning, and I've got to get things ready. Lock that door behind you when you go, would you?"

Abby's mood was buoyant. She walked arm in arm with Philippe back up Main Street and stopped in front of the Black Witch, where motorcycles lined the curb. When Philippe offered to buy her a drink, Abby decided it would be more intimate to have a drink on the farmette patio. Something inside her told her it was now or never. She took his arm and pulled him away from the Black Witch doorway.

"I made a promise to Jean-Louis. Would you like to help me keep it?" she said.

"But, of course."

"Tonight?"

"I would do anything for you," Philippe answered. His expression reflected a sweet tenderness.

The warm night air blowing through the open windows cooled Abby's flushed skin, one reason she loved this drive from town to the farmette on hot summer nights. Another was the way the limbs and leaves of the tall eucalyptus trees lining the road danced in the moonlight to cast ghostly shadows across the asphalt. Even the scents on such a hot night were pleasing: the fragrance of the earth, warmed from the heat of the day, mingled with the perfume of wild indigenous plants and trees, like pitcher sage, wild thyme, the Jeffrey pine, sagebrush, and the California spicebush.

"What do you think of it here, Philippe? Do you like Northern California?"

"I like wherever you are."

Abby felt flirty inside but tried not to show it. Philippe looked at her often, sometimes studying her for many minutes at a time before turning away when she looked back at him. The sexual tension between them could not be denied, yet they said little on the moonlit ride from Las Flores to the farmette. Sugar greeted them with a nonstop welcoming bark at the gate. Abby retrieved a rawhide bone from the metal garbage can just off the patio.

"Now, settle down," she said, scratching Sugar behind the ears. Sugar tugged the bone out of Abby's hand and trotted off, apparently content to gnaw on her treat far from the reach of human hands that might try to reclaim it.

"Ready?" Abby asked. "Watch your step."

She led him to the apiary at the end of her orchard. From a distance, the hives appeared under the pale lunar light to be ethereal columns squatting on a platform, as though they might have once supported the ancient stone throne of a long-dead ruler. Abby had positioned the two stacks of white Styrofoam boxes evenly along a straight line, with roughly a foot of space between them. They were positioned in front of the fence, with six feet of unobstructed space in front, and were protected by a wooden roof, which kept rain and moisture off the hives.

Abby leaned down and placed her ear against one of the two hives to listen to the soothing hum of her bees. "They are all inside. It's warm tonight, and the bees are cooling the hive. The honey flow has started."

"Ah, oui?"

"Put your free hand on top of the hive there," Abby instructed.

"You are certain about this?" Philippe asked, taking longer than necessary to do as she asked.

"Absolutely. You won't be stung. Did I ever tell you that Jean-Louis had no fear of them? He loved not only the honey, but also the bees." Placing her palm on the other hive, Abby reached for Philippe's hand to give him courage. As her heart and mind focused on the task of putting her feelings into words, Abby spotted a guard bee fly up into the moonlight in front of her face, buzzing her, as if to greet the beekeeper; and then, just as quickly, it retreated to the bottom of the hive and disappeared. A lump formed in Abby's throat. She swallowed hard and felt her eyes tearing. Her resolve hardened. She would not leave until she'd said the words. Finally, mournfully, she whispered, "Sweet bees, I have come with sad news. Our beloved pastry chef, Jean-Louis, has passed away."

And with that, all the sorrow Abby had tried to hide through gallows humor and emotional restraint rose like a swarm lifting upward in uncertain flight. Her mournful sobs were soon buried in Philippe's chest. He held her tightly, stroking her hair, murmuring, "The sweetest thing here, Abby, is not the bees or their honey, but your heart."

Tips for Correlating Bees' Flower Sources to Honey Type

- Dandelions—the honey is golden yellow in spring

- Orange blossoms—the honey is pale yellow in late spring

- Buckwheat—the honey is dark aubergine in early summer

- Eucalyptus—the honey is pale amber in summer

- Star thistle—the honey is dark yellowish green in late summer

- Wild thyme—the honey is medium amber in late summer

Chapter 16

Help your chickens through the annual molting
process (when they lose feathers and stop egg
production) by feeding them 20 percent more
protein and reducing their stress.

—*Henny Penny Farmette Almanac*

Abby abruptly awakened, alarmed, not knowing why.
She soon realized the arm draped over her tummy
wasn't hers. She sucked in a surprised gasp. Philippe reclined beside her—one arm over her and the other cradling
his pillow. Sugar had positioned herself in a ball, her back
against the soles of Abby's feet. Abby relaxed and thought
about how the three of them had ended up on her bed . . .
together.

After dinner and pie following the graveside service, she
and Philippe had sipped cordials under the stars on the
farmette patio. Her choice had been a late-season muscat;
his, a brandy. When Philippe had complained of sleepiness
due to the meal and an alcohol buzz, Abby had pointed
the way to the bedroom. After all, she didn't feel much like
clearing the couch, which was covered in boxes of unopened bee supplies and the jars and egg cartons that Lucas

had given her. While Philippe rested, Abby had reclined on a large pillow next to him. She had stroked Sugar as she'd explained to Philippe where the case was now headed. Within minutes, Philippe and Sugar had drifted off to sleep. Soon after . . . she had, too.

A grin parted her lips as Abby realized that at some point Philippe had reached over to draw her close. Trailing her fingers along his arm, she soon felt the fabric of his shirt where he had turned up the cuff. *Oh, jeez. We're still fully dressed in our funeral clothes.* She suppressed a chuckle. So much for the long-awaited kiss and the sizzling whatever else that might have followed. She liked him, but he would soon leave for New York. He was a city boy, after all. Maybe this was the way things were meant to be.

Her thoughts settled peacefully as she listened to Philippe's soft breathing and Sugar's snoring. Beyond the window, the tinkling wind chime seemed to compete with the rustle of the fig tree leaves. A frog let go a trio of throaty croaks. All pleasant enough sounds, but what had awakened her? On the other hand, what did it really matter now?

Houdini crowed. Never quite sure why he felt the need to crow at all hours of the night, Abby wondered if he was experiencing a testosterone rush or if he was sounding the alarm about a prowling skunk or raccoon. Or maybe he had just heard another rooster cock-a-doodle-doing and was responding. *Whatever.*

Guiding her fingertips along Philippe's hand where it rested against her tummy, Abby touched the angled ridges of his knuckles and traced the prominent vein that ran along the top of his hand to the boundary of soft hairs covering his forearm. She felt utterly content, so much so that not even Houdini's crowing could interfere with the secret pleasure permeating her being, except . . . Houdini hadn't stopped crowing. *What is bugging that rooster?*

A soft scuffle sounded on the gravel path alongside the house. Abby strained to hear it. For a long interval, she listened, on high alert, but the sound had ceased. She heaved a heavy sigh and settled back down. Then . . . a bottle rolled on the patio's stone surface. Abby sighed in exasperation. *Those pesky raccoons are definitely back.*

Checking on the raccoons wasn't a good enough reason to leave the comfy bed, but as she thought about their tendency to riffle through anything and everything, Abby remembered the antique cordial glasses. She had left them on the patio table after Philippe had told her how sleepy he felt. The set of crystal, a gift from her grandparents, had been etched with an Edinburgh thistle pattern. So whether she wanted to or not, Abby felt she had to get up and save those glasses from the nocturnal bandits.

Easing Philippe's arm off her midsection so as not to awaken him, Abby rolled to the edge of the bed, then felt for the flashlight and the fuzzy pink house slippers she kept under the bed. With the items firmly in hand, she quietly tiptoed to the kitchen sliding-glass door. The sudden slap of Sugar's tail smacked her leg.

"Not this time," Abby whispered sharply, dropping her slippers and sliding her feet into them. "I still haven't recovered from your last go-round with those raccoons. You guard Philippe. Now stay."

The night-light under the microwave mounted above the oven gave off enough light for Abby to see on the counter the jar in which she kept a few baked dog biscuits in the shape of a bone. Retrieving one, she waved it under Sugar's nose. The dog wasn't interested. Abby laid the dog biscuit on the floor. Sugar ignored it. Stealing over to the patio door, Abby quietly unlatched it and opened it just a little. She held on to Sugar's collar to keep the dog inside while she peeled herself out through the narrow opening. Sugar whined. She left the heavy glass door slightly ajar, certain that it was too heavy for Sugar to push and that the opening was too narrow for her to squeeze through. But Sugar was still able to sniff the raccoon scent in the night air. Immediately, she rose on her hind legs and began pawing and whining.

"Settle down!" Abby whispered. *Who am I kidding? Like you are ever going to listen to me.* The moon had set, taking with it that glorious silvery light it emitted, but the stars remained bright against the dark sky, and the breeze was gentle and warm. Abby almost wished that Philippe would awaken and that they could sit for a spell and maybe talk of dreams the way she and Clay used to do. *Nah, let him sleep. He's probably as physically exhausted as he is emotionally.*

She found the glasses right where she'd left them. Now to get them inside before the raccoons caught sight of her. But how to do it? Sugar was just waiting for that door to open. She was sure to dash right between Abby's legs or jump up and knock the glasses from her hands. Already, Abby could hear a commotion on the side of the house. If the raccoons had knocked over that stack of five-gallon buckets she was planning to fill with frames of honey, it meant they were just around the corner. If they saw her, they could get mighty aggressive.

Not wanting to deal with Sugar while she carried her antique stemware or to alarm the raccoons in any way, Abby conceived another plan. She turned off the flashlight and reached for the glasses. Rather than trying to wiggle through that patio door and risk dropping them, Abby cradled the glasses to her chest and struck out barefoot through the wet grass. She headed past a row of white tea roses to a wooden bench. It was positioned between thickly canopied nectarine trees; the trees' round, dark silhouettes looked like ancient beehives. After finding the basket of rags she'd left on the bench, Abby wrapped the stemware and slid it between the layers of cloth. She wedged the basket under the arm of the bench, eager to return to bed.

Hands seized her from behind. Abby's heart thudded against her chest. Though she was filled with terror, the cop in her fought back. Her attacker clamped a hand reeking of stale tobacco over her mouth. Joining her two hands together for strength, Abby thrust her elbow toward her attacker's face to break his hold. It didn't work. She realized that he was taller, stronger, and that he outweighed her. She twisted her body, trying to break free. Her slippers came off as he pulled her through the roses to an open area of grass.

She was now in his stranglehold. Terror filled every fiber of her being. Abby squeezed her index and middle fingers together for strength and plunged them into the hollow of the man's neck while she rolled in her shoulder to lengthen her arm and wrest herself away. Thinking she was free of his iron grip, Abby pivoted, intending to hit him with an eye gouge, followed by a groin kick. But before she could execute either maneuver, he sucker punched her in the face. Knife pricks of pain shot through her left cheek. Falling, Abby screamed in pain. It came out more as a breath than a sound. The man flipped her over. Dragged her farther. Straddled her.

"Don't fight me." His hand was again on her mouth. "You're going to like it!"

Abby twisted her head. She prayed Philippe had heard her. Any second now, Philippe would flip on the lights, step outside. He would see she was in trouble. She could hear Sugar. The dog was agitated.

Pain. Dress ripping. Sugar barking. Wake up, Philippe! Help!

Sugar pawed the door. Lunged through the opening. Snarling and barking, she flew at the stranger. The man's grip loosened, but he held on to Abby as they rolled in the wet grass. Sugar was unrelenting. The man let go. His arms and hands flailed against Sugar. The dog had his sleeve in her mouth. Sugar's head twisted . . . made staccato movements . . . back and forth, like she was playing with a rag doll. She released his hand and bit his face. Then, when his hand flew up defensively, Sugar snapped at his fingers.

Abby crawled from the melee, screaming, "Philippe! Gun . . . bedside table!" She looked back at her attacker. The man had risen to a semi-sitting position, in a fight for his life as he wrestled with Sugar.

"Call him off!" he yelled.

Abby lunged forward. Crawled toward the patio.

The man screamed, "I'll kill it!"

Finally . . . Philippe appeared. "Mon Dieu! What is happening?" Apparently realizing the dire situation, he somehow remembered the garbage can where Abby kept rawhide bones for Sugar. Philippe lunged toward the garbage can and grabbed the large river rock anchoring the lid. He hurled the rock at the attacker. It hit the man's shoulder. Abby's attacker fell back in slow motion. Sugar, who had retreated momentarily, quickly pounced back on the man, snarling, her teeth exposed.

Abby crawled faster than a rabbit, pitched upward, and sprinted past Philippe as he reached for her. She raced to the bedroom. Grabbed the gun. Raced to the patio. Aimed up. Pulled the trigger.

Sugar yelped, darted a few feet away, and cowered as Philippe took cover inside the kitchen.

With her weapon trained on the man, Abby said in a steely voice, "Move, and I shoot to kill." She walked backward and, without taking her eyes off the man, reached inside the kitchen to flick the outside light switch to the up position. The patio light went on. She could see her attacker now.

Heavyset, and wearing a T-shirt, a leather vest, jeans, scuffed combat boots, and a blue bandanna, he appeared to be a skinhead in his midtwenties. His clean-shaven face bore a long scar: it ran from under his left eye to his chin. Blood seeped from bite marks on his cheek and hand. He hawked up a mouthful of blood.

"Keep your hands where I can see them," Abby ordered. To Philippe, she said, "Call the cops. Phone's on the kitchen counter. Police are on speed dial."

While Philippe worked the phone, Abby stood rooted in a shoot-to-kill position, one leg in front of the other, both hands on her weapon. "Who are you?" she asked.

The man stared at her in silence.

"Fine . . . Save it for the cops."

From inside, Philippe asked her for the address; dispatch was on the phone.

After a few minutes, the skinhead spoke. His tone was still arrogant. "I'll answer your questions if you let me go."

"It doesn't work like that." Abby kept her gun trained on him, not even moving when the raccoons began to scurry across the yard. The mama coon paused near the man, rose up on her hind legs, then dropped back down and retreated with her cubs to the abandoned property behind the fence. Philippe, visibly shaken, stepped out onto the patio and leaned against the wall. Sugar panted hard and then ran inside. Abby guessed it was to quench her thirst at the water bowl.

Minutes passed. The sky grew lighter. The stars dimmed. Houdini began his crowing routine. The next eight minutes seemed to Abby like an eternity. Then she heard wheels screeching on her gravel driveway. A car door slammed. *Can't be the police. They can't get here that fast.*

A man called out her name several times. Abby recognized Lucas Crawford's earthy baritone voice.

"I'm back here, Lucas."

"I heard a shot," Lucas said, stepping around the corner and onto the patio. "What's going on here?" His eyes were trained on Abby, but then they shifted to the man on the ground, before finally resting on Philippe. "Couldn't tell where it came from. Worried me," Lucas said. He seemed to be sizing up the situation. "You got blood all over you, woman. You need medical attention."

Abby nodded. "It's on the way."

"You friend or foe?" Lucas asked Philippe.

"Friend, *naturellement!*" Philippe replied.

"Right answer," said Lucas. He turned to glare at the stranger sitting on the ground. "So what's the story here?"

The man on the ground scowled in silence.

Abby doubted the man would talk, but she took comfort in the take-charge attitude that Lucas was showing . . . and also in the sound of approaching sirens. When the man refused to answer her when again she asked his name, she decided to fill Lucas in. "He attacked me. Fearing for my life and limb, I got my gun and fired off a round."

"You want me to beat the daylights out of this piece of crap?" Lucas asked. "I could do it before the cops get here." Abby couldn't see it, but she guessed that Lucas had locked eyes with her attacker and was engaged in a stare down. Finally, Lucas said to Philippe, "I would have thought you would have already done that."

"Let the police handle it, Lucas. From the sound of the sirens, I'd say they're almost here," Abby said.

Philippe was still holding Abby's phone and jumped slightly when a text ringtone sounded and the screen lit up.

"That's Kat's ringtone," Abby said.

"What does s-w-y-p mean?" Philippe asked, reading the phone screen.

"So what's your problem?" Abby answered. "That's what it means. Kat must have heard about the trouble here from our dispatchers putting the call out for units to respond."

"There's more," Philippe said. "There's a one-eight-seven at the Crow Ridge cutoff."

"One-eight-seven is the code for homicide. So who was murdered?"

Philippe shook his head, stared at the phone, and said nothing. After a few seconds passed, the text ringtone sounded again. "Eva Lennahan," Philippe said.

Abby let go an audible gasp. Her thoughts spun. *Our prime suspect? Oh, that's not good.* Her lips tightened. She shook her head in disbelief.

At the sight of two police officers running onto the patio, Abby heaved a sigh of relief and gave them her gun. She would gladly let them do their job securing the scene and taking her attacker, whoever he was, into custody. She knew that once the scene was secured, the cops would let the paramedics in to check her out. She felt wracked with pain from the assault, particularly the blow to her cheek.

The sun rose through the thicket of trees behind the chicken house. Houdini began his crow-off with a neighboring rooster farther down Farm Hill Road. While

Philippe petted Sugar and Lucas helped the male cop hand-cuff and lead the skinhead to the patrol car, Abby gave her statement. By then, the place was swarming with cops, first responders, firemen, and paramedics—all of whom knew Abigail Mackenzie as formerly one of their own. When the female officer asked about discharging the weapon, Abby carefully explained how terrorized she had felt, how she had feared for her life.

"I was standing about here, facing him, when I made the split-second decision to fire off a round. He'd threat-ened to kill my dog," Abby explained. "I imagine the cas-ing went down five to six feet to the right, most likely parallel to the roses, perpendicular to the patio. It's got to be somewhere in the grass there." She tried to stand but suddenly felt quite weak. Maybe she just needed coffee.

As if reading her mind, Lucas returned, put a warm, re-assuring hand on Abby's shoulder, and said, "You look like you could use a cup of joe, Abby. Your pot in the kitchen?"

Abby nodded. "You can find the canister of beans, al-ready ground, in the upper cupboard nearest the sink." She sank into the rocking chair on the patio.

Philippe drew close and knelt at her feet, his hands on the handles of the rocker. "Ma chérie, are you in pain? Your face, it has a deep cut."

Before Abby could respond, a paramedic, dressed in a blue uniform with reflector stripes on the sleeves and a lapel badge that spelled DOTTIE, rushed over to treat her. "Excuse me, please," she said to Philippe, who moved aside. The paramedic dropped her medical pack on the patio table and leaned down to have a closer look. After opening the pack, she took out some tweezers to pluck out bits of debris from Abby's cheek. That done, she turned back to her pack and began removing items, such as alcohol prep pads, hydrogen peroxide, iodine, antiseptic cream, gauze, and tape.

Philippe moved to the other side of the paramedic. He watched intently as the woman pushed aside her stethoscope and pulled on latex gloves to examine the laceration on Abby's cheek.

"Could you give us a little room here?" the paramedic asked Philippe.

"Oui," Philippe said. "I am not leaving you, Abby, but I do not want to be in the way. And the sight of the blood, it makes me queasy," he said sheepishly. "I will check on the bees and give you a few minutes. Hmm?"

"Thank you, Philippe." Abby watched him stroll in the direction of the apiary.

"Are there other cuts on your body?" the paramedic asked.

"Scratches, mostly on my extremities, from my rose-bushes," Abby replied.

"How did you get the cut on your face?"

"During the attack, I was punched."

"Oh, that's awful. I hope that lowlife gets what's coming to him. What about pain in your head and neck? How does it feel when I move it from side to side like this?" Using her hands, the paramedic gently moved Abby's head from left to right and up and down.

"Feels kind of stiff, like I've been manhandled." Abby managed a weak smile.

The paramedic checked Abby's pulse and listened to her heartbeat and breath sounds. Waving a light into and away from Abby's eyes, the paramedic began asking a series of questions. "Do you know your name? The president's name? Where you are? What day it is?" Abby knew they were standard questions paramedics used to assess a patient's orientation and level of consciousness.

After correctly answering Dottie's questions, Abby said, "Look, I know the drill, but I don't need c-spine. I don't need transport. I'm fine."

The paramedic reached into her bag and pulled out a small sealed package. "These should help with the pain. Refusing transport is your right; however, your cut could use a stitch."

"No, I really don't want to go to the hospital." Abby didn't feel it necessary to explain why she hated hospitals. She just did. And not just because of the failed surgeries on her thumb, but also because in her former line of work, it was the place of endings. Cops died. Perps died. Witnesses passed away before they could testify. Oh, sure, plenty of local women went there to give birth, but Abby had never seen that. She just didn't like the place. It was that simple.

"Okay, but if you are going to decline our offer of a ride in the ambulance, you'll have to sign a release form," the paramedic told her as she finished taping the butterfly closures across the cut on Abby's cheek. As soon as Abby had signed the release, the paramedics left along with the first responders, cops, and firemen.

Lucas strolled out from the kitchen with a mug of coffee and handed it to Abby. He went back into the kitchen, brought out the pot and two empty mugs, and set them on the table. "For your other friend," said Lucas, adding in a disapproving tone, "The one who lets a lady rescue herself." He poured coffee for himself in one of the mugs and sat down on a patio chair. Abby didn't say anything. What could she say? *That's not fair. . . . Philippe was asleep in my bed. Uh-oh, might not be a good idea to tell him that.* Abby inhaled deeply, stared up at the clusters of red berries on the towering pepper tree, and said, "Great coffee, Lucas. Thank you for making it."

"I can cook, too," he replied.

She smiled.

Sugar had gotten her drink and then had remained at Abby's side after the attack. She had growled occasionally, as if to continue expressing her dislike for the man who had attacked Abby. Now that he was gone, the dog, who had been panting like crazy, had taken an interest in Abby's house slippers. The slippers were old. And letting the dog chew them was a small enough gesture of appreciation for Sugar saving her life.

Abby and Lucas quietly sipped coffee, watching Sugar. The mutt quickly abandoned the shoe chew to chase a hummingbird that had zoomed past, apparently to lap nectar from the tubular flowers of the trumpet vines.

"I've been thinking," Lucas said. "I've got a single-action revolver in my gun safe that I could loan you until you get your gun back."

"Really? It's a tempting offer, Lucas." Abby thought about it for a moment. She liked the idea but suspected that she might not be able to handle it as easily as her own gun.

As if reading her thoughts, Lucas said, "I'd be happy to offer some pointers."

"I'd need target practice, for sure," Abby said, thinking it could be fun to shoot cans off a fence with Lucas or fire at the range. But then again, a single-action revolver required manual cocking. Lucas would pretty readily pick up on her gimpy thumb action. Still, how cool it was that he had offered to loan her *that* gun. A shot from it could take down a 250-pound attacker, even if he was high on drugs.

"Think about it. Let me know," he said in his deep country-singer voice.

Abby stared at the hills, which were now ablaze with color and which, only hours ago, would have looked like camelback humps in black. Her thoughts returned to the skinhead. She wondered who he was and why he'd come all the way out to her farmette to attack her. She was dying to call Otto to find out what the cops knew, but she would make the call when she was alone, after Lucas and Philippe had gone. This was personal.

"Looks like you got yourself a pointer there, judging from the liver spots." Lucas stretched out his long, jeans-clad legs and crossed his feet, one worn cowboy boot over the other, and sipped his coffee.

"Well, Sugar actually belonged to someone else, but . . . her owner isn't coming back," Abby said, then took a swig of her coffee and thought that it had never tasted so good. But as she thought about Sugar, it seemed to her that the poor dog really had no one but Abby. Abby had a debt to pay to Sugar. And just like that, she decided she would care for the mixed-breed canine for the rest of the dog's life. *What is that . . . ? Fourteen . . . fifteen years?*

"I could use a good bird dog," Lucas said. "Take her off your hands . . . train her. Get you a proper guard dog, if you want."

"Well, I appreciate your offer, Lucas. I really do. But I think Sugar and I are destined to be together. "

His light brown eyes stared straight out over the back property. "Glad to hear it. A woman living alone out here . . . Well, you know how I feel about that."

"Yes, and I appreciate that you came straight to my farmette as soon as you heard the shot. A lot of folks live along Farm Hill Road, but you are the only one who checked on me. You're a wonderful neighbor, Lucas. I hope you know that."

He took another swig of coffee and locked his soulful eyes with hers. After a long beat, he said softly, "Maybe sometime we could—"

"Your bees, they are happy today, Abby," Philippe cried out exuberantly. "And the coffee smells great." He strolled back to the patio, a broad grin creasing his face, apparently unaware that he had interrupted Lucas in mid-sentence.

"Lucas brought a cup for you, Philippe. Right there." She pointed to the white mug on the table.

"Merci, mon ami." Philippe gave an appreciative nod to Lucas, reached for the mug, and poured some coffee in it. After tasting it, he put the mug back down. "Oh, sadly, the coffee, it is not hot enough."

Lucas rose and strolled into the kitchen to put his mug in the sink. Philippe sank into Lucas's chair. When Lucas returned, he put a hand on Abby's shoulder.

"Feel better, Abby. You know where to find me." A few moments later, his pickup engine started, and the gravel crunched under his truck tires as he pulled away.

"I think I've seen him before, Abby. Who is he?" Philippe asked.

"He raises beef on a ranch near here, one that's part of an old Spanish land grant." Abby's thoughts were drifting elsewhere. What was it Lucas had said? *Maybe sometime we could . . . What?* What was Lucas about to say when Philippe interrupted? Abby made a mental note to ask Lucas the next time she saw him.

Although her cheek throbbed and her body felt weary, Abby wanted to get Philippe back to Las Flores so he could finish packing up his brother's apartment and ship the boxes back to New York. And she also wanted to find out the details of Eva Lennahan's murder. She also wanted to talk with Otto about that skinhead and find out what the police knew. The pain reliever the paramedic had given her would soon kick in, and so for now, regardless of how she felt, she would work her agenda.

"I'll just change out of my dress and drive you to the funeral home, where you left your car." Abby used her most cheerful voice. Despite her tone, the smile evaporated from Philippe's face.

"Must we?"

"I think we must."

Sugar's Favorite Doggy Treats

Commercially made dog biscuits often contain preservatives and other additives to keep them fresh and tasty for as long as possible. When you make homemade treats for your dog, you can cater to his or her personal taste by adding liver, bacon, cheese, or another flavorful ingredient. The following basic recipe is perfect for such modification. Cut the dough with a bone- or heart-shaped cookie cutter, or any desired shape.

Ingredients:
2 cups flour (all-purpose or whole-wheat or a mixture of both)
½ cup rolled oats
1 tablespoon wheat germ
½ cup chicken broth
1 large egg
1 tablespoon canola oil, plus more for greasing the baking sheet
2 tablespoons mashed cooked liver, minced cooked bacon, or grated cheddar cheese (optional)

Directions:
Preheat the oven to 350°F. Grease a baking sheet with oil.

In a large bowl, mix together the flour, oats, and wheat germ until well blended. Add the chicken broth, egg, and oil, and liver (or bacon or cheddar) to the flour-oat mixture and mix well.

Roll the dough out to a thickness of ¼ inch on a lightly floured surface. Cut the dough with a bone-shaped cookie cutter or with the cookie cutter you prefer. Place the biscuit shapes on the prepared baking sheet.

Bake on the center rack for 30 minutes, or until the biscuits are light brown. Remove the biscuits from the oven and transfer them with a spatula to wire racks to cool.

Store the biscuits, once they have cooled completely, in an airtight tin at room temperature for up to 2 weeks.

Chapter 17

Time spent in a garden is a lot like yoga; it
slows the breath, quiets the mind, and guides
you to the truth.

—*Henny Penny Farmette Almanac*

While Philippe played with Sugar in the orchard area, Abby took a quick shower and changed into a lime-colored silk blouse with embroidery trim in a yellow paisley pattern along the edges of the capped sleeves and hem, straight-leg jeans, and black Mary Jane flats. She brushed her hair into a ponytail and twisted the end back under a rubber band to make a thick knot. After a quick application of mascara to her light lashes, she chose a soft shade of peach lip gloss and smoothed a fingertip of it across her lips. The use of blush was not possible because of her injured cheek. She decided that a drop of rosemary and lemon oil dabbed against her temples couldn't hurt; the herbalist who sold it to her had emphasized its qualities for enhancing mental clarity and concentration. And today Abby needed all the help she could get as she met with Otto at the police station to talk through the loose ends of the pastry chef's murder. The evidence boxes were already loaded into the Jeep and she was eager to return them to the police.

Strolling onto the patio, into a light breeze, she imagined the wind carrying away the ugly vibe of the skinhead who'd attacked her. Since buying the farmette, she'd always felt safe and peaceful there, as though the more she nurtured the land, the more it nourished her spirit. Her assailant had stalked her like prey, and the memory of it would always be with her. But for Abby to live in fear meant he had taken her power, and she wasn't about to let that happen.

Although the farmette was a peaceful place, it was never quiet—what with the squawking of jays and the endless hoarse cawing of crows, which had taken up residence in the tall pine near the front of her property. Now, as on most other days, Abby watched them flap, flap, flap overhead without gliding as they flew from the massive sugar pine to the eucalyptus grove at the rear of her property.

Philippe stopped his game of fetch with Sugar to watch the crows, too. He and Sugar walked over to the patio.

"This place, Abby, it is special," he said. "I feel content, and that surprises me. I have always felt more at ease in cities."

"Well, it just means you'll have to visit Sugar and me as often as possible," Abby said. She held his jacket in one hand and jiggled the car keys in the other. "Ready?"

"Oui." Philippe dropped the stick he'd been throwing to the dog and brushed his hands together a few times, apparently to rid them of dirt from the stick and Sugar's slobber. "Did you know Sugar can do tricks?"

Abby smiled. "What kind of tricks?"

"Fetch."

"Really? Does she find the stick and bring it back?" Abby wondered why Sugar had never fetched for her.

"Well, no. She goes after it, but she does not bring it back."

"Then, technically, I don't think it's a trick. But we'll work on it, won't we, Sugar?"

Sugar trotted over and stretched down on her forepaws, looking up at Abby with large brown eyes. She wagged her tail happily, as if in anticipation that she would accompany the humans during an outing, which she already sensed.

Abby already felt guilty for not wanting to take Sugar to the police station, and her heart melted as she looked at Sugar's sweet face, with its expression of trust. She knelt and scratched the short hairs behind Sugar's ears. "Good girl. I love you for protecting me, Sugar."

"What about me?" Philippe asked. "I threw the stone."

"Of course you did!" Abby said, looking over at Philippe and smiling. "You hit him squarely on the shoulder. Your aim was perfect."

"Well, not exactly," Philippe admitted sheepishly. "I was aiming for his head."

Abby laughed and stood. "But at least you nailed him, and not Sugar or me."

Philippe gave her a quick hug. "You know, Abby, when I first saw this place, I couldn't understand why you would choose to live out here. I thought how difficult it would be for me to live without art galleries, the opera house, and a symphonic hall all within walking distance or, at the very least, a taxi ride away. But I think I understand. It is your paradise, n'est-ce pas?"

"I suppose it is. Not quite paradise, but there's nowhere else I'd rather be."

After a beat, Philippe said, "When I return to New York, come with me. I'll introduce you to my parents. They'll love you. And we will get to know each other better, ma chérie."

Abby felt a momentary rush of excitement. *New York. The Big Apple.* A place she'd always wanted to see someday. But how on earth could she possibly get away now, when she had fallen behind with her planting and renovation projects? She said nothing but swallowed hard.

An awkward moment ensued. Abby maintained her silence, pondering how to respond to his invitation. In the silence, an unwelcome tension arose between them. Abby sensed it, and her stomach tightened. Finally, she touched his arm and said tenderly, "You know I'd love to . . . someday . . . but I can't leave the farmette now, not with seeds still to go into the ground . . . and the harvesting of stone fruit for canning . . . and the honey flow just starting. Then there's Sugar, who needs training, and those plywood countertops, which need replacing, and the bathroom renovation . . . all before the rains come . . . our season of winter."

"I understand, Abby. I do." Philippe stepped back and gestured to the house. "I'll just wash my hands and be right out."

Abby knelt and hugged Sugar. She fought back tears. Why shut him down like that with a litany of excuses? She felt like kicking herself. When had anyone as handsome and as charming as Philippe Bonheur ever invited her to his home to meet his family? Never. Not even Clay, who supposedly had truly loved her, had done this. Maybe Kat was right and she just needed to open her heart to those around her, to start having a social life, and to enjoy the men she met for as long as the relationship worked. If she didn't get out more, there was a good possibility she'd end up alone.

The unspoken tension created a gulf between Abby and

Philippe that remained as they left the farmette and drove toward town. However, as soon as they passed some vine-yards, Philippe broke the silence, telling Abby that he was beginning to appreciate the provincial charm of small-town life. As he extolled the virtues of rural life from his per-spective, Abby felt the tense muscles of her body relaxing.

"Really?" she said.

"C'est vrai." He flashed one of those charming smiles at her, and she relaxed even more.

As she listened to Philippe free-associating, Abby con-cluded that he was considering the possibility of returning to visit her and Sugar, perhaps around Thanksgiving or Christmas. It would give him a good excuse to leave the family gallery in New York and check on their other gallery in San Francisco. He could spend part of the time enjoying her company.

"How would you feel about that, Abby?" he asked.

"Sounds lovely, Philippe. It gives me a reason to finally get the kitchen finished." She felt happy that he'd given her a second chance to say yes to the possibility of a rela-tionship . . . or at least to a visit, which had more to do with the birth of new possibilities than with another ending.

Abby guided her Jeep into a parking spot in front of the police department. Philippe placed one evidence box in Abby's arms and took the other. Inside they met Nettie, who was still on crutches, and she led them to the office of the Otto Nowicki, the acting chief of police in the absence of Bob Allen.

"Hello, Abby. Mr. Bonheur," said Otto, extending a pasty white hand to Philippe, who juggled the box so that he could shake Otto's hand. "Kat told me to expect you two. She also laid out your theory, Abby, but we have a problem. Your prime suspect is recently deceased."

"I heard about it. I don't think it's an insurmountable

problem," Abby replied. She looked briefly around the office and realized there was not a single uncluttered surface on which they could put the boxes. She set the evidence box in her arms on the floor, next to Otto's small desk. Philippe followed her lead and sat down.

Abby knew these four walls all too well. The space had been promised to her by Bob Allen, along with a promotion, which had never materialized. "Too good," he'd told her. She was too good at what she did to leave the streets, whether she liked it or not. The truth be told, he felt threatened by smart women in positions of authority. Chief Bob Allen made no excuse for believing as he did that only men could serve effectively as police chiefs, since men wouldn't want to take orders from a woman. But that was then. . . . She didn't need to think about that anymore.

"Heard about your attack this morning. You okay?"

"Yes," Abby replied. "My attacker got a name?" She sat down and leaned forward in her chair. "Can you tell me why he singled me out?"

"His name is Roy Sweeney. Ring any bells?"

"I know a Harlan Sweeney, a rough-around-the-edges guy who practically lives at the Black Witch when he isn't in his double-wide, watching episodes of *Street Outlaws.*"

"Well, I interviewed Roy Sweeney. He's Harlan's cousin by marriage on his father's side. He's been staying with Harlan since being paroled a month ago. Roy told us that your friend Mr. Bonheur attacked him with a rock and that he was just defending himself."

"Well, the rock part is true," Abby said, looking over at Philippe, who was shaking his head, apparently in disbelief. "But did he mention that he was trespassing on my property, casing it in the wee hours of the morning, that he tried to rape me, and that he threatened to kill my dog?"

"He left those details out. It shouldn't surprise anyone

that he's got a rap sheet with a lot of priors . . . assault, burglary, illegal drug possession, sexual assault. Now, with the probation violation and the attack on you, his future doesn't look too bright. He's got himself boxed into a corner."

"Has he lawyered up yet?" Abby asked.

"No."

Abby smiled at Philippe. "That's a good thing, because Otto can ratchet up the pressure on him. I'm wondering if he had anything to do with Eva Lennahan's murder."

Otto looked at Abby with a poker-faced expression. "You know I can't talk about an open investigation." He rapped his fingers on the desk, as if thinking about something. Then, after a beat, he rose and said, "Excuse me, Mr. Bonheur. Would you give us a moment?"

"Mais oui," Philippe replied, rising from his chair.

"I'll be right out, Philippe," Abby said.

Philippe followed the chief to the door just as Nettie hobbled up.

"I'll take him to the waiting area," she said to Otto and Abby.

After closing the door, Otto sat back down. "So we've got a history, you and I, and let's just say you've helped me out more than once. So keep this to yourself, Abby. The vic—that is, Eva Lennahan—was a town council member who was running for mayor. You know that, right?"

"Yes. I know of her. Met her once," Abby answered.

"Her campaign manager called us after she went missing."

"Okay. So her campaign manager, not her husband?"

"No. He left for the Caribbean yesterday. My sources tell me that he's in bad shape, grieving and all."

"Well, I knew he was planning to go there for his birthday," Abby said, "with Chef Jean-Louis, but that's neither here nor there. You were saying about her campaign manager?"

"He knew her password to a phone location app and tracked her phone pinging off the tower closest to the Redwood cutoff."

"Well, besides the tower, there's nothing up there but brush, steep canyons, and a serpentine road that twists through the mountains."

"All the way up to Vista Point," Otto said, finishing her thought. "She had been at a fundraiser at the Las Flores Inn. No one saw her leave."

"Why was she up at the Redwood cutoff, then?"

Otto shook his head. "It's anybody's guess. Perhaps she was lured up there by someone she knew."

"How was she killed?"

"Strangled, looks like, with her own scarf, according to the coroner."

"You said her campaign manager tracked her phone. . . . Did you find it with the body?"

"No, we didn't."

"Anything taken from the scene? Her purse?" Abby asked.

"Her purse had been riffled through. No money in the wallet. A credit card was dropped on the seat, and a lipstick on the floorboards. A woman like her always has cash and cards. Her killer probably took the rest of her cards and her phone. Her campaign manager said he had searched everywhere and had finally resorted to pinpointing her location by tracking her phone. It was triangulating at the Redwood cutoff. That's when he called us, and we sent a cruiser out to check on her. But the campaign manager called back to say the phone had begun pinging off a different tower, one in the south county, city of Baxter, and after that in Juniper Ridge, heading out of the county."

"You know what this means, don't you, Otto?"

"Yep . . . Our person of interest took her phone and is on the move."

"Find her phone, and we find our guy," Abby said.

"We've notified law enforcement in the south county. Put out a BOLO. They've established roadblocks. Our perp is trapped. Shouldn't be long now."

"Hope so. Whoever killed Eva Lennahan, I believe, was involved in helping her kill our pastry chef, too. Eva was probably killed to shut her up. That's what I think."

Otto was grinning widely. "Knowing that we're going to close this case makes me hungry. How about let's head down to the break room? I'm off that diet," he said. "Didn't work, anyway, and Nettie brought in some chocolate chip cookies this morning. Hungry?"

"Not really, but I'll walk with you," Abby said.

Stepping out of Otto's office, Abby heard Kat's voice coming through Otto's radio. "Ten-nineteen with Harlan Sweeney in custody . . . ETA . . . five minutes."

Abby suppressed an urge to high-five Otto. She felt giddy with excitement. Abby knew how things would proceed now. Harlan Sweeney would be interviewed before being booked into the county jail. Abby just hoped the evidence would support a charge of capital murder. He was in this up to his elbows, with Eva Lennahan most likely calling the shots, until she pushed him the wrong way or Abby's investigation caused him to be concerned about being found out. But Abby knew these were just her suspicions. Otto would have to back him into a corner if he was going to trip up Harlan Sweeney with his own statements.

They entered the break room. Otto poured himself a cup of coffee, added sugar, and then made a beeline for the cookies.

Watching Otto pop a cookie in his mouth and wash it

down with sugary coffee, Abby said wryly, "Well, some things haven't changed."

"Carbs reduce my stress," Otto confessed, reaching for another cookie. "Want one?"

"I'll pass. More for you."

Abby suggested that Otto push hard on Roy Sweeney. "Those two have a linkage in more ways than as blood relatives," Abby said. Leaning against the wall, she added, "I'm thinking he's weaker than his cousin Harlan. Implicate them both in Eva's murder, and I think Roy will sing like a songbird."

"Roy will say he was busy when Eva Lennahan died, and he'd be right," Otto said. "In a strange twist of irony, you, Abby, will be his alibi. He'll say he was defending himself against your friend Mr. Bonheur here, who tried to kill him with a stone after he mistakenly walked onto your property and roused your dog."

Abby asserted, "Well, the dog . . . Sugar was protecting me from that thug."

The sound of approaching footsteps interrupted the conversation. Her question intended for Otto, Nettie called out, "Which interview room?"

"Number two," Otto called back. "I'm thinking it's going to be a long day," he said.

Kat marched a disheveled Harlan Sweeney in handcuffs past the break room and toward the interview rooms. Another officer, whom Abby didn't know and who, she surmised, was a new recruit, judging from his youthful face, followed Kat and the handcuffed Harlan.

"Good luck," Abby said. "Philippe and I will be waiting for news."

Otto nodded and gave her a half smile, which, Abby knew from working with him, meant that he was already thinking of the order of the questions and his approach to the interview.

It was 6:12 p.m. when Abby got a text from Kat asking her where she was. Abby replied via text that she and Philippe were at his brother's apartment, packing the last items to be shipped to New York. Fifteen minutes later there was a knock on the door. Leaving the bags of left-over bubble wrap, packing paper, and clear tape, Abby offered to answer the door.

"Hey there, girlfriend. Could we talk for a minute in the cruiser?" Kat asked, glancing past Abby toward the open door to the bedroom, where Philippe was tucking books of a similar size into cardboard boxes.

"Sure," Abby said. She called out to Philippe, "I'm going outside for a moment to chitty-chat with Kat. I'll be right back."

He smiled and, flicking his fingers sideways, waved her on.

On their way to the cruiser, Kat said softly, "Otto and I thought you'd like to be the one to inform Philippe that Harlan Sweeney has confessed to murdering Chef Jean-Louis and also Eva Lennahan. And it went down, Abby, just like you said. Harlan Sweeney heard Etienne spreading that ridiculous lie about Jean-Louis and figured Eva could use it to her advantage."

"How did someone like Eva know a thug like Harlan Sweeney?"

"Mutual associates. The night the chef died, Eva met Harlan in the alley behind the bar and the pastry shop, where they sat in her black Mercedes and hatched their plan to kill the chef."

Kat opened the cruiser door and slid into the driver's seat. Abby climbed in on the passenger side and waited as

Kat scrolled to an image on her laptop. "Do you know what this is?"

Abby looked closely at a picture of a gold medallion hanging from a chain. "Looks like a man's necklace. Saint Honorius, I think. Where did you get it?"

"Harlan Sweeney had it in his pocket, along with Eva's credit cards, when I took him in."

"That looks like the medal the chef always wore."

"That's what I thought. And it has a nice fat fingerprint on it that could be Sweeney's."

"Assuming Jean-Louis was wearing it when he was killed—and Harlan Sweeney removed it from the body— this could be the proof that you'll need to prove he's a murderer, just in case he tries to retract that confession." Abby studied the medallion closely. "See the imagery there? It tells you that this man is Honorius, or Honoré, as they say in French. In his right hand, he holds a paddle for sliding loaves of bread into the oven. On the table are the loaves. He's the patron saint of bakers."

"I figured there was no need to research this, since you'd probably know what it is. You've got more trivia in your brain than anyone I have ever met."

"Why, thank you."

"So, this is how we think it played out," Kat said. "Eva Lennahan paid Harlan Sweeney five thousand dollars to help her murder the chef. The Black Witch was about to close when Eva sent Sweeney back in to buy a couple of glasses of brandy. Eva—who suffers from asthma and carries capsules of diphenhydramine around with her—heavily spiked one of the drinks. She knocked on the pastry shop back door, told the chef that she wanted to talk and that she'd brought drinks in honor of his upcoming birthday."

"Okay. I'm with you so far."

"According to Sweeney, Eva told the chef she wanted discuss the upcoming Caribbean trip her husband had scheduled. Of course, she knew that Jean-Louis would be going with him, and that infuriated her. Once inside the pastry shop, Eva made small talk until the chef could no longer fight off sleep. She had used several high-dose capsules, and it took only about twenty minutes, Sweeney said. At some point, she motioned for Sweeney to come in. He overpowered Jean-Louis, then strung up the chef with a long piece of twine that Jean-Louis kept in a bucket in his shop kitchen. Apparently, he recycled the twine taken from the daily newspaper bundles."

"What about the messy kitchen? It was so unlike Chef Jean-Louis to have his work area in such disarray."

"All part of the staging, during which Eva lost her earring."

"Dora must have arrived at the back door for her coffee shortly afterward," Abby said. "Poor woman. I can only wonder what she must have been thinking as she cut the body down and removed the twine from around his neck."

"As I told you already, we found the chef's apron and the rest of the twine in a plastic bag in Dora's shopping cart."

"I cannot even imagine how she must have felt seeing him like that. It had to be traumatic for her," Abby said, reaching back to adjust her ponytail. "If money was Sweeney's motivation to murder the chef, what motivated him to kill Eva?"

Kat shook her head. "He is such an idiot. He was afraid she'd talk. But he was the one doing the talking. He likes booze. Drank too much and spilled to his cousin what they'd done." Kat met Abby's gaze. "Don't you remember me telling you when we met him in the bar that night that his kind mouthed off too much and that would be his undoing sooner or later?"

Abby nodded. "His cousin Roy Sweeney might have been next on his list. It's crazy." She looked toward the apartment. Philippe was standing in the doorway, the light behind him. He was leaning against the door frame, hands in his pockets, grinning and shaking his head, apparently finding it humorous that the two women were hunkered down, heads together, in conversation . . . in the cruiser.

"I need to get back, Kat," said Abby. "But I have to know why Roy Sweeney attacked me."

"As a favor to Harlan, who was giving him shelter and a helping hand. Those two were not too happy about how you were turning up the heat on the investigation just when they hoped it would go down as a suicide. It was payback for your interference."

"What a hot mess!" Abby said. "But thank goodness, it's all over."

"Yeah. I hear you." Kat leaned down and looked past Abby out the window. "When is Philippe flying back to New York?"

"I suppose soon, now that his brother is buried and the Sweeneys are in jail," Abby replied.

"He'll be back," Kat said. "He seems to appreciate you. If he doesn't come back because his heart tells him to, then he'll surely return to visit his brother's grave, and let us not forget, the trial of his brother's murderer. . . ." Kat heaved a tired sigh. "Well, that's it, girlfriend. I think I'll head home now, take a shower, have a sandwich, and call it a night."

Abby leaned over and gave Kat a quick hug. "You're the best," she whispered. "Thank you, Kat."

"Thank me? No, I think we should all be thanking you. This case was closed until you gave us a reasonable theory and evidence to reopen it."

Abby grinned and allowed herself to feel a moment of personal pride before getting out of the car and waving good-bye. Philippe had strolled away from the apartment's doorway and was walking toward her.

"Everything all right?" he asked.

"More than all right," Abby answered. "It's over, Philippe. Two people took your brother's life. One is dead, and the other is in police custody."

"And the police, they can prove it was murder?" Philippe asked as they headed back to the apartment.

"Yes. Well, they'll give the case to the DA to prove in court. But the murderer is going away for good."

Philippe ran his fingers through his hair. "*Fantastique!*" Once they were back inside the apartment, he closed the door and look at Abby tenderly. "What about the man who hurt you?"

"That hooligan is in custody, too."

Philippe sighed and pulled her into his arms. "There is only the silverware to pack now. Let's finish this tomorrow, Abby. You are welcome to stay in town tonight, or I could accompany you home . . . make sure you get there safely."

Abby turned over the options in her mind. "Both are lovely choices, but home is calling. Sugar will be waiting for me, and I want to check on the bees and my chickens."

Philippe stroked her hair and whispered, "I've never met anyone like you, Abby. Whatever happens, I hope you'll always remember that for me you are a woman *extraordinaire.*"

Abby relaxed into his embrace. As she tilted her head up to look into his eyes, he leaned down and touched his warm, soft lips to her, at first kissing her slowly and then devouringly. Maybe Sugar and the chickens could wait a while longer; it wouldn't be dark for a few more hours.

She melted under his kisses. He responded with a passion lit, apparently, by an inner fire. After gently pushing her against the wall, he pulled the elastic band from her hair, swooped the mass from her shoulders and began to kiss the length of her neck, earlobe to décolletage. As he reached for the top button of her blouse, his cell phone rang.

"Mon Dieu!" He fumbled with the button, ignoring the cell. When the phone continued to ring, he said in a voice edged with exasperation, "Let me answer and be done with it." After pulling the phone from his pants pocket and glancing at the screen, he frowned. "C'est mon père."

Abby sucked in a long breath and exhaled as Philippe answered the call from his father. She scanned his face for signs that the call brought good news or bad. When his expression darkened and he wiped his palm over his mouth and stepped away, turning his back to her, it became apparent that he needed to some space.

"Right," she murmured and headed toward the kitchen to finish packing the utensil drawer. After a few moments, Philippe strode into the kitchen, still holding the phone to his ear.

"Eh bien! Je prends le premier vol demain." He sighed heavily. "Moi aussi."

Abby watched him pocket his phone and stare at the floor, a forlorn expression claiming his features. No longer did he look like the devastatingly handsome man about to make mad, passionate love to her. He looked vulnerable and sad, as if he'd lost his only friend. Abby dropped the forks, rushed over, and threw her arms around him, laying her face against his chest. They held each other in silence.

"What's happened?" she asked finally.

Philippe kissed her head. He cleared his throat and in a husky voice said, "It's my mother. This Parkinson's disease—it has ravaged her body. It has robbed her of her mind. The pneumonia has cleared, but this is the second time she has had it in three months. My father says she doesn't eat. She sleeps most of the time. Her tremors continue, even in her sleep. She thinks her husband is her brother. My father believes her time is coming to an end. He's inconsolable." Philippe curled a finger under Abby's chin, then tilted her face upward. "I must go, Abby, back to New York tomorrow." His eyes caressed her face.

"Of course," Abby said, trying to convey understanding and strength in her tone. "Your family needs you."

He bit his lower lip and nodded.

"The last of the packing is done. I can meet the shipper for you tomorrow . . . get all these boxes out of here, so you don't have to think about anything but your parents," Abby offered bravely.

Philippe nodded.

"So," she said with hesitation, "I guess I'd better let you get on with packing your suitcase and checking flights leaving for the East Coast."

"Not so fast," Philippe said. "That can wait until morning."

"Oh, I see," Abby said, but she didn't see. Surely he would not want to waste a minute more than necessary in Las Flores.

"Is it all right if I stay with you and Sugar tonight?"

Abby's eyelids batted in sudden disbelief. "Really? Well . . . what I mean is . . . I'd love that."

He grinned. "I intend to see to it that no one interferes with your sleep tonight . . . unless, of course, it's me."

Heat crept into her cheeks. "How gallant of you."

*   *   *

The ride home seemed shorter than usual. Abby explained how the killer had been caught through GPS tracking of the cell phone belonging to Eva Lennahan, the wife of Jean-Louis's lover, Jake. And how Etienne had started the tragic spiraling of events leading to murder with his malicious lies. "Oh, I almost forgot," she said. "The cops have your brother's Saint Honoré medallion, but they have to keep it for evidence. You will get it back after the trial."

Philippe nodded. "I cannot thank you enough, Abby, for all you've done." For the remainder of the ride home, he seemed deeply absorbed in thought, and Abby did not intrude.

Sugar met them at the driveway gate. "Down. Get down," Abby said, kneeling to stroke the dog's head and nose. Sugar licked her face, giving her multiple doggy kisses. "I know you're glad to see me. I'm glad to see you, too . . . and *so* glad to be home." Sugar ran from Abby to jump up on Philippe, pawing at his waist.

"No, no," Abby commanded, but Philippe seemed not to mind Sugar's excitement at being reunited. As they walked to the back of the house, Abby said, "She won't let me out of her sight, Philippe. Will you play with her while I make us some mint tea? We can relax for a bit, and then I'll make dinner. Okay with you?"

"Ah, oui. That sounds good, Abby."

Abby smiled and walked inside the kitchen. It felt just like the old days, when Clay was around and the two of them moved in an easy rhythm of work and winding down. She kicked off her shoes but just as quickly picked them up for fear that Sugar would chew on them the moment she spotted them. Abby walked down the hallway and tossed the shoes in the bedroom closet, then closed the door securely. Back in the kitchen, she gave Sugar a rawhide bone to take outside.

After dropping ice cubes into two tall glasses, Abby turned on a burner, added water to a saucepan, and put it on to simmer. She strolled back outside and headed in the direction of the mint patch, where she plucked a handful of fresh green leaves. Back in the kitchen she paused to sniff the sweet scent of the summer mint before dousing it with cold water and then tossing it into the saucepan. After the mint had simmered long enough for the water to extract the flavor from it, Abby poured the tea over the ice cubes in the glasses, then sweetened each with honey. She cut up some honey cake into bite-size pieces and put everything on a tray, which she carried out to the patio.

As soon as Abby appeared with the tea and cake, Sugar trotted over, tail wagging. After handing a glass to Philippe, Abby sank into the old rocking chair. Philippe adjusted the cushion of the other chair, took a piece of the honey cake, and sat down beside her.

He put a bit of cake in his mouth. "Mmm," he said. He reached for Abby's hand.

She rocked slowly, secretly feeling delight at the warmth of Philippe's hand around hers. He didn't speak. Like her, he seemed to be soaking up the peacefulness of the early evening. She gazed at the eucalyptus trees next to the old house on the back acre. Branches swayed as the blue-green leaves rustled in the wind, which had begun to kick up, as it usually did around sunset. If the wind continued its summer pattern, the breezes would blow for a while. The mourning doves had descended from the olive tree to feed from the giant pottery saucer of birdseed that Abby kept filled near the back fence. A lone scrub jay screeched as it chased a flock of smaller birds from the firethorn bush sprawling between the two properties.

As the muscles in her body began to lose tension, Abby felt contentment take hold of her spirit. The rhythms of nature comforted her. All was right again on the farmette. More than right . . . Philippe was here to share the wild beauty of this place.

They sat in silence, the rocker quietly clicking on the stone surface of the patio. The sounds of the ice cubes groaning and plopping as they melted and moved to the bottom of the empty glasses reminded Abby that every day should end in such sublime sweetness. Torn between wanting to preserve the moment and knowing she should be getting up to make dinner, Abby looked over at Philippe. He was resting his head on the back of the chair, eyes closed. Abby heard a faint buzzing to the left of the patio, off near the bee apiary. The sound stirred Sugar off her haunches and into a state of alertness.

Philippe opened his eyes. He sat upright and turned toward the sound. After a moment, he pointed toward the wooden fence that partially cordoned off the apiary from the rest of the farmette. "There."

Abby followed the line of his finger. She spotted a tiny swarm, no larger than a child's fist, coalescing beneath the birdhouse she'd hung on the fence. "Well, bees, thank you for waiting," Abby said, rising from the chair.

"What can I do to help?" Philippe asked, standing. A grin crinkled his face as he stood at the ready. "I shall be your knight in shining—"

"You're not afraid of being stung again?"

His smile evaporated as he thought for a moment. "Do you have an extra bee suit?"

Smiling at his exuberance, Abby shook her head.

Seemingly dismayed, Philippe stared at her.

"The swarm is tiny, Philippe, and it's so late in the day that they might just go back inside the hive," Abby explained. "But, in case they're indecisive, I've already placed a super close by with frames of wax and honey for when they are ready to make a move."

Philippe drew a half step closer and put his arms around her. When Abby tilted her face upward, his gray-green eyes locked on hers. "Then, will you stay here with me?" he whispered huskily. "I am not indecisive like your bees. I am ready to make the moves."

Abby sucked in a breath and let it escape in an effort to calm the sudden erratic beating of her heart. "What about dinner?" she teased. "Have you no appetite?"

"Au contraire. My hunger, it increases . . . for you." Philippe flashed a sexy grin, slipped his hand under her blouse, and trailed his fingers along her waistline at her back. "Ma chérie, let us do what the bees do."

The warmth of his touch against her flesh kindled sensuous feelings within Abby, feelings she no longer wanted to resist. Pricks of electricity arced through her body. "And, pray tell, what is that? Taking flight?"

"Non. Making something sweet," he whispered, "of our time together."

"In that case . . . ," Abby mumbled as Philippe's lips pressed hungrily against hers. *We won't need bee suits.*

Old World Honey Cake

Ingredients:
1 cup honey (preferably dark and thick), plus 1
    tablespoon for brushing the cake
1 teaspoon ground cinnamon
½ teaspoon ground nutmeg
½ teaspoon ground cardamom
2 teaspoons baking soda

½ cup softened unsalted butter
1 cup dark brown sugar
4 large egg yolks
½ cup natural Greek yogurt
½ cup cottage cheese (small curd)
1 tablespoon fresh orange zest
2½ cups unbleached all-purpose flour
½ teaspoon salt
10 dates, pitted and diced
1 cup walnuts, finely chopped
½ cup seedless raisins
12 cup slivered almonds, for garnish (optional)

Directions:

Preheat the oven to 300°F. Grease a 10-inch tube pan.

Combine the honey, cinnamon, nutmeg, and cardamom in a small saucepan and bring it to a boil over medium-high heat, stirring often. Stir in the baking soda, remove from the heat, and let the honey-spice mixture cool.

In a large mixing bowl, cream the butter with the brown sugar. Beat in 1 egg yolk at a time. Fold the reserved honey-spice mixture into the butter-egg mixture and set aside.

In a small mixing bowl, mix together the yogurt, cottage cheese, and orange zest.

Sift half (1¼ cups) of the flour and the salt into the reserved honey-spice-butter mixture. In a medium mixing bowl, combine the remaining 1¼ cups flour, the dates, walnuts, and raisins. Fold the date-walnut mixture into batter. Fold the yogurt mixture into the reserved honey-spice-butter mixture.

Pour the batter into the prepared tube pan and

bake for 1½ hours. Test for doneness by inserting a toothpick into the cake, which should have no batter on it when extracted.

Cool the cake for 15 minutes before inverting. Invert the cake onto a wire rack, and brush it with the remaining 1 tablespoon honey. Sprinkle the cake with slivered almonds, if desired. After the cake has completely cooled, store it in an airtight container in the refrigerator for 24 to 48 hours before serving.

Serves 8

Acknowledgments

My deepest gratitude goes to Aaron Pomeroy for his insights into law enforcement. I also want to thank his wife, Heather, as well as their daughters Madison and Savannah, for their feedback, suggestions, and hilarious stories, which continually inform and enrich my own storytelling.

Thanks also to Ken and Lynne Davis for sharing with me their knowledge about guns and police work.

A special thank-you to my friend, fellow globe-trotter, and dog lover, Katerina Lorenzatos Makris, whose knowledge about our four-legged friends and dog rescue work worldwide boggles the mind. Thank you for your enthusiasm, energy, and invaluable feedback.

I owe a deep debt of gratitude to Botros (Peter) Kemel and Wajiha (Jill) Nasrallah for teaching me about keeping bees and harvesting honey, and for fostering in me a love of beekeeping, which has resulted in the establishment of my own hives.

I want to thank Anne Marie Behan for her years (and stories about) working as a paramedic, and Abbie Serrano for her service in law enforcement and for inspiring my sleuth, who bears her name, albeit with a different spelling.

For her unwavering support of the Henny Penny Farmette and the vacant midcentury house she owns, which inspired threads of rising tension in this narrative, I extend a warm thank-you to Jeanne Lederer.

To my husband, Carlos J. Carvajal, and my son Joshua, I give my heartfelt thanks for your love, patience, and support throughout the writing of this book.

And finally, a hug and a kiss to my agent, Paula Munier, who tells me the truth, but always lovingly . . . and to my editor Michaela Hamilton, who saw promise in an untested novelist and took a chance.